THE SCARLET ROSE

A Beauty and the Beast Retelling

VALIA LIND

SKAZKA PRESS

~ The Skazka Fairy Tales ~

A Beauty and the Beast Retelling

THE SCARLET ROSE

Valia Lind

For Queens of the Quill,
Thank you for always inspiring me

NOTE FROM THE AUTHOR

You may wonder why I decided to write a retelling of the Russian Beauty and the Beast fairytale. The answer is quite simple: it's the fairy tale I grew up on. It's my heritage, the Skazka of my childhood.

My mama has always encouraged me to read, and these fairy tales were the stories that were introduced to me at an early age. I grew up in St. Petersburg, Russia, and I remember spending time in our apartment, devouring every story I could get my hands on.

The Russian fairy tales are what taught me about magic. They're the ones that opened my eyes to the possibilities. So, I wanted to bring that to you, dear reader.

This story is inspired by the original material but also by my own life. There are pieces of my childhood woven into the pages of this book as I bring the Russian culture to you within this story.

I have included a glossary of Russian words at the end of the book for your convenience.

I hope you love this story as much as I do, and I hope it can bring a little magic into your life.

With much love,

Valia

He had listened by their gate
   Whither he'd been led by fate,
   And the words that he heard last
   Made his heart with love beat fast.

                  — ALEXANDER PUSHKIN

PROLOGUE

GAVRIIL

On the warmest night of Autumn, when the breeze was full of laughter and music, the prince of the wolf kingdom was cursed.

I used to think my father's influence created walls too high for spells and curses to penetrate. As it turns out, believing something doesn't make it true. I didn't know my fate that evening. I couldn't have planned for what came next.

"Gavriil, pay attention," my father, the king of *Volkoyskova Korolevsta*, snaps, bringing my attention back to him. I've been staring out over the courtyard as the castle prepares for a revel. A sense of foreboding reaches toward me through the open window.

"You are not listening. We have to strike fast. The land north of us is prime for the taking. I need you to lead the assault."

"Must we truly do this now, Father? I have been on the road for days, and need some rest." I turn to face him. He crosses the room in the blink of an eye. His hand is on my cheek, backhanding me before I can sidestep him. Not that I would. The sting of his slap is much less painful than the sting of his whip.

"You will do as you are told. I did not raise you to be a weakling."

I take a step back from him, curling my hand into a fist to keep it from reaching toward my tingling cheek. That would be a sign of weakness. I am to take whatever punishment he deems best with my back straight and my head held high.

"After the revel, you are to take an army to the borders of *Vodnovo Tsarstva,* and you are to seize it. By whatever means necessary."

He doesn't wait for a reply. Pivoting on his heels, he leaves me alone with his commands. I take a deep breath, turning to glance out the window once more.

My father has always been a hard man, but even more so in the last twenty years, since he decided to pillage and conquer our corner of Skazka. He has raided countless villages, murdered more creatures residing in the magical forest than I knew existed, yet, he wants more.

When Skazka fell to the rule of Baba Yaga years ago, there was no order. My father made sure to take the opportunity such anarchy created for him.

He has raised me to be his shadow, his sword when he's too busy to swing it. I'm the harbinger of death to every person and creature in these parts. The forest of Skazka is alive with creatures of folktales and dreams. Since my father began his conquest, it has also become a forest full of nightmares.

"There you are." The soft voice comes from the doorway, and I turn to watch my half-sister walk into the room. *Princessa* Larisa is here for the revel, sent by her kingdom to act as a liaison. She's beautiful and fair and good, the complete opposite of who I am. Especially of who I've become.

"He's ordered me to go after the water kingdom," I say by way of greeting. I watch my sister's features darken. She hates him as much as I do, but at least she's allowed to.

"You don't have to do this, Gavriil," she says, but I'm already shaking my head.

"You know I do. We're not kids anymore, Larisa. We can't just hide in the garden until his wrath has passed."

"When you are king—"

"What then?" I turn on her, my voice full of bitterness and anger. "You think I can fix all the damage I've done?" Larisa has always seen the good in me, but I doubt there's any left after the orders I've followed. "The land bleeds and weeps and magic seeps from it. Creatures are in hiding, villages are suffering. I can't undo decades of wrong."

"But you can try." Larisa reaches for me then, her gentle fingers squeezing my upper arm. I wish her faith in me was justified. But I know better. While I was busy trying to keep myself alive, I became my father. Not in looks, but in my soul. I have become the very thing I hated most.

Larisa opens her mouth to say something else, but then there is a loud bang and the whole foundation of the castle shakes.

"What was that?"

"I don't know." I grab her hand and tug her behind me. We reach the stairs, and Yevgenii, my captain of the guard, is there with his second in command.

"Your Highness, we need to get you to safety," he says, but I'm already shaking my head.

"Take *Princessa* Larisa." I push her gently toward Dina. The woman steps up immediately to usher Larisa down the stairs.

"Gavriil."

"I'll be fine. Yevgenii, come with me."

We leave the women behind as another boom shakes the castle. Paintings rattle in their golden frames, a chandelier swings overhead. My feet carry me toward the grand staircase and when I reach the top, my eyes zero in on my father.

He stands at the foot of the stairs with some of his guards spread out around the main entrance. But what draws my eyes is the strikingly beautiful woman in the midst of it all. She seems to carry her own wind as it ruffles her hair and clothes. The very fabric of her dress seems to glow, an otherworldly magical glow that is blinding and beautiful at the same time.

Suddenly, her eyes find mine, and I'm frozen at the top of the stairs as her lips curl up in a sinister smile.

"There is your pride and joy now." Her voice is melodic and mesmerizing. I find myself moving down the stairs before I can stop myself. "A king is nothing without his kingdom. But what is a king without his weapon?" she asks.

I narrow my eyes at her riddle, trying to chase the fog away from my mind. But I can't seem to look away from her. I can't control my impulse of growing closer.

"This is between you and me, you old hag. Your quarrel is with me."

My father's description makes no sense when thrown at the beautiful creature in front of me. Suddenly, I'm on the main floor, and she's in front of me as if she materialized there. My father yells something, but I can't hear anything as I stare into her pitch black eyes.

She runs her hands over my face before walking around me like she's circling her prey.

"Beautiful boy with a hardened heart. Can we make what is inside appear on the outside?" She laughs then, a cackle that sounds like an old dog dying. It sends a chill down my spine. I will myself to move out of her grasp, but I can't. As I tear my gaze from her, I realize, no one can move. Yevgenii is somewhere behind me, frozen, just like my father.

"What an interesting dilemma. A boy with a beautiful face and a dangerous mind. *Ya bi tebya pokushala.*"

A chill creeps over my skin as her words wash over me. "I would eat you." At that moment, I know exactly who she is. Baba Yaga, the nightmare of children's stories, the very same creature who feasts on innocent flesh and drinks chaos like blueberry chai.

She runs a finger down my cheek before she steps closer and licks where her finger made a path. I shudder but can do nothing else. "Alas, this is a different kind of game. One you will enjoy far less."

She steps back then, and without a word, raises her hands straight into the air. The breeze she carries with her becomes a tornado, sweeping through the hallways, dancing all around us. I can't seem to breathe as the air is

5

sucked right from my lungs. Then a roar like I've never heard before sounds all around me. My eyes find my father as he screams. I can't reconcile what I'm seeing. His body slowly turns to stone, he screams in pain as his flesh hardens.

Baba Yaga is suddenly at my ear, her voice whispering over the maddening wind and the screaming.

"You are his pride and joy, but you are not him.
If your heart can be turned, you will be saved.
But time will pass in agony.
Your days will be filled with pain.
He will suffer as you suffer.
And when he crumbles, you will become a beast.
Do not despair, princeling.
There is hope in this spell.
If you find the one who turns your heart,
All will be well."

My mind fills with all the lessons from my childhood, of witches and *volshebnits* and curses cast. The magic of her words spreads around her like a blanket, reaching toward every corner that I can see.

A different kind of a chill travels up my spine, the curse weaving its way into my blood.

My body shakes, tightening my skin and stretching out my limbs. What looks like fur appears and disappears over my hands in quick succession. I drop to my knees, screaming at the change happening inside of me.

Through the pain, I find what's left of my father. He's an already crumbling statue made of stone. There's no doubt in my mind. The moment he crumbles, the curse will be complete, and I will be dead.

The woman cackles once more, pulling my attention to her, spinning and spinning and spinning. A mortar appears beneath her, taking her away, until the wind and the magic are gone, and I am left alone in the hall.

The horror of what transpired grips my heart, hopelessness filling the empty space around me. I was a monster before the curse, and now, a visual representation of it is left on my skin. I am left all alone with an unbreakable curse upon my kingdom. If I must find the one who can turn my heart, there is no end in sight. For who is brave enough to turn the heart of a monster?

❧ I ❧

As usual, my day is starting off with a fight.

"You can't seriously be wearing that, Nikita," Masha comments, glaring at my outfit. I glance down at my black pants before meeting her eye.

"What's wrong with it?"

"Everything. This is a party. Can't you, for a second, pretend to be a girl?"

"I don't have to pretend. I am a girl. But that doesn't mean I have to dress like you."

My sisters are in new dresses. Masha is in a green one, Olga in pink. They like bright colors and lace and flowers. And showing way too much skin, which is fine. For them. I love dresses as well, but only when I choose to wear them, not because it's expected of me. Masha and Olga are two years apart, but they resemble each other as if they were proper twins. Their brown hair is professionally styled to fall around their shoulders in big waves, the highlights

9

make them look sun kissed and ready for fun. My long brown hair is up in a high ponytail, as usual.

"You are hopeless. We have an image to uphold."

"What is this? 1700s Russia?" My sister rolls her eyes. "It's the 21st century, Masha. I'm wearing a tailored blouse and black dress pants. I look professional and nice. Look, I even put on my heels. "

"Those are not heels. They're wedges."

I'm not sure why I'm even bothering to defend myself. Masha and Olga are two peas in a pod while I'm a random weed that decided to grow in their garden. That's actually a pretty good analogy, since neither of my sisters can stand me. They'd pluck me right out of their garden if they could.

"You look like you're going to a business meeting," Olga comments, walking back into the room while putting in her earring. Her neck-breaking heels echo against the hardwood floor.

"Perfect then, considering this is a business party."

I'm pretty sure they've forgotten that part. They heard "party" and that's all that mattered. But this is important for our papa. Especially considering how tense the dealings with the magical world have been lately.

I'm still trying to wrap my mind around the magic part. It's only been a year since papa told us, but it's still too fresh in my mind. Especially since I haven't seen any physical evidence. I like my facts like I like my shoes. Sturdy and tried. My sisters may hate my wedged booties, but if I need to run, I am more than capable. My shoes make me feel powerful when I walk into a room. Considering I need all the confidence I can muster up, they're helpful.

"You are hopeless," Masha gives up, making me grin. She'd probably have a coronary if she knew about the concealed knife at my lower back, under the shirt. I've always felt safer with a weapon, and since this party is one hundred percent a front for the organization members to get together, I'm not leaving anything up to chance. But I don't say any of that, I simply say, "Thanks!"

I think I'm about to get another talking to as Masha opens her mouth when papa walks in. He's wearing a dark grey suit, his hair slicked back at the temples. It's getting a little long at the top. We'll have to get him a haircut soon. I know for a fact that he's carrying a weapon as well. After all, he's the one who taught me to be cautious. When his eyes meet mine, I know he likes my outfit.

"Ladies, shall we?"

WHEN WE ARRIVE AT THE HOUSE, IT TAKES ME A MOMENT to take it in. Many of the Bratva syndicate members have multiple houses and move more often than not. This is a new-to-me house, and I have to admit, it's a beauty.

The brick structure is dark, contrasting against the white and gray trim around the windows. The staircase that leads up to the front door is built for royalty. From what I know of architecture, it looks like a Neo-gothic style, leaning heavily into the decorative patterns and lancet windows. These types of homes aren't usually for the public, as many of them around Moscow and St. Petersburg have become museums or public houses. If I were to make a guess, I'd say our host paid a pretty *ruble* to make this a private property.

There's a valet at the bottom of the stairs. He takes our car as we make our way up to the double doors. My sisters loop their arms through papa's so they have someone to hold onto as they wobble on their heels. I bring up the rear. Honestly, I'm good with not being escorted in. It gives me a chance to study the people as we step inside. My sisters know how to make an entrance, and I don't miss the appreciative looks thrown their way. I also don't miss the holsters of guns peeking out from the suit jackets of nearly every man we pass. I'm definitely not the only one who came prepared.

A butler waits at the front doors, leading the guests into what appears to be a ballroom. The room is large, with high ceilings and floor to crown molding wallpaper. A huge chandelier hangs overhead, the crystals sparkling in the light. Even though Moscow has had modern electricity for years, these people went for ambiance. There are candles lit along every wall, the flames making the golden sconces sparkle just like the chandelier.

The hosts of the party, Mr. and Mrs. Balakin, greet people as they enter the ballroom. I was kidding earlier about this being 1700s Russia, but now I'm thinking I was right on the money. These people are all about presentation. Proper presentation creates the kind of atmosphere they can control. Right now, that atmosphere consists of them presenting themselves as the most powerful.

"Artur Ivanovich, welcome to our home," Mr. Balakin greets us, shaking my papa's hand. "Ladies, beautiful as usual." Each of my sisters receive a kiss on the hand and cheek and a bright smile. When I step up for my turn, I put out my hand first, diverting the typical kiss on a cheek to a handshake. Mr. Balakin doesn't hesitate to oblige with a small smile.

"Nikita, always a pleasure."

There's a part of me that knows he's simply humoring me. I don't miss the way he doesn't use my patronymic name—Arturovna— the formal form of address and a show of respect in our culture. Most of my papa's associates see me as someone who only plays at being a businesswoman— a term they use loosely in the organization to keep a sense of mystery about them. But that's okay with me. They underestimate me, and it makes me work that much harder to prove them wrong.

"You have a beautiful home," I say, because it's expected of me. Since they have moved in recently, the compliment I give is an appropriate one. Not that anything I say is pleasing to them. Mrs. Balakin smiles at me, but there's no warmth in it. Both of them have already dismissed me. Mrs. Balakin's attention is on my sisters now.

"Masha, darling, you will be happy to hear that Ilya is home from his travels. He is most eager to see you."

I watch my sister's face as she tries to keep the excitement to a minimum. Her one goal in life is to marry rich, and Ilya Balakin is one of the richest. Clearly, I'm not the only businesswoman in the family because my sister has the perfect expression on her face. Just excited enough, yet aloof. It truly is an art. Mrs. Balakin looks thrilled. She whisks Masha away as Olga gets distracted by the dance floor. Because of course there's a dance floor. And a slew of young, scrappy, gentlemen wanting to dance with my fun-loving sister. That truly is the only difference between Masha and Olga. My oldest sister is here to ensnare a rich husband, Olga simply wants to dance with as many people as she can.

"Artur Ivanovich, whenever you're ready."

I'm close enough to hear the quiet words directed at my papa. He glances at me to give me the tiniest of nods.

We have this system down to a science. He'll head off with Balakin first, with me taking a walk about the room to see if anyone is whispering anything we should be aware of. There always seems to be a rush of gossip anytime the top members of the Bratva exit the room. After I do the recon, no one truly pays attention to me, I follow papa to the meeting.

Even though cell phones and computers are a part of our lives, The Bratva likes to keep their important documents handwritten. Every contract is signed in person for maximum intimidation. It's why these meetings happen like this, disguised as parties or family dinners.

I move off, walking slowly but purposefully around the dance floor. The room houses a hundred bodies easily. There is a buffet to one side, against the wall, and a few tables set up near them against the adjacent one. Most of these events have a formal dinner, but once in a while, they forgo the dinner and have only a buffet. No matter the type of a party, there must be food.

"If it isn't Nikita Arturovna." The voice comes from over my shoulder. I turn slowly, coming face to face with none other than Ilya Balakin.

"Are you trying to suck up to me?" I say, instead of a

greeting, which earns me a broad grin. I don't miss him using my patronymic name. He's the only one who ever does. His eyes glitter now as he looks down at me. The man is handsome, and he knows it.

"Always."

"Shouldn't you be over there smooching it up with my sister?"

"Ah, come on, *milaya*. You know I enjoy your company much more." I hate his use of the endearing nickname. We have never been anything but two rivals, but he has a tendency to talk to me like I'm one of his weekend girls. He's had plenty.

"Don't let my sister hear you say that," I mumble. I never understood Masha's obsession with Ilya. To me, he's just like any other boy toy walking around here, not big enough for his breeches. Then again, he is set to inherit the lead chair in the organization when his father steps down. His attitude just comes with the position I suppose.

"What do you say, should we give this dance floor a whirl?"

"No, we most certainly should not." This time I make sure I speak loud enough for him to hear it. There's no teasing in my voice, just cold rejection, but he isn't deterred.

"Come on, Niki. Live a little." I roll my eyes as he lowers his voice, adding an extra layer of flirtiness to it. "Give Ilya a smile, why don't you?"

My eyes grow completely cold at his misogynistic comment, and I'm moving back before he realizes what I'm doing. He reaches for my hand. I can tell by his predatory stare that he's not about to take a no for an answer.

There's a reason I won't be found alone with Ilya in a room. Well, maybe if I had my knife on me.

I sidestep him like a pro.

"A little rejection is good for the soul, Ilya," I call out before I move, putting a throng of dancing people between us. Even while we were talking, I kept listening for any gossip. Unfortunately, I heard nothing of interest. Without a backward look, I'm by the side door and through it. He always assumes I'm playing hard to get, considering no one has ever said no to him. I have to make sure I keep my guard up, in case he tries something later.

A corridor opens up in front of me with a door to the left and a door to the right. I don't have to wonder which way they went. What gives it away are the two goons standing at the third door, a little ways from the ballroom. They're in dark suits, also armed for battle. I notice a small gun holster on one leg, the pant leg scrunched up around it a bit.

"Hello, boys," I greet them. "My father is expecting me."

I try to move past, but they block the path.

"No one is allowed."

"Didn't you just hear what I said? My father, Artur Ivanovich is expecting me."

"He's expecting his son." This conversation has happened before because papa has a tendency to use my nickname. The goon grabs my arm roughly, ready to drag me away. But just like with Ilya, I know this dance. My hand grabs for my knife, yanking it out of the sheath. At the same time, I bring my knee into his groin, pushing him back against the wall. The knife comes up to his neck as I pin him in place, glancing at the other goon as he tries to move forward, but freezes, surprise clearly all over his face.

"Well, it's too bad my father only has daughters." I nearly growl, enjoying the shock on the goons' faces. "Nikita "Nik" Arturovna Belenova at your service." I see the moment the goons make a connection. I drop my hands, taking a step back, a small smile on my face. "Step aside."

They do not hesitate to move, letting me slip in quietly. The room is shrouded in shadows and cigar smoke, a staple in any syndicate member's office. The dark furniture, brown and leather, is pushed in between the bookshelves that cover the walls all around me. A movement on the desk catches my attention, but it's there and gone before I can register what I saw. At first, I swear it's a tiny doll-like creature, hovering over the open notebook. But it can't be. Living doll-like creatures don't exist, and they certainly don't fly. The noxious cigar smoke must be distorting my senses.

I sheath my weapon as my eyes narrow on my father. He's sitting in front of the desk, his legs crossed in his most nonchalant pose. But I see his shoulders are tense. There are two other businessmen present, and then there's Mr. Balakin behind the desk. No one pays me any attention.

"It's a dangerous way to go, but it's our only option," Mr. Balakin says.

"Skazka isn't a welcoming place, Sasha." One of the men speaks, but I can't see his face from where I'm leaning against the wall, concealed by the shadows.

"We don't have a choice, Pavel." There's sharpness to

Balakin's words. In that one sentence, I can see just how desperate he's become. Whatever situation he has gotten himself into, it affects all of us. That means someone will have to pay the price, and there is no way it will be Balakin. His position allows him to pick on those below him, to do his bidding and take the hits.

My papa's job would probably be best described as a merchant. He moves products across our realm and that of Skazka—a magical realm full of fairytales and nightmares. A place I didn't even know existed until last year. What kind of product and who exactly he deals with has been a mystery to me since the day I started dealing with the ledgers. Everything is in code. The only thing I truly know is that we're deep within the syndicate. My mama's medical bills, coupled with my sisters' love for a rich lifestyle, has put us in the red. He's been doing his best to keep us afloat, but it's not enough. When I take his place in the syndicate, I will make some changes. It's not a life I would've planned for myself, but I will do whatever it takes to protect my family.

One day soon, he'll have to explain it to me. He took the first step when he finally came clean about where exactly he goes on his many travels. Until then, I didn't know magic was real. Truth be told, I'm still not one hundred percent convinced, considering I've never seen any tangible evidence. Or been there.

When my sisters found out, they made a list of a million things they wanted papa to bring back. I simply want his safe return. Every time.

"It's Artur's turn." The voice pulls me out of my musings, and I focus on my papa. That's why he looks so tense. They take turns going into Skazka, since it's not exactly a 'buy a plane ticket and spend a few hours at the airport kind of a trip.' As far as I understand it, it involves a deal with a magical creature and a portal. And of course, the syndicate has those on demand. I don't even want to know what kind of bargain was struck to make that happen.

"Then it's his decision."

"No, it's not!" Balakin stands suddenly, slapping his hands on the table. My stomach drops, the dread rising. "He goes, that's final. *Ne spoirit!*"

Balakin isn't simply concerned, he's nervous. Whatever part of Skazka he's sending my papa, it's not a place he would want to go. I glance over at my father and find his eyes on me. For the first time since my mama died, I see something there—something I didn't think I'd ever see in my papa: fear.

✿ 2 ✿

"They can't truly make you go!" It's the next day, and I'm pacing in papa's study while he goes over some paperwork on his computer. Thankfully, while papa's study is a close replica of Balakin's, with its dark furniture and floor to ceiling bookshelves, there's no cigar smoke to irritate my eyes.

Papa pushes a few more buttons on the computer, before sparing me a glance. I've finally convinced him to keep at least some of our contacts and information logged digitally, even though the rest is pen and paper. I glance at the phone sitting silently on the desk, wishing it would ring and tell us that papa can stay. I hardly slept last night, tossing and turning and trying to get the fear I saw in papa's eyes out of my mind.

"You know they can, *dochenka*. I work for them, not the other way around."

"It's not fair. If the land is as unsettled as you say it is, then it's too dangerous."

Last night, I wouldn't leave my papa's study until he explained to me exactly what was happening.

Apparently, Skazka has been going through a few power struggles lately. The land north, *Zeleyonoe Tsartsvo*, along with *Holodnoye Korolevstvo*, are ruled by a fair and kind queen, but only recently. The rest of Skazka is in uproar. Some kingdoms are completely in chaos, missing their rulers and any sense of what is up and down. Of course, as luck would have it, those are the kingdoms closest to the trading routes.

"You seriously just told me there's a bandit king, or whatever you want to call him, and his many minions are pillaging the land, and you're going into it like nothing is the matter? Because sure, there's no way you'll be attacked on the road or taken prisoner or get eaten alive by one of those magical nightmares I've been reading about. And you can't even take your gun because the portal nullifies it. *Da.* This is totally fine."

I'm out of breath as I finish my rant. Papa watches me quietly before getting up from his seat and walking over to me. Taking my hands, he leads us to the couch near the windows. I don't understand how he's so calm when I feel like my heart is going to explode out of my chest.

"*Dochenka*, I see you've been reading up on Russian fairytale lore. But you need not worry about your old man. I have been through many of these journeys over the years, and I've come away unscathed. It's why Sasha will send me into Skazka, when he won't send anyone else. He knows I can handle myself."

"I know, Papa. But—now that I know where you go on these journeys—it's a place I can't follow."

"You don't have to take care of everyone, Nikitochka," he says, squeezing my hands.

"Maybe not. But I do take care of you."

"Just like your mama" He smiles, that sad kind of smile that is reserved only for Mama.

I was barely five years old when she passed away. I don't remember her like Masha and Olga do, but I do remember that she loved Papa deeply, and he loved her. He still does.

"I'll take care of things on this end," I finally say. He reaches over to bring me into his arms.

"What a strong and smart girl you are, *dochenka*." He whispers the words into my hair, and I cling to him for a brief moment before I pull back. This feels too much like a goodbye, and we don't say those to each other.

"It's time."

⚜

WE LEAVE THE STUDY BEHIND AFTER PAPA MAKES SURE I have all the necessary logins; in case something comes up. I don't remind him that I already run most of his business on paper. He needs to appear in control as much as I need to see him presented as such. He's right, I have been reading up on Skazka lore since finding out the land is real. Not that many Russian libraries hold the "History of Skazka" in their stock, but what they do have are fairy tales. Since the land is filled with the creatures from every page of those fairy tales, they're as close to a history book as I can get. Knowing what kind of creatures lurk in the forest of Skazka does not put my mind at ease.

"Papa, we have requests!" Masha power walks into the

foyer with Olga close on her heels. Today they're dressed in more of their flowy dresses with their signature colors of green and pink. Also, as usual, their shoulders are exposed, and while the skirts are full around their legs, the slit Masha sports on the left side leaves little to the imagination.

"Seriously, he's going off into a near war, and you want presents?" I snap, but papa places a hand on my shoulder.

"It's okay, Nik. It is my custom to bring something back, you know this."

"I know it, but I don't like it," I grumble, receiving a hatred-filled glare from Masha before she turns her eyes to papa. One of these days, Masha will poison my dinner, I have no doubt.

"I've thought about it, and I think the best gift you could bring me is a golden tiara. I saw one of the girls wearing one at the party, and it was all the rage. It would look stunning with my green gown for the New Year's party."

Papa doesn't even bat an eye.

"Of course, Masha."

"Oh, Papa!" Olga steps up, clearly encouraged by Masha's outrageous demand and papa's acceptance of it. "I would like a crystal mirror. You know, one of those hand-held beauties, adorned with the purest crystals around the glass? I heard Skazka carries loads of them, and everyone has one."

"Well, if everyone has one." My anger is really growing with each request. Olga also throws a glare my way, but I simply roll my eyes.

"No problem, Olga," Papa replies, because of course he

does. He is a good father and will always go out of his way to please his children. He's always been like that. I just wish my sisters didn't take advantage of him like they do. It's what got us into a lot of our debt in the first place.

"Ah! Perfect!" Olga nearly squeals, rushing over to give papa a kiss on the cheek. Then she's out of the room. Masha follows suit with a kiss on the cheek, and a brief, "safe travels!" Before she's also gone.

"Well," Papa turns to me, as I hand him a coat. He smiles at my preparedness. "What is it that you want from this trip?"

"For you to return safely to us."

"Nikita." He shakes his head, shrugging his coat on. "Always the selfless one. What if I told you that bringing you a gift makes me happy? Would you ask for one then?"

"That was sneaky," I reply, folding my arms in front of me as I pout at my papa.

"Who do you think you get it from?" He taps his finger on my nose like he used to do when I was only a toddler running around here. The feeling of foreboding suddenly crashes over me like a wave, but I don't let it show.

"Fine. Bring me back—a flower. The most beautiful scarlet flower you come across. That will be enough for me."

And that would mean that when he has found the flower, he would be on his way home, to deliver it before it wilts. He smiles, as if he knows exactly what I'm doing, but I don't care.

"Wish me good luck?"

I step to my tippy toes and place a kiss on his cheek, just like is our custom.

"Look after your sisters, Nikitochka," he says before he leans over to place a soft kiss on my forehead. "I'll be seeing you soon."

Then, he pulls his coat tightly around himself, opens the front door, and leaves.

3

It's been nearly a week and no word from Papa. I've contacted all his known associates, including Mr. Balakin, but he's been screening my calls. Just another way to undermine my position in the Bratva.

"Would you stop worrying so much? You'll get wrinkles," Masha calls out from her spot on the couch. She's watching some reality television show while Olga sits beside her, painting Masha's nails. That's right ladies and gents, my oldest sister is so lazy she can't even do her own nails.

"Oh, you mean I'll look like you?" I reply, which earns me a gasp.

"I do not have wrinkles!"

"Have you looked in the mirror lately?"

"Nikita Belenova, you—"

But I've already stopped listening to her. The only person who can tell me anything about my papa is refusing to answer my inquiries. There's possibly a way I could get around that, but that involves me calling the one person I'd really rather not. I check my phone again. There's nothing. It seems I have no choice. I've purposely blocked and then deleted his number, which means I need to ask Masha for it. She's about to hate me even more than she does already.

"Masha, I need your phone."

"What? No! First you insult me and then you need me? That's not how this works."

"What do you mean? That's exactly how sisterhood works. Now, please. Your phone."

"Who exactly are you calling?"

Ugh, she's not going to like this.

"Ilya."

"What?" Her voice goes up an octave as Olga groans.

"You're ruining your nails," my middle sister whines.

"Well, Nikita is ruining my relationship with Ilya! She can't be calling him. He already pays her way too much attention."

"He only does so because I refuse to acknowledge his advances. You should try not falling all over yourself in front of him, and I bet you he'll be right over."

Masha opens her mouth to protest, but then stops herself. She knows I'm right. Ilya doesn't want me. He wants to conquer a prize. That's all it is for boys like him. Rich, spoiled, and Masha's perfect type.

"I promise to mention how much you are not interested in him if you give me his number," I say. This time, Masha hands her phone over. Quickly, I dial on my phone before giving hers back to her and step out of the room.

"Make sure you don't mention me!" she calls out. I only roll my eyes. She's so obsessed with getting her claws into Ilya she forgot for a second that she hates me.

"Hello?" Ilya answers on the second ring, and I can only assume he still has my number in his phone.

"Hello, Ilya."

"Color me surprised, Nikita. I thought someone had stolen your phone, or you were held against your will. It's neither of those, right?"

"Sorry to disappoint, but no, I don't need a knight in shining armor right now."

"Dang it. I look so good in armor, atop a white horse."

I shake my head, thankful he can't see the look on my face. I'm pretty sure my hatred for him is on full display. And I most definitely would like to punch him in the face, as usual. But I'm not here to burn bridges. I need his help.

"Ilya, I need a favor."

"Ah, of course. Always the businesswoman." But there's a smile in his voice as he says it, so I have hope.

"Papa has been gone for a week. Is there a way you can see if your father has heard from him?" It's difficult not to sound desperate, but I manage. Somehow.

"As far as I know, there haven't been any reports from Skazka."

"And how much do you know?" It's a fair question, considering I have no idea where he stands within his father's dealings. My papa didn't tell me about this magical world until recently. I suppose there's a sense of maturity the children have to reach before such a secret can be shared. From what papa has told me, the realm of Skazka guards the secrets of our realm as well. Not everyone is privy to the knowledge that there are portals available to travel between worlds.

"I've been in on all of his meetings."

That surprises me, but maybe it shouldn't. After all, Balakin is grooming Ilya to take over his side of the business. Ilya is his only son, although from what I've been able to scout when it comes to the power struggle within the syndicate, Ilya may be taking over the business sooner rather than later. He's power hungry and ambitious enough not to be patient. Considering I have no idea what has Balakin so spooked, I can't predict the outcome of this battle between father and son. I have no doubt there will be one.

"Thanks, Ilya," I say now, ready to hang up.

"Wait, hold up, Nikita. That's it? That's all I get?"

I nearly groan into the receiver, but I think he'd enjoy that a little too much.

"What else is there?"

"Come to the club with me."

Why am I not even surprised he asked? The Club is the one place in town where all the richest of the rich hang out. It's much like anyone would expect one of these places to be. Glamorous outfits, expensive drinks, strobing lights, and loud music. I've been once, even though I'm not allowed until I turn eighteen, which is happening in two weeks. But even so, I have absolutely no desire to go.

"Ilya, I'm really not in the mood to party right now."

"Come on, *milaya*, it'll take your mind off things."

The way he says that—as if my father is just a thing—

solidifies the fact that Ilya and I will never see eye to eye on important matters. He'd probably leave my papa rotting in Skazka if it was beneficial to him. On the business side of things, I have to keep him as an ally, so I can't exactly go off on him. But it still makes my blood boil.

"I think my sister is calling me, I have to go. Thanks again." I hang up before he can say anything else.

Giving myself a moment to feel, I lean against the wall, hand over my heart. My stomach is in knots as every terrible possibility of what could have happened to papa races through my mind. Sometimes, having a vivid imagination is a curse because I can picture a million ways fairy tale creatures can rip him to pieces. He has never been gone for more than two days without contact. Now that I know he goes to Skazka, and that's not the hindrance—traveling to another realm—I'm not sure what the problem could be. Because there clearly is one.

I take a few more breaths, doing my best to stay calm. There's no point in panicking. My next step has to be to go see Balakin in person. Most likely, he'll refuse to see me, but I can be inventive when necessary. Stepping away from the wall, I turn to the mirror next to me. My hair is slicked back in its usual high ponytail, my eyes haunted from worry and lack of sleep. I do a quick assessment of the rest, deciding that the dark jeans, mustard yellow sweater, and my boots are presentable enough for a meeting with the head of Bratva.

Before I can take two steps toward the front door, a scream shatters the quiet air. I rush into the living room to find my sisters staring at something on the other side of the couch. They're holding onto each other for dear life.

My heart quickens as I slowly approach the dark blob. That's when I see it's not a blob at all. The material is pulled back, and I find our father in a crouch on the floor wrapped tightly in his coat. He glances up at me, and my heart nearly shatters. There are tears in his eyes, and in his hand is a single scarlet rose.

❧ 4 ❧

I help him to the couch before thrusting a warm cup of tea into his hands. It takes a while before he seems like himself again. He sips the tea as I place another blanket over his shoulders.

"Papa, what happened?" I ask, crouching in front of him. The color has returned to his skin, and he looks a little better overall. "Where have you been?"

At first, I don't think he'll speak. He seems shell-shocked. So am I, to be honest. For the first time since I found out about Skazka, I saw evidence of the magic it carries. I'll have to dissect that later. I watch as papa thinks for a long, tense minute. Then the words pour out of him in the same way mine do when I'm overly stimulated.

"I was attacked on the way back to the portal. There are paths marked for travelers such as me, and the bandits knew about them. Of course they did. The land is not stable. They wanted my things, but I wouldn't go down without a fight. They chased me into the forest, far from the marked path, and when I lost them, I lost my way back as well. I wandered and wandered and then I stumbled onto the most beautiful of castles, deep in the Skazka forest—"

"A castle?" Masha interrupts, leaning forward. She and Olga have been sitting quietly on the love seat, staring at our papa like they've never seen him before. I'm still trying to wrap my mind around the fact that he appeared out of thin air. I suppose they are too. They haven't seen real magic at play, only been told about it. All three of us are riveted by papa's words.

"A castle, Masha, like I've never seen. There are gardens all around it, so different than the forest I left behind. Somehow, frozen in time. But then, there, in the midst of the trees and the bushes, was a garden of roses. Vines and vines of them, thriving in a nearly dead place." He pauses, his eyes finding mine. "The most beautiful scarlet flowers I have ever seen."

"Oh, Papa." My chest growths heavy with emotion as I glance over at where the flower sits inside of a small glass. It looks magical, as if it holds a piece of Skazka within its petals. I want to hate it on sight, but I can't deny its beauty.

"When I reached for one of the roses, a roar as terrible as a dark night filled the air, and he was upon me. A beast and a man, both and neither. Stuck somewhere in between."

"What are you talking about?" Olga says.

"A cursed creature, like I've never imagined before. He took me into his dungeons, called me a thief, which I suppose I am. Sentenced me to servitude, doomed to live at the castle."

"For a single rose?" That comes from Masha. I too have a million questions, but I'm not sure where to start. I suppose a good place would be at the knowledge I now know for myself.

Magic is real.

That wasn't some code the organization put together to protect its secrets. It wasn't an inside joke, or a way to control people with the fear of the unknown. It's actually something that exists. I have no idea how to feel about that.

"The magical world is a cruel place, Masha." Papa's words bring my attention back to him. "The creatures who live there are made up of darkness and fear. You remember those old stories, passed down for generations."

"Papa, you can't mean sorceresses and spells and such?" I ask, remembering all the research I've done on the realm of Skazka recently. Some stories I remembered from childhood, but many were forgotten over time.

"I absolutely do!" He turns to me, his eyes bright with excitement or fear, I can't tell. "They're cruel creatures, cunning and sneaky. They'll take you for all you're worth."

"Papa." I take his hand in mine, trying to calm him. "How did you get away?"

He doesn't respond right away, and I feel that dread setting in once more.

"Papa?"

"I didn't."

There's a moment of silence, as we all try to wrap our minds around that one. If he didn't escape, that means he was let go. But if what he's saying is true, that wouldn't come without a price.

"What did it require?" I ask, surprised my voice comes out steady. Masha and Olga are completely useless at this point as they simply sit and stare at our father. I don't blame them. They're not the ones who've been making the difficult choices for this family for years. They see the glitz and the glamour, but I see the hard truth. I know how the business world works. A decision must benefit both parties or the contract won't be drawn. What is life if not a business transaction?

"Please don't tell me you made a bargain with one of the creatures?" I speak low, watching my father for a response. I know I guessed right the moment the words leave my mouth. I've read about bargains and riddles, ways innocent people find themselves in the snares of magic. "Papa, what did you do?"

"I was only given leniency to return to say goodbye. I snuck that stipulation in before accepting the bargain." He sounds more like his old self just then, a businessman making a deal. "I am to return, in nychthemeron, after my affairs are handled."

"A day? He gave you a day?" Masha exclaims, standing up in outrage.

"Girls, my precious girls. You will be okay. Nikita has the business side handled. You will want for nothing."

"I don't want Nikita! I want you! Who will escort me to the formal outings? How will I ever find a husband with no father figure to parade me around? You are supposed to be here. I deserve to be part of that world, and I can't do that without you."

Of course she's thinking about herself. Olga is whining that she'll never see the world now, and all I want to do is scream at them to shut up. Anger rises up inside of me, but papa knows me better than anyone. He holds my hand, and in turn, me in place. I feel a pressure against my skin, and I glance down to see an unfamiliar ring on his pointer finger.

"I have brought you the gifts you requested." Papa points to the satchel we left discarded in the middle of the floor. Immediately, the whining stops, and my sisters move to it at once. But I am more interested in the ring.

"What is this?"

Papa glances down, a dark shadow falling over his face. Even before he answers, I have an inkling.

"This is how I got here. A blood contract. I place this on my ring finger, and a portal carries me back to the castle. I am sworn into his service until the end of times."

None of this makes sense. Anger at this creature rises inside me to match the anger I feel for myself. If only I had asked for something else. I look over at my sisters as Masha places the tiara on her head, while Olga let's her admire it in the mirror. Such simple ambitions, and it was mine that ruined us.

"I don't understand." My eyes are still on the ring. "Why would he bind you like that?"

"It doesn't matter, *dochenka*. Tomorrow I will be gone, and you will take my place in the Bratva. I know it's not what you wanted." I go to protest, but he waves his hand. "It's what you want now, but I have put you into that position, and I am truly sorry you had to grow up a mafia protege. I am so proud of you, Nikitochka. Don't let anyone, ever, minimize your importance just because you aren't the head of the house or because you are younger than most. You will take care of your sisters, and you will take care of the business."

He's not really asking, but I nod my head anyway. He glances at my sisters, but my eyes drop back down to the ring. The shiny silver glitters up at me, as if it knows what I'm thinking. I give my father a quick squeeze on the hand, leaning over to place a quick kiss on his cheek. In that one movement, I take the ring with me. I rise to my feet, not giving myself a chance to think this through. I promised my mama years ago that I would do what's best for this family. As I am the youngest child, I think Mama thought I wouldn't remember my promise. But I've kept it, all these years. It's why I shadowed my papa to meetings, it's why I learned all I could about ledgers and contracts and how to handle a weapon, if the opportunity requires it.

I gave up my dreams of becoming a musician because I knew my papa needed me.

What I'm doing now is simply keeping that same promise.

"Nikita?" Papa is instantly on alert as I move away from him quickly, putting as much furniture between us as I can.

"A blood bargain, right?" I ask, with a small smile on my face. Papa's eyes drop to my hand. He jumps to his feet, tangled in the blankets.

"No!" He tries to get to me, but there's a table and chair between us now.

"Yes."

I place the ring on my finger and then the air ripples around me. My father's stricken face is the last thing I see.

There is a sense of coming apart, as if all my cells have detached from my body before they all spring back together again. I land on my hands and knees, gasping for air. My body is sore, as if I've come from a long workout. My head is heavy. No offense to magic, but I think I prefer a good old car or a plane for traveling.

As I force the air into my lungs, I push up onto my knees. Looking up, I find myself in what looks like a foyer, except it's probably bigger than my whole house. There's a door to my right, which leads outside, I'm sure. On the left is a set of stairs that lead up and spilt into two sections at the top. Each takes a path in opposite directions.

Pushing myself to my feet, I do a quick review of my body, but everything seems to be intact. Rearranging my shirt, I realize I don't have my knife on me. Well, this is a problem.

I look down at the ring as it sits comfortably in the

palm of my hand. I'm not sure when I took it off or if that's how it works once it's done performing its duty. Instead of placing it back on my ring finger, I follow my papa's example and put it on my pointer finger. I have no idea if this ring is still operational or not, but right now it doesn't matter. Even if I could leave, I'm not going to. I have a debt to settle with my papa's jailer.

First, I need to find him.

I do another quick three-sixty, my eyes cataloguing the plethora of windows that seem to make up one side of the foyer. As I take a step closer, I notice the golden trim running along the walls and framing each glass pane. The color is dull somehow, as if the gold has forgotten how to shine.

The place seems to be completely deserted.

Ignoring the huge marble staircase for now, I decide to stay on the ground floor as I begin my exploration.

I walk down one of the corridors and notice how everything is in shadows. Heavy spiderwebs and dust cling to every surface. Large windows adorn one side of the hallways, providing a tiny amount of light. The curtains are drawn, exposing a darkened landscape beyond the castle. Taking a step toward the window, I try to make out what surrounds the castle, but a heavy fog obscures my vision past a few feet. The curtains are floor to ceiling, at least nine meters up—30 feet, I correct myself instantly. I've been dealing with some business overseas, and papa has made sure I can convert the metric system when necessary.

The thought of him brings a pang to my chest. I can feel tears welling up in my eyes, but I blink them away.

There is no way in this realm or my own that I'm going to show weakness here. I'll find time to grieve later.

Making my way through the hallways, I'm amazed by how little light there is. There are dozens of sconces on the walls, lining the walkway. Typically, they would be lit. But they sit idle with no fire in sight. The only light I have to guide me is the small sliver of it that's coming in from the windows.

Overall, the decor isn't that different from what I find in great houses of Russia. There is framed art that covers the majority of the wall space, in between the doorways. Glancing inside, I can barely make out the shapes of the furniture, so I stay in the main hallway.

The only difference that jumps out at me are the floor decorations. Statues of people line the hallways, crowding around me as I walk. I stop near one, curious to see more. The lifelike quality to the design is fascinating. I've never seen anything like it. There are many of these, spread out across the whole hallway, as if there were actual people in this corridor and these statues are now representing them.

When I reach the next room, the door is open, and I can see a bit of light inside. It appears to be a typical sitting area. Couches are spread out strategically across the space and drink carts are pushed to the edges. A fire is lit in the fireplace, the only source of light. The walls are also covered in art and decorative molding, but I can't make out anything specific with the lack of light.

There are no windows in this room, but because it is a sitting room, it should open up to another. Stepping inside, I walk across the room, and yes, there's a door.

Instead of returning to the main hallways, I push the

door open. The moment I do, my breath catches. This looks more like a study, with floor to ceiling bookshelves all around the rectangular space. There is a lamp, just one, shining from a side table. That one piece of modern technology leaves me completely flabbergasted.

My feet shuffle toward it as I lean over to look at the bulb. The lamp may look modern, with a golden finished stand and a circular glass top, but instead of a lightbulb, a tiny flame burns within. The glow is multiplied by the glass. It makes this room feel enchanted and terrifying at the same time.

Carefully, I make my way toward the books, running my fingers over the spines. I've always loved books, and my papa has a collection that can rival anyone's. He brought home tomes of stories from every one of his travels. It's like a gift he gave to himself.

My mama loved to read. I think he continued the tradition to feel connected to her, even all these years. When I was younger, he read to me in his study. The curtains drawn and one candle burned on the windowsill, as if that candle was mama's spirit and she was there with us. Now, they're both gone.

Closing my eyes, I give myself a split second to feel it all before I shut it down. This is no place nor time to reminisce about what I've lost. Mentally, I know my papa isn't dead, but he might as well be, if I am to stay here for the remaining years of my life. This castle, with its dark hallways and unnatural fog, is too quiet and too alien.

But it doesn't matter. I chose this, I made the decision to come here. Papa is needed at home. He'll be able to take care of my sisters like I never would be. He's sacrificed so much for us already. I couldn't let him do this as well. Especially not when it's my fault he was in the predicament in the first place.

Making my way around the small library, I look for another exit. That's when I notice a sliver of light behind one of the bookshelves. I place my hands on the shelves, pulling them toward me. A hidden door swings open. The brightness in the new room is sudden and makes me squint. As my eyes adjust, I realize it's not even that bright, just a dozen lit candles, mostly situated on the opposite wall. But in comparison to the other rooms, it's like daylight.

This room is larger than the other two and emptier. My eyes find the one piece of furniture in the space. It's a piano. A familiar longing fills me at the sight. Slowly, I make my way toward it. It's a beautiful specimen of design. Dark and sleek, it's also completely void of the dust I see covering every other item in this place.

I haven't played the piano in ages, not since I started working with papa. Mama wanted all her girls to learn. Masha is the only one who stayed with it, but only for recognition. More than once, she's been invited to play at family dinners at the Bratva's member's houses. Olga was too restless, and I was too focused on the business. Then again, I didn't need much learning. The music flowed through my fingers easily. I remember the melodies Mama taught me, even after all these years.

Raising the cover, I run my fingers over the keys ever so gently. A melody sounds in my ears, a long forgotten lullaby, as if I've been playing it all this time. When my right hand picks out the notes, it's like second nature. The sound of the piano is too loud in this too quiet of a house, and it echoes all around me.

"Who are you?" A growl comes from the shadows, making me jump. There's so much venom in that one question, it makes me want to shrink back into myself. But I won't. This must be the creature papa spoke about, the one who bargained for his life. So, I pull on all the years of dealing with difficult individuals, and I turn slowly, my shoulders back, toward where the voice came from.

"Your prisoner," I reply. I think I shocked him. My voice is strong as it reaches out into the darkness. When he still says nothing, I raise my right hand, wiggling my fingers to show off the ring.

"You are not the older man I gave that ring to." The creature finally speaks, his voice more of a growl as it rumbles in his chest.

"You are very observant," I snap, my patience waning. This is ridiculous. It's not like I want to be here, I have to be because he made my papa enter into a bargain with him. If anyone should be annoyed here, it's me.

"The ring does not work on anyone but him. You cannot be here."

"Well, observant, but clearly not that smart. You made a blood bargain. I am his blood. I'm his daughter."

Okay, so maybe I shouldn't be antagonizing the creature that is holding me prisoner, but I get on the offensive when I'm scared. And right now? I'm full of terror. It would be stupid for me to lie to myself. The creature is hidden by the darkness, beyond the ring of light the candle provides. It makes him that much more menacing.

"Daughter. That was not the deal."

"Too bad. My father is needed with his family."

"He should not have sent you."

"He didn't. I chose to take his place, without his input." My anger is rising as I squint into the darkness to try and make out the shape of the creature. "You know, it's very inhospitable of you to be hiding in the shadows. I should at least see my jailer."

There's another moment of silence, and it's so quiet I wonder if he left. But I hold my ground anyway, just in case this is another trick. My body is shaking on the inside, but outwardly, I look as cool as a cucumber.

"If you are to stay here," he speaks up again, and I almost pat myself on the back for guessing right. He was studying me, deciding what to do with me. "You are to follow explicit rules. Do as you are told. Don't leave the palace grounds. The thief, your father it seems, was bargained into a service. Every morning, you are to head to the study and continue the research."

"Research?"

"There are instructions on the desk. You must follow them to the letter."

The way he says that seems like he's done talking to me. There's a rustle of movement, as if he's turned to go. But I'm not finished.

"Wait, what do I do in the meantime? Where do I eat? Sleep?"

There's a slight hesitation on his part, an extra beat of silence in an already silent room. He's thinking, and I don't interrupt, waiting him out. Honestly, I expect him to throw me into the dungeons my papa mentioned. It would really fit this persona the creature is presenting. But then, he surprises me.

"Follow the path you just took back out to the main hallway. The kitchens are farther down, on the right, past the dining room. I will leave you a path to your rooms from there."

"Why can't you just show me?"

But there's no response to my question because he's already gone. I take a deep breath, calming my racing heart. I wonder if he could hear it. My breathing slows, and I give myself a small pep talk in my head. This is something I can handle because I can handle anything. I am not a weakling, and I do not cower. I am here because I am protecting my family. I am determined to succeed. From what I know of blood bargains—and it's not nearly enough —they can be broken in two ways. Release from the bargainer or death. There are consequences when the points of contract aren't followed. So, I will do what I'm told. And if the opportunity presents itself, I will kill the creature and escape with my freedom.

❧ 6 ❧

I follow his instructions and find the kitchen with no problem. I guess I should say kitchens because there are two? Kind of. There's the main one, which houses the large burners and countertops for fifty people to work off with no fear of bumping into anyone. But then there's also a smaller one that looks more like the kitchen we have at our house.

I'm not exactly sure what the necessity of that is, but then again, I've never lived in a castle before.

It kind of hits me right then and there that I live in a castle now, like one of those heroines I read about in my papa's books. All I'm missing is a handmaiden and a puffy dress and I'd be set to go. In all honesty, I would love one of those dresses. I may not like my sisters' dress styles, but I do love dresses. Especially when they look like I'm meeting the Queen or something. I've simply never had the opportunity to wear them. And I've learned that the men in the organization do not take women very seriously, especially if they're wearing a flirty dress.

My mind is apparently filling itself with the most random of thoughts as I look through the kitchen. The room is square shaped with an island in the middle. The counter runs along the wall, in an "L" shape before it comes to an end at a burner. There are cupboards on the top and bottom of the counter. I pull open a few to find dishes and pots and pans.

Maybe the most surprising aspect of it all is the fact that the kitchen has a refrigerator. I'm not sure what I was expecting from a magical land, but it wasn't a modern convenience such as a fridge. The amount of knowledge I don't have about this place is astounding. Walking over, I pull the door and find it stocked with all kinds of food. The light comes on, just like a regular fridge. I can't help myself when I lean around the fridge to look behind it. There's no electrical outlet that I can see, or wires, but it hums as it works, the cool air escaping as I hold the door open.

I definitely need to brush up on what is and isn't possible in Skazka. A magically run refrigerator is going on the list of things I'd like to research. At least I do know that I'll be able to make myself some bacon and eggs, if I desire to do so.

The one thing I do before leaving the kitchen is find a glass and fill it with water. I take a few sips, feeling better as the simple action settles me. Every movement I make seems to echo in the quiet. It's very unnerving. At home, there's always some kind of noise. My sisters moving through the house, music playing, or papa on the phone with someone. Even the cars on the street added a buzz to the space around me. I've never realized just how used to the white noise I am, but now I can totally tell the difference.

Taking my glass with me, I walk back out the way I came only to find the area a bit more lit up. In the span of a few minutes, the creature apparently turned on some lights. Well, one or two lamps similar to the one in the study, which he seems to have in every room so far. There are also various candles. As I walk out of the dining room into the hall, I realize what he meant by he'll show me the way. He has left a candle burning along the wall to lead me, so I follow the tiny light.

When I reach the main foyer where I landed, I see candles on the stairs and then up on the landing to the right. Seeing no other choice, I follow his guidance, only pausing to study the marble banister. The middle part of the banister has some kind of design. I bend down to see it better. A vine full of leaves is carved out of stone, weaving in and out of the pillars that hold up the top part of the banister. I run my fingers over it gently, mesmerized by the beautiful work. I may be a cold-blooded mafia heiress, but I can appreciate real beauty.

When I reach the top of the stairs and turn right, I realize this place really likes statues for decoration. Much like downstairs, they're pushed closer to the wall, lining the way. They don't follow any sort of rhyme or reason when it comes to design, people and animals in various poses. It makes the hairs on my arm stand at attention, so I rub my skin with my free hand.

Much like downstairs, the walls are lined with art. But

there are more shadows here, since there are no windows in this corridor, and it's difficult for me to see. I pass quite a few doors before I find the one with the candle right in front of it. Picking it up off the floor, I push the door open and step inside. But I don't actually need the candle to see. There are quite a few burning all around me, filling the room with a soft glow.

It looks fit for a queen.

The gold trim I noticed throughout the castle is present here as well. When I take a closer look, I see that they're vines, just like the staircase. In between the trim, the walls are covered, but not with hanging artwork. Wallpaper that is an art all in itself covers the walls. A garden spreads out around me with trees painted tall, reaching for the ceiling, and flowers covering the meadow. A chandelier hangs overhead composed of small clear crystals with a row of candles on top of each tier. They're not lit.

There's a bed to my left, a spacious one with a canopy over it. The sheer material of the canopy is glittering in the low light, like a sky full of stars. A vanity rests on the other side of the room, near doors that lead into the bathroom. Another set of doors are near the front of the room, near the bed, and I can only assume it's a closet. I take all of that in at once, but what captures my attention immediately are the windows. There are three total, and they take up most of the wall in front of me. The closest two to me curl slightly inward. The middle curtains are open.

Immediately, I'm at the window. Curiosity of what the world outside looks like nearly overwhelms me. I've walked up a number of stairs, and I hope to see something beyond the fog that covers the outside on the ground floor.

My hope is dashed because I just find more darkness, only broken apart by the millions of stars shining above me. It seems impossible so many of them can fit in one sky, but they're a blanket of beauty, and I can't help but stare.

The space below me is in shadows. I can't find the moon to light it in any way. If I concentrate hard enough, I can make out a fence and a dark forest at the edge of it. A wall of trees. From what I can see, it seems the fence and the forest spreads out in both directions before it gets lost to the fog. It creates a sense of isolation, even more so than the knowledge that I seem to be the only one in this castle with the creature. There are no servants from what I can tell, which is also very strange.

So far, everything is strange. As I turn back to the room, I see the door on my left does lead to the bathroom like I guessed. Stepping inside, I find a bathtub, a sink, and a modern looking toilet, But the room is still lit by candles. Turning the handle, water pours out into the sink. Just like the fridge, it has to be magical.

This place is a contradiction, and my inquisitive mind wants to discover all the answers. If I'm stuck here, I might as well make the best of the terrible situation. Plus, the more knowledge I have about this place, the more ammunition I have in my pocket to make things work in my favor.

Walking back into the main room, I do another quick study. There's a bench in front of the vanity and a plush chair in the corner. Moving toward the bed, I strip one of the pillowcases off the pillow and march back over to the doors. They're double doors, the beautiful dark wood carved with flower designs. Giving myself a moment to admire it, I realize this whole castle is filled with flower patterns, but the doorknob is a head of a wolf.

Beautiful and terrifying.

I take the pillowcase and wrap it in an eight shape around the handles before tying the ends together. Then, I grab the chair, dragging it over to the doors to anchor it under the door handles as well. Since I have no idea how powerful the creature is, I have no idea if this would stop him. But it would at least give me a few seconds of heads up.

I do another quick search of the room, but I find nothing I can use as a weapon. Hopefully, since he made the bargain with papa, he's not coming to murder me in my sleep. He definitely seems to need me, and if I can't trust him, I can at least trust that.

As sudden as a hummingbird, exhaustion weighs on my body. All this time, I've been holding onto my resolve to move, to do things, but now that I'm somewhat secure in this room, I feel the tiredness in my bones. I glance into the other room near the bed and see that it is indeed a closet. I will have to explore it more fully later. Right now, I'm going to wash my face and try to get some rest. Walking over to the bathroom, I splash water over my skin, and pat it dry with the small towel placed near the sink. The cup of water I brought with me from the kitchen is placed on the bedside table. Then I climb into bed, fully dressed, with my shoes still on.

I lay on top of the covers. Even though I'm tense, I can feel the pull of the comfort the bed provides. In a castle full of darkness and emptiness, this room seems alive somehow. There are no spiderwebs here. The bedding underneath me seems fresh. I file that information onto the list of things I need to ask about and research. But not right now. I have to force myself to rest if I'm to go up against the creature.

This place would be beautiful if it wasn't a prison to me. But then again, even the most beautiful places can feel like prison. It's all in the attitude.

I turn on my side, facing the door. This is just another obstacle I need to overcome. I can do this. So, I close my eyes, and I force myself to relax. Even if I can't sleep, I need to rest. I have no idea what tomorrow will bring.

❦ 7 ❦

Surprisingly enough, I slept. It was only for a few hours, but I feel better than I did yesterday. Well, as well as I can, I suppose. Checking the door, I find it undisturbed before I head to the bathroom. Moving through my typical morning routine—even without my regular items—makes me slightly more balanced. Once I've brushed out my hair and washed my face, I feel more in control. With my hair back in its signature ponytail, I feel ready to face him. As ready as I can be.

I take a moment to study myself in the mirror, checking to make sure nothing is out of place. My brown eyes seem bigger. My skin is flushed with worry or antici- pation, I can't tell. I run a finger over my eyebrows, making sure the hairs are facing the same way. Just like my papa I am blessed with thicker ones, and I also have his strong nose. But I also have my mama's full lips, which are currently set in a grimace. Taking a deep breath, I move away from the mirror.

I'm still wearing my dress pants and blouse from last night. I will have to figure out a way to wash these. Maybe I can find some clothes around the castle that will fit.

Remembering that I never checked out the closet, I head there first. When I step inside, my breath catches. The room is large. Clothes hang all around the perimeter of it with only a break for a full length mirror. There's a cream-colored round ottoman in the middle, as if I need a place to sit while I pick out clothes.

Running my hands over the material of the clothes, I pull out a few. There are dresses of every color—leaning heavily on the greens and blues—and various designs, as well as shirts, skirts, and sweaters. I even find sweatpants. This room is definitely stocked for someone like me. That raises more questions.

A part of me wants to pull out all the clothes and try them on, but instead of changing, I keep my current clothes on and head out of the closet room. Right now, my human clothes are my armor, and I'm about to go to battle.

I drink the rest of my water before untying the pillow-case and venturing out. The place is slightly brighter than last night. I wonder if there are open windows on this side of the castle, letting in more light. Not that it's that much lighter. The darkness seems to hang right around the corner, as if it can spring at me at any time.

Instead of exploring, which is what I want to do, I decide to head to the kitchens and make myself breakfast. That's officially my first point of concern: taking care of myself.

He did leave the candles burning, or he relit them,

because I have no issues finding the kitchens. As I walk, however, I feel a tension on my skin, as if I'm being watched. Discreetly, I study my surroundings, but it's nearly impossible to see past the statues that are residing in front of the walls. The space behind them is pitch black. When I stop to listen, I don't hear any movement. It might be my paranoia, but I'm not about to stop that. I have to be on my highest alert.

Once I reach the kitchen, I pour myself more water and then look through my options. While he does have a refrigerator, there are no toasters or a microwave that I can find. But the stove is gas lit, and I remember seeing pots and pans yesterday.

It takes me about ten minutes to find matches before I can light the stove. Much like in my house, the bread is in the refrigerator, keeping the mold away. Pulling it out, I butter the bread, then fry both sides of it, deciding on simple toast instead of a full out breakfast. The curious side of me is eager to get to the study and see what this whole research thing is about.

The one thing I wish I could find in this kitchen is coffee. Or even tea. Unfortunately, I see nothing but pitchers of water and some weird looking juice that I'm almost positive isn't good for drinking anymore. I even check the other monstrosity of a kitchen, but I guess Skazka doesn't believe in coffee or tea. Or maybe the creature has hidden it in order to torture me. Maybe not, but I kind of want to take everything personally. It'll continuously fuel my resolve to get out of here.

Leaving the kitchens behind, I head toward the study. I

keep expecting the creature to show up, to make sure I'm doing what I'm told, but he doesn't seem too worried about it. Maybe he can see the curiosity in me. Or he might be spying on me from the rafters. Either way, it's not like I'm really doing this for him. I just want answers. And if I can use his orders to my advantage, then why not.

The study is officially the brightest place in the castle. He didn't simply light the candles, he also turned on the lights. There are two chandeliers on opposite corners of the room, hanging from the ceiling. They were hidden by the darkness last night. So clearly, the castle has some sort of electricity, between this and the refrigerator. But he's conserving it for reasons unknown? Or maybe it doesn't work all the time. Or perhaps he's hiding from his own reflection. I mean, if papa's word is to be believed—which it absolutely is—he's not a normal looking creature. He might be afraid of his own shadow at this point. I need to stop obsessing about the way he looks.

Pushing all thought of the creature away, I head to the desk. There, just like the creature said, are papers on top of the book piles with handwritten instructions.

"Read through the books on the desk first, making a note of any mention of curses or the breaking of curses."

Of course, how did I not think of this before? He's searching for a way to break the curse put on him. Papa mentioned the curse, but I guess it slipped my mind in all the excitement. It makes sense. Someone did this to him, and he wants a way out.

Now the bargain with papa is more understandable as well. The creature is desperate for answers, and somehow, he needs outside help to get it. Maybe he can't read. But no, that couldn't be it, could it? I have so many questions now, my mind is spinning.

He's a puzzle I want to solve. I've always been good at puzzles. That's why papa brought me into the organization at such an early age. I saw things the way others didn't. I could find answers when others struggled to see the questions.

"You are supposed to be working." The voice comes from the open doorway, nearly giving me a heart attack. I suppose asking him to wear a bell is out of the question, but he's going to get me to an early grave if he keeps sneaking up on me like that. He's beyond the light, hiding in the shadows again. Today, he doesn't sound as scary. Maybe it was anger that made his voice rumble in the way it did last night. This morning, he sounds almost...human.

"Good morning to you too. What lovely weather we're having, eh?" The sarcasm is automatic. My sisters call it very "unladylike," but I never cared. And I care even less now. I must have stumped the creature again because it takes him a few moments to reply.

"You are unlike anyone I have ever met," he finally comments.

"Oh, is that right? Bring many girls back as prisoners, do you?" Instead of trying to squint into the dark hallway to see him, I focus on the books on the desk. There are quite a few to go through. I didn't know curses were so well documented. Then again, I've never been in a magical realm before.

"You would be smart to watch your tone with me."

"Or what?" I look up, placing my hands on my hips. "You'll lock me up in the tower?"

He grows quiet once more. I glance down at the desk to hide my smile. I guess my personality is good for one thing at least: confusing magical beast creatures into silence.

Deciding I actually do want to do some research, I take a seat behind the desk and pull a book toward me. My curiosity is really at its peak. Now that I know magic is an actual real thing, I want to learn as much as I can about it. Especially if it'll help me get back home one day.

"Will you be difficult the whole time?" When the creature finally speaks up, I don't bother hiding my smile.

"Absolutely. Difficult is what I do best!"

He growls then, and it's the most animalistic sound I've heard him make. My mind can't seem to conjure up what he looks like, not with the tiny bits of information I'm getting from him.

"Why don't you come in here and help me research?" I ask, completely nonchalant. He growls again, but this time, it's that 'I know what you're trying to do' type of a growl.

"Come on, you can't be hiding in the shadows the whole time I'm here, can you? I have so many questions. Why were you cursed? You are cursed, right? That's the whole point of this research. And what about other people, servants and friends, in the castle? Where are they? Can you give me something to work with here?"

I let the steam run out of my words, waiting for a response, but none comes. He probably left right in the middle of my question attack, but honestly, who knows?

He seems of the difficult sort himself, so I doubt he even had any friends before he became whatever he is.

If he wants to be like that, so be it. I'm not here to socialize anyway. This little library might yield me more answers than he's expecting, and I intend to use that to my full advantage.

❧ 8 ❧

I spend all of my morning pouring over books. There is so much fascinating history hidden between these pages. The land of Skazka isn't all that unfamiliar to my home world. We carry many of the stories hidden inside our fairytale books. Because that's what Skazka is. It's a land full of all the fairytale creatures I read about as a child. But never in my wildest dreams would I have imagined it being a real place, a-fear inducing one at that.

There have been many wars fought in these lands, kings and queens rising against each other. Sorcerers searching for power. Everything centers around power and magic here. The power aspect I totally get. The organization works like that. It's all about who has the upper hand, who holds the majority of votes. It's how decisions are made—the most powerful scare the others into submission.

But here, those searching for that ultimate power are aided by forces I can't even wrap my mind around. There are those who wield fire or water or change seasons with a flick of their hands. It's a land where forests are alive and plants speak a language that can be understood by some. Curses are a sure way to get something one wants or to punish someone who may or may not deserve it. There are many curses. Enchantments to bring on dreams that turn into reality, potions that cover a person in sores and lesions. A spell that causes the receiver to break their nails every time they do anything with their hands, or one that takes a person's vision every time they look at someone they love.

Cruel and dark. Just like papa warned.

I stay hunched over the books for hours, soaking in the knowledge of something I didn't know existed. But now, I can't get enough. There are artifacts that help with powers. If I could get my hands on one of those, I could go up against anyone, my prison guard included.

I glance down at the ring I'm still wearing on my finger. This has to be one of the magical artifacts, but besides putting it on my ring finger to travel here, I have no idea what other secrets it holds. I tried it earlier in the day, seeing if it would take me back to papa, but it did nothing. Still, I can't part with it.

"You need to eat something." The voice startles me, making my stomach tighten. Thankfully, I don't show much of an outward reaction. I've been anticipating him all day.

"I'm not hungry," I reply without looking up.

"It's hours past lunchtime."

"Don't tell me you're concerned about me." I place my hands on the desk in front of me, looking up into the open doorway. I'm not sure how he knows what time it is. I've seen no clocks in this place.

"If you keel over, you are of no use to me."

"Ah, of course. How could I confuse your selfishness with concern." I turn back to the book, dismissing him. Truth be told, I *am* hungry. But I'm not about to let him know that.

"It will do you good to remember your manners."

"It will do you good to remember that I don't cower in the face of bullies."

I look up, glaring straight into the darkness beyond the doorway, daring him to come face me head on. This is getting repetitive and tiring. I'm waiting for him to cross that invisible line he's created between us and face me like a man. Or a normal person, at least. But he doesn't. I wait him out, but he's gone again. Or maybe he's always in the shadows, watching me. Either way, I turn back to the books.

It's another hour, maybe more, before my stomach growls. I have to go find food. There are no clocks in the study, but at least I have a body that tells me what it needs.

Following the now familiar path to the kitchen, I make myself a sandwich, thankful there's ham and cheese in the fridge. I'll have to figure out a healthier food menu eventually. Or who stocks the food and if I can get them on my side. For now, I take my sandwich and leave the kitchens behind.

At first, I turn back in the direction of the study, but then I decide against it. If I'm to stay safe, I need to know what I'm up against. That means exploring my area of residence, at least as much of it as I can. I have no doubt I won't make it far. The creature is probably close enough to jump out at me if I suddenly do something he doesn't like.

I give my surroundings a quick study, to make sure he isn't about to jump out now, and then I turn in the opposite direction from the study. This part of the house isn't lit up, clearly showing me that he doesn't want me here. But oh well.

When I reach what looks to be a small foyer, I push the door open. On the other side, I'm met by daylight. Well, I wouldn't quite call it daylight. Maybe the last moments before the sun finally sets below the horizon, but it's brighter than any place I've seen besides the study.

I step outside, eager for some fresh air and to see how far the wall extends. There are gardens all around the castle, as far as I can see. I walk back the way I came, but this time on the outside of the castle, studying it as I go. The stone structure is much taller than I anticipated. It must hold another three floors above the one where I'm staying. It looks grey and stained by years of neglect. I come upon the front of the castle with the huge double doors I landed in front of when I first got here. On each side of the doors stands a sculpture of a wolf. Magnificent creatures, the statues are taller than I am. When I step closer, I can see the details are similar to that of the statues inside but not quite at the same level. Maybe two different sculptors created them.

Turning away from the front of the castle, I look out into the gardens. The fog dances around my ankles as I begin walking. Trees line the walkways, slumbering as if it's the middle of winter. The air here is cooler and heavier somehow. What once were bushes adorn the areas in between the trees. The pathways branch off into multiple directions. I'm sure the gardens are set up like a maze of sorts, weaving in and out.

I walk slowly, turning left and right, not even concerned with the fact that I have to find my way back. When I look over my shoulder, the castle rises above me as dark on the outside as it looks like on the inside. I can see fog hugging it like a blanket wrapped around someone's shoulders. It would be a beautiful structure if it didn't look so sad. I'm not sure why I'm qualifying it as sad, and not something else, but it's the first thought that comes into my mind.

Turning back to the gardens, I continue my exploring. I doubt I'll find anything but the dead trees and what used to be flowerbeds, but I can't stop walking. It becomes a need, almost, and I give into it. Just a little. Then, I come to an area with a gate. The gate itself is surrounded by dead trees planted so closely together, they resemble a wall. I almost turn and go back, but something pushes me forward.

Unlocking the simple latch, I step inside. What greets me isn't at all what I'm expecting. The miniature garden within a garden is alive. Vines grow up and down trellises, enveloping this space with its beauty. For every green vine that I see there is a flower blooming.

Scarlet roses fill the space and the air, their fragrance settling on my skin like a soft touch. It's the most beautiful garden I have ever seen. It's such a contrast to the rest of the castle and its occupant.

Reaching out toward one of the flowers, I run my fingers over the petals, careful not to disturb it too much.

"You have found it."

The voice comes to me through the bushes. I'm getting used to him appearing suddenly so much so that I'm expecting it. I definitely was in this case.

"This is the flower you punished my papa for."

"He chose his own fate."

That one statement unleashes a fury of emotion within me. I spin around, focusing my attention on the direction the voice is coming from. Here, in this strange garden, I can see almost a shadow of an outline. He's much taller than I expected him to be, maybe close to seven feet tall, if not more. His shoulders are broad, and he could probably crush me with his bare hands. But I won't be intimidated.

"Papa was only bringing me back a gift I asked for. You punished him for loving me like he does."

"Then I suppose it is fitting you are here instead of him, for it was your fault for asking for such a frivolous gift."

"I didn't want to ask for anything but his safe return!" I nearly shout, advancing on the shadowy outline. "But he insisted. So, I asked for the gift my mama would've, something that was theirs—" I stop myself abruptly. Emotion is making it difficult to breathe, and I will not cry in front of this creature. I will not allow myself that show of vulnerability. Instead, I narrow my eyes and take a deep breath to steady myself.

"You wouldn't understand what it means to live a life of sacrifice on behalf of another person. You just sit in your castle with your magical garden and hallways full of candles and smoke, and you bargain with the lives of others for your own amusement. You do not know what it means to care. Or to love."

"You know nothing of who I am, little girl!" His roar echoes around me, shuddering the very ground I stand on. "Your naivety of the world is laughable at best. You simply put on a brave face, to fool those around you. But you are only fooling yourself."

"Were you such a charmer before you were cursed too?" I snap, but his words hit too close to home. I want to say that I am brave, but I play at that much more than I should. Even now, I'm terrified. I can't tell if I'm being brave or foolish. Maybe a little bit of both.

"I didn't choose this for myself!" His voice rises as an echo around me, and for the first time, it truly sounds like he's lost control of his emotions. But it's only years of dealing with men who speak in anger that I don't flinch. That I don't back down.

"Cool. Such a sad tale. But now, you have to deal with this situation. So, you can be a jerk and wallow in your misfortune, or you can do something about it. That's something you do have a choice over!"

There's only a wall of roses between us now. I can hear his uneven breathing from the other side. He's angry, that much I can tell. But maybe he's something else as well. He said I'm not truly brave, and he may be right. But one thing I will never do is cower in front of spoiled men—beasts—whatever he is.

"Why do you think you're here?" He finally speaks up, and his voice is calm once more. "It's not because I enjoy your company."

"Well, that one is on you." I shrug, trying to calm my racing heart. In the span of two days, he's managed to rile me up like no one else ever has before. It's something I'll have to learn how to deal with if I'm to gain the upper hand.

The one thing I can say is that I think I might've actually broken through his carefully erected walls. Since the moment I showed up, he's spoken in the most proper of ways, keeping his words calculated, using no contractions. But just now, that went out the window, and I count that as a win. Maybe that's why I decide to push my luck.

"Why is this garden so important to you?" I ask, keeping my voice lower, calmer, as I watch him through the vines. I know it is. He punished a man greatly for one flower. He doesn't reply immediately, and I think he might not at all. But then he does.

"It's the only living thing here."

That makes no sense. The only living thing?

"Are you some zombie creature?" I ask, "Because if that's the case tell me now. I don't want to be stumbling upon your severed arm or anything like that."

There's a moment of silence, then a sound I haven't heard before. For a second, I think it might be a laugh, but that can't be it. A terrible monster of a creature doesn't have a sense of humor.

"I am not a zombie, but I am alone in my living state. The garden is—"

"I get it," I say when he doesn't continue. "It's your connection to the world."

"Yes."

His one word is soft, almost a whisper, but I think it might be the most real he's been with me. Not that I expect him to spill his heart out after only meeting me, but even his quest for the curse breaker doesn't feel as genuine as that one word. Three letters, and it's filled with such sadness.

He moves away then, his shadow disappearing, not waiting for me to ask any other questions. I give the roses one last look before I too pull the gate closed and leave it behind. If he and I never agree on anything else, we do agree on this one thing. That kind of beauty should be preserved.

❧ 9 ❧

Much of the next week goes by in the same manner. I wake up, I make myself breakfast, I spend hours in the study pouring over books. The creature only shows up to remind me to eat since I have no way of keeping time in my darkened dungeon. He never stays around long enough for me to yell at him some more. I think, and I can't be one hundred percent sure about this, he might be scared of me. Or maybe he's scared of what he'd do to me if he let his rage free. I see the signs. It's a bit sad that I've learned to recognize them.

Giving in to my predicament, I have started dressing in the clothes provided in the closet. Nothing flashy, mostly just single color outfits—mostly black and sometimes green maxi dresses. They fall down to my feet, a simple cut that leaves my shoulders open, so I make sure to have a sweater with me. The castle is drafty. If I'm being honest, I'm itching to try on some of the ballgowns. But I won't. That seems too much like giving in—or giving up.

I keep a piece of paper tucked under the stack of books where I track the time passing. My eighteenth birthday is days away now. While I've never been sentimental about birthday celebrations, this one means something. It's the year the organization can finally recognize me as an equal. Well, as equal as a woman can ever be with their misogynistic ways.

Something I've always hated about the organization, and worked to change, is their outlook on who is important and why. Women in the organization have always been just as powerful, if not more. I need more than two hands to count how many times Mrs. Balakin used her cunning skills to change Mr. Balakin's mind about something. I've witnessed it myself. But they're never recognized as such. they never get to sit at the big boys' table.

When Papa began bringing me in on the meetings, there was a huge uproar. My sisters could not wrap their minds around why I would be interested in such a business in the first place. That threw a few extra wrenches into our already rocky relationship. Especially because, according to Masha, men didn't like strong women. Maybe the men she liked didn't, but if Ilya is any indication, he's been fascinated with me for years. I guess now that I'm gone, he might turn his attention to one of my other sisters. He needs my papa on his side. Especially if he's taking over for his.

I slam the book in front of me shut, pushing thoughts of my family and my life away. There's no use crying over spilled milk, right? Or burnt *pirogies*. What's done is done. I made the decision; I am living with the consequences.

My shoulders are tense and achy, so I stand, stretching

as I do a quick turn about the room. It's not that these magic books are boring. They're quite fascinating in fact, and I'm learning much more than the creature probably wants me to know.

For example, I have learned that if I run away, if I go back on the blood bargain papa made with the creature, I will die. More specifically, my blood will boil me from the inside. A lovely picture, isn't it?

That took the wind out of my sails in regards to simply killing the creature and running. Although, I'm not sure how I'd be able to get home without his magic ring. I'd be lying if I said I didn't try it on my ring finger two days ago. Even with the threat of my body boiling from the inside, I needed to know if it would work. It still doesn't. But I won't take it off. There's an ingredient to the magic that I'm missing. As far as I know, it's not in any of the books I've read so far.

Deciding I've had enough of reading for the day, I mark my spot just in case and move to leave the room. I've been running in the mornings, trying to keep my stamina in check, and I'm thinking of doing another run now. But then, I pivot, heading toward the hidden doorway, pulling it open. He's never closed it properly, so I didn't have to figure out the mechanism to make it work if it was locked. Thankfully.

The piano sits right where I saw it last, and it still carries no dust on it. It makes me think that he's in here more often than not, but I've never heard any music in this dreary place.

Pulling the bench out, I take a seat before raising the cover from the keys. The same melody as before fills my ears. This time, I don't hesitate to let my fingers run over the keys.

The movements come easily, like I've been doing this nonstop for years. The song is an old lullaby my mama sang to me when I was but a baby. It may seem strange to remember a sound before you even remember your name. But I've carried this song inside of my heart for as long as I've been alive. As I play, it's like I can hear my mama's soft voice singing it once more.

The notes run over my skin like tiny drops of rain, showering me in memories and love. My eyes fill with tears, hovering at the edge, but I won't let them spill. I haven't cried in years, and I'm not about to start now in this strange place with not a soul who understands.

"I told you to stay out of here." The words come from over my shoulder instead of from the door like I expect them to, but I still don't flinch. He always finds me, even if it's been hours since I've last heard him. There must be dozens of passageways in this castle. That's the only way I can see him moving so stealthily around it.

His presence doesn't surprise me, but his soft words do. I expected anger because that's all he's shown to me, except for that brief moment in the garden.

"I don't think you did. Do you play?"

I'm trying to be civil as I swallow my sadness. I don't actually expect an answer. He's very picky about which parts of him he lets me see. Or don't see. At this point, I have no idea if he'll ever show his face, but he surprises me.

"I used to. It was the one—" He stops, and I nearly groan out loud.

"Don't you think it's past time for us to have any

secrets? We literally live in the same house. If you're afraid I'll move out, I actually can't." I try to lighten the mood, but I think my joke does the opposite. He grows quiet again. It takes everything in me not to turn around and face him. For some reason, I think I'd be able to see his face, if only because the shadows aren't as dark on this side of the room. But I'm afraid that if I do, he'll leave and whatever this common ground that we've been gaining, it'll be gone.

"I'm not a nice man," he finally says, sighing. It's the most human thing I've heard him do since I got here. It makes it seem like he's not that much older than me. I've always thought he's some kind of ancient creature. But maybe I'm wrong.

"Is that why you were cursed?" I dare the question.

"Yes and no. This curse is a punishment, for my father and for me."

"Will you tell me about it?"

It feels strange, talking like this. He seems so different from the harsh creature who barks orders at me. But he's trying—I think that's what this is about—and I'm not about to turn him away. It's like the melody touched him, the same way it has touched me, pulling him out of his dark despair and into the here and now.

"The story isn't all that different. My father, the king, was a cruel man who showed no kindness toward his people and wanted nothing but power and riches."

"I know a few of those."

"He crossed the wrong *Volshebnitsya*, and in turn, she hit him where it hurt the most. Me."

"She cursed you because of his cruelty?" I'm trying to

wrap my mind around the kind of individual, or I suppose a magical sorceress, who would do such a thing.

"I was his pride and joy because I was exactly like him. When the time came for him to step down from the throne, he knew I'd keep pillaging and conquering, just like he did."

Pillaging and conquering.

Two simple words, but they bring with them so many images. I've read about these types of kings in the books the creature has me studying. They leave behind burned villages and starving families.

"You did that?"

"No, but I would've. I never stopped him. I basked in the conquers that came with each of his decisions, no matter the consequences. I would've been just like him when the time came for me to call the shots."

For some reason, I don't think so. I know all too well what children do in order to follow in their father's footsteps. But at the end of the day, they still make their own decisions. Maybe the creature wouldn't have been as bad as what the magic woman thought he would be. Or maybe it doesn't matter.

"You're thinking I'm not like him." The creature interrupts my thoughts. "For someone who is as hard and calloused as you are, you still want to see the good in people? Why is that?" He sounds almost in awe of me. I pause, thinking the answer might mean more to him than either of us realize.

"Because," I begin, with a small smile on my lips, "we are not all black, and we are not all white. We are made up of good and evil. My mama taught me as long as there is balance in the world, it will keep turning and the good will continue to win. I choose to believe that."

He doesn't say anything for a moment, but then, I can feel him right at my back, his breath ruffling my hair.

"You really think I can be good?" His voice is low, almost like a caress at the back of my neck. My skin breaks out in goosebumps.

"I don't know. But there's always a chance."

There's another moment of silence before I ask, "Where is he now? The king?"

"Punished, like the rest of us." There is sadness in his answer, and something else I can't identify.

He moves away then. I can feel his body heat retreating. I want to turn around more than anything, but I don't. Something major has happened here, and I want to hold on to that.

Just when I think he's gone, he speaks again. "Gavriil. My name is Gavriil."

The small victory is exhilarating and is more than I hoped for.

"Nikita."

There's another pause and then I dare to ask the question that's been plaguing me.

"Why do you need me anyway? You have a library full of books."

He doesn't reply right away, and then he does. "I can't read."

"Wait, what?"

"It's part of the curse. It takes parts of me."

And then he leaves, leaving me with more questions than answers and his name echoing inside my mind.

❧ 10 ❧

I t's another three days before he makes himself
known to me again. Although, I think he's always in
the piano room when I go in there to play. Yesterday,
there was sheet music left on the bench. It's been years
since I've actually looked at written notes, but this gives
me something to do, and I dive into it headfirst.

Notes are much like the numbers in my papa's ledgers
—something for me to figure out. My memory is sharp
when it comes to music, much more so than I hoped for. It
makes it easier to get through a whole piece of music in
one day. I play until I have it memorized, the ups and
downs of the melody, the story it tells between the notes.
My fingers fly over the keys as if they were made to do so. I
soak up the moments I have in the piano room like a
drowning man gasps for air.

Even though he hasn't spoken to me in days, I can feel
Gavriil's presence, like an object on the very corner of my
peripheral vision. If I turn too fast, I'll send the world spin-

ning and him running. So instead, I play, giving both of us the gift of music.

He's a contradiction that I would love to understand. When I first came here, I saw the mean streak in him and hated him for what he forced me to do in order to protect my papa. But since then, we have found a bit of common ground, mostly in the form of songs. I have no idea what to think about that. I'm afraid to break our silence because I want to hold onto those moments when I'm playing. It has become my oasis.

While my life has become a routine, my eighteenth birthday is only two days away. After a long day of research, I'm in the piano room when he comes to me. My stomach coils in warning when I hear movement at my back. It's only the fact that I've come to expect it that I don't jump in my seat.

"Tonight is the full moon." There is no polite greeting. He simply dives right into whatever order he's about to issue. " You are to be in your room before the moon rises and to stay there for the duration of the night, no questions asked." Just like that, he's given an order after ignoring me for days. I can hear him moving away then, but I won't stand for it. Jumping to my feet, I twist around. He jerks back into the shadows.

"What is this about? You're locking me up?"

"Yes. I said no questions."

"And I say, too bad. You can't just order me around."

"You are my prisoner." The words are delivered with no emotion behind them, and I narrow my eyes.

"Yes, please remind me of that some more so I can be extra miserable about still being here," I snap. My breathing is heavy, and my heart is ready to jump out of my chest. He's so close. I think if I reach out, I might touch him. But he's covered in shadows, and I can't make out any of the features, only the feel of him and the heaviness of his gaze on me.

"It is for your own safety," he finally says, taking the wind out of my sails. He sounds genuine, and I'm not sure how to take that.

"What am I hiding from then?" I ask.

"I can't explain it—"

"So try."

"No."

"Yes."

"Nikita—"

It's the first time he's said my name, and the sound makes me gasp. I feel those three syllables rush over my skin. I nearly can't control the shudder. Before I can think too much of it, I move toward him.

My movement springs him into action, as if he too was frozen momentarily by the sound of my name on his lips. But then, there's a whoosh of fabric as it obscures my view, and the door between the piano room and the study slams shut.

"Not fair!" I rush over to it, slapping my palm against the wood a few times and try the handle. "You can't keep running from me."

"I'm only trying to keep you safe."

"I can take care of myself. Now open this door!"

"I will, but you must go to your room. You must! Promise me you will. Promise!"

It's the tone of his voice that finally gets to me. He's

scared or nervous or something that I haven't heard before. The sense of urgency is unmistakable. I stop banging on the door, placing my forehead against it.

"Okay," I say, suddenly tired to my very core. "But you have to promise that you will let me out. You can't keep me locked up there forever."

The fear that he might—simply lock me up and throw away the key because I am no longer useful to him—steals my breath. There isn't a scenario where I would survive that kind of captivity or find a way out. It's the one thing that would kill me, I just know it. Even though this castle is my prison, I'm still free to move around it. As eerie as the castle is, filled with the shadows and the statues and the slight song the wind brings when it blows too hard, I can still go where I like. But being completely isolated, completely locked up, it's a fear I didn't think I had until I'm presented with it. And right now, I hold my breath waiting for his response. When it comes, I feel like I can think again.

"I promise."

The words are but a whisper, but I believe them. When the door clicks, I grab the handle and pull it open, but he's already gone.

❧ II ❧

I am a woman of my word, so I put the sheet music away, grab one of the books from the study and head to the kitchens. After making myself eggs for dinner —yes, I'm eating extra healthy nowadays—I head toward the bedroom.

The castle seems even heavier with darkness tonight, thicker in a way that causes me to grab an extra candle, even though I already know the way. As I walk, the candle illuminates a small portion of space around me before it gives way to the dark. My eyes find the statues in the hallway leading to my room. I can't help the shudder that rushes over me as the candle's light flickers across the stat-ue's face. It makes it look almost as if it's breathing. My heart stumbles over itself as I hurry my steps.

Stepping inside my bedroom, I close the door, leaning against it as I catch my breath. I try to remind myself that the castle may feel haunted, but I've seen no evidence of it besides the creepy looking architecture and floor decor.

And the unnaturally heavy fog that never dissipates. Sometimes the heavy gothic atmosphere gets to me, and because the creature made such a big deal about tonight, I'm on edge. That has to be it. Pushing away from the bed, I relight a few candles and take a survey of the room.

It's strange being in here before it's time to head to bed. I spend very little time in my bedroom. It is mine, though, that much is obvious. Stacks of books and papers litter almost every surface. I'm still researching for Gav—the creature—but now I'm also reading for myself.

I can't get used to calling him by his name. Something happened back there when he spoke it to me like he was sharing his greatest secret. Something changed between us. But if I allow myself to use his name—I think there's no going back from that. And I have no idea how to feel about that.

No matter how much he's been different with me lately, or how much we've bonded over music, he's still my prison guard. I can't forget that. Even though sometimes I do and then I just think he's as sad as I am.

I didn't think I was, but being here, away from the business of helping papa in the organization, I now see that what I've tried to do for years is keep myself from feeling. I knew what was required of me and I did that. It's easier to work toward a goal and not think about all the outside factors. Or feel how those factors affect me.

But now, being here, my whole life gone, I see that outside of working for the Bratva, I had no other ambition. Not that becoming the first female boss is a bad ambition. It just lacks—heart. My mama would be saddened by that fact.

I used to have a passion for music and art. I wanted to write songs and play at gallery openings. But once Mama passed away, none of that mattered anymore. I had to become like my papa if I was to survive in our world. The only promise I ever made my mama was to protect Papa, and I've done so my whole life. He protested at first, but then, when the grief became too much, he stopped doing what the organization required, and I took over. He didn't even notice at first, but then I was running everything for him. When he finally realized he couldn't live in his grief, it was too late. I was in too deep and so were our debts to the syndicate. We learned and we adapted. Now I'm doing that all over again.

A noise catches my attention, bringing me out of my musings. Slowly, I get off the bed, leaving my book behind. The noise comes again, and this time, I think I identify it. It sounds like a shuffle of feet. But that makes no sense. The only other living thing in this palace is the creature, and he doesn't sound like that when he moves. I've learned to recognize his movements, if only to help myself not have a heart attack every time he suddenly appears.

I know I promised him to stay in my room, but my curiosity is nearly overwhelming. The only thing I can think of is those bandits who attacked papa have found this place and are now looting. But no, that doesn't make sense either. They'd have to get through the wall, and the locked doors, and the mind-boggling fog, and the creature himself. There's no way he'd let them get that far.

My hand reaches for the door handle that I've stopped wrapping my pillowcase around a few days ago, but I hesitate. The creature and I have built a very fragile wall of trust and coexistence. If I ruin that by letting my curiosity win, my stay here will be anything but nice. I have no doubt about that.

The smart move would be to stay in here, to keep my word. Even though it's the hardest thing, that's what I do. Dropping my hand, I take a step back as the noise gets even louder. I think I might hear voices, but that definitely can't be true.

Just then, the door handle rattles. My eyes zero in on the tiny movement as I stop in the middle of my room. Quickly, I race to my bed, grabbing the kitchen knife I stuck under my pillow a week ago. It's been the only weapon I could find within these walls, and it really makes me wish for my dagger. I know this knife won't do much damage, but it will blind someone if I stab them in the eye.

I stand as still as possible, gripping the knife, as I keep my gaze trained on the door. The handle rattles again, and this time, it pushes the door open. It swings inward, just a tad, as if whoever is on the other side is testing the waters.

"I come bearing no ill intent," the voice calls out, and I nearly drop my knife. The voice doesn't belong to the creature. It belongs to a woman.

The door swings farther in, and a body slips in. The woman is much younger than I anticipated, maybe in her late twenties, but tall. She must be close to six feet, lean and strong. She's dressed in dark pants, a dark long sleeved shirt, and combat boots. She reminds me of an action hero, and I'm impressed on sight.

"I know this may seem very strange to you, and a bit anxiety inducing, but I simply had to come see you."

She smiles, and with that small gesture her whole face

transforms. With her hair braided in two and that smile on her face, she looks younger.

I'm still in shock—I honestly didn't think I'd ever see another human being—but I know that I need to gain some ground back. Right now, I look as surprised as I feel. That gives her an advantage. Clearing my throat, I raise my chin a little before I speak.

"Not to sound rude, but who are you and what are you doing in my room?"

She gives me another quick smile, as if in approval of my tactics before she replies.

"I'm Dina, the second in command in the king's army."

My mind tries to wrap itself around that.

"If you are part of the king's army, where have you been all this time?"

"Here, in the castle."

"I don't understand."

Dina nods, giving me a sympathetic smile.

"I can see how all of this is confusing. I'm sure His Majesty made absolutely no effort to try and explain."

It shocks me how casually she speaks of the creature, but I try not to show it.

"No, he didn't. He told me to lock myself in the room and not to come out for anything."

"Stupid man," Dina mumbles, and with those two simple words she endears herself to me. I try not to smile. "He's always been so secretive, which is so stupid on his part. How much do you know?"

"I know he was cursed by someone who wanted revenge on the king. That he's—whatever he is—until the day he dies unless he can break the curse. That's why I'm here, I guess. That part still doesn't make sense. I've been doing research for him."

"It's hard to understand why he would bargain for someone to live here, and I won't make excuses for him. But please do understand, he does need you. Maybe more than he realizes."

There's passion in her words, and I can see she cares about the creature greatly. While I've seen moments of him being almost kind, I can't wrap my mind around the fact that he inspires this kind of loyalty. But maybe, just maybe, she'll be able to give me some answers. I don't dare to wish for all.

"Can you tell me how you're here now?"

She nods, motioning for us to sit on the window seat. I keep the kitchen knife out, but I do lead her to the couch.

"Prepared, are you?" She nods toward the knife.

"Always. It's the best I could do."

"Do you know how to handle yourself with a weapon?" She's not unkind in her question. Most people back home are because they could never imagine me good with a blade.

"Yes. I trained with one of the goons back at home."

Dina nods. "Good, a woman should always know how to handle herself in any situation. A fight, included."

"I agree." I don't say anything else, waiting her out. She smirks, knowing exactly the tactic I'm using.

"I like you, Nikita." When I make a face, she shrugs. "His Majesty told us your name. Well, we gave him little choice in the matter."

I raise my eyebrows, and she continues. "If you may

have noticed, the castle is particularly fond of statues as its main means of decoration—"

She doesn't have to keep going because it clicks automatically.

"You're them? The statues? But how?"

"You are smart." Dina smiles, but there's a bit of sadness in her eyes. "We are cursed, along with the royal family, to spend our lives in this cycle, until the curse is broken."

"Cycle?"

"Every full moon, we are given a twelve-hour window in which we come alive again."

"The whole castle?"

"No. Those who would hurt His Majesty the most. Most of the staff stay frozen. But those of us who are closest to him, we come alive. It's a kind of torture, reminding him of what he can't have. And as he grows more—" She catches herself, taking a deep breath. "Myself, his captain of the guard, and his half-sister, the three of us have always stood by his side and now, we get to torture him with our presence."

I give myself a moment to digest that. Whoever this magical person is, who cursed this kingdom, she sure knew what she was doing. It's the oldest trick in the book. Torture your captive with the wellbeing of their closest family and friends. It's hitting someone right where it hurts.

"Why did he want me to stay here, away from you?"

"I'm not sure, Nikita. I think—he may be trying to protect himself and you."

I let that sink in as well, glancing out into the night sky.

The moon shines bright, nearly as bright as the sun does during the day in my home realm. I haven't seen the sun here, as it is always covered by the fog, but somehow, the moon pushes through. I should feel more excited, getting these bits of information, but I don't. I just feel sadder.

In the weeks that I've been here, I haven't found anything in those books that could be of help to the creature. Not even close.

"Dina—" I stop because I'm not sure how to ask what I want to know more than anything. I doubt she would answer honestly, even if I straight out ask her. But maybe...

"You want to know about him, right?"

"I do. He hasn't—he hasn't shown himself to me. Is he...deformed? Sick? He won't let me see him, and it's driving me insane."

Dina doesn't reply right away as she too looks out the window. I don't expect an answer, because she doesn't owe me anything. But then, she opens her mouth to speak, and I sit up a little straighter.

A roar, louder than I've ever heard it, sounds from somewhere deep in the castle, shaking the walls around us, and then it is followed by one word.

"Dina!"

❧ 12 ❧

We jump to our feet, facing the door just as it bursts open. I expect the creature to come through, full of the anger we heard in his roar, but it's another man I've never seen before. He runs into the room, slamming the door behind him.

"Dina, you had to, didn't you?" he asks, shaking his head as he leans against the door.

"Of course I did. Look at her."

The man turns his eyes on me, and I'm shocked by how incredibly blue they are. His hair is dark. He's wearing an outfit similar to Dina's, except there's a splash of gold across his torso, as if he's wearing a sash.

"I am sorry we are not meeting under better circumstances," the man says. "I am Yevgenii Alexandrovich, the captain of the guard for the crown king and prince." He inclines his head in a nod, and I feel like I need to curtsey or something.

"I'm Nikita Arturovna, the bargained upon prisoner of the crown prince."

Dina snorts beside me, and I glance over at her to see her trying to keep from laughing. At least she thinks I'm funny. When I glance back at Yevgenii, there's amusement in his eyes too.

"I see what you mean, Dina."

I'm definitely missing something here. They're speaking a language I understand but saying things I do not.

"Mind clueing a girl in? And what's the deal with him?" I point to the door as another roar sounds behind it.

"He's just being a little angsty," Yevgenii says, which earns the door another bang. I'm surprised all over again at the casual way the captain of the guard speaks about his prince.

"I am not angsty!" the creature shouts. This time, I can't help but chuckle. He sounds so pouty. But the moment the sound escapes my lips all eyes turn to me, and the creature grows quiet.

"What?" I glance between the two who are in the room with me.

"Nothing," they answer in unison. I narrow my eyes, but they turn away, both of them tense. For some inexplicable reason, I'm the only one in the room who isn't afraid of the creature. He may sound angry, but to my ears, there's no danger in it. I wonder when I've arrived at this point, where I think that I can read his moods.

Suddenly, I have an idea. I march to the door with purpose, keeping my eyes on the captain of the guard. He gives me a confused look as I place a finger over my lips. Then, I simply motion for him to move aside. Understanding comes over his features, and he opens his mouth to protest. I shake my head, using my eyes to plead with him. Yevgenii looks over my head at Dina and the two share another bit of communication I can't interpret. Then, without a second's hesitation, he pulls the door open.

Stepping out, I expect to come face to face with the creature, but the hallway is completely empty. There must be a thousand ways into the secret passages between these walls because he disappears way too fast. Or maybe he's only beyond the shadows, and I can't see him, but he sees me. I make sure to roll my eyes at the darkness, just in case. Dina and Yevgenii step out behind me. When I turn to face them, they look almost contrite.

"I'm sorry, Nikita," Dina says. "He's not a horrible person, he's just been raised by one."

"I understand that." Because I do. "But what's the point of running from me if he wants my help?"

Dina and Yevgenii exchange another look. Before they speak again, I already know they're not divulging any secrets.

"That's his story to tell."

I nod, glancing back and forth down the hallway once more. He really isn't making it more appealing to help him when he acts like that. But that gives me an idea. I'm here helping him, even though it's against my will, but that doesn't mean I have to focus only on him. Giving the two soldiers in front of me a smile, I say,

"Since he doesn't want to be around me, how about we

find something for us to do? Like, let's see if we can try some ways of getting you out of your suspended stasis?"

"What do you mean?"

"Well, now that I know you exist, I may be able to use that information to help you. It's worth a shot, right?"

I'm still kind of trying to wrap my mind around the fact that the statues I pass on my run every day are actual people, but this is not the time to freak out about it. Honestly, the whole idea is kind of freaking me out a little, but I decide that putting my focus on actually helping these people is more beneficial. Plus, I'm a little desperate for company.

There's that look between the two again. This time, I realize it's because they have a relationship that surpasses simple employer and employee one. There's warmth in their eyes when they look at each other, and that makes me want to help them even more. When they turn back to me, I already know what their answer will be.

"Lead the way, *umnaya devushka*," Dina says, grinning.

❧ 13 ❧

We head for the study first, and once inside, Yevgenii and Dina do a quick flip through the books I've been studying. I have notes upon notes regarding curses, but I've never been able to find one specific for the creature. However, their whole predicament is something more tangible that I can use, considering how specific their stasis is.

"You've done a lot of work," Yevgenii comments, reading over one of the pages.

"Don't tell *him* this, but I'm a huge fan of research. While I haven't been able to find anything that might help his situation, there might be something that helps yours. Can you tell me a little about it?"

Dina and Yevgenii exchange a look. I don't need to be a mind reader to understand that it's a difficult conversation for them. I can't even imagine. I open my mouth to tell them they don't have to when Dina speaks up.

"It's a strange state. We can't feel anything, or move,

but we know we're alive. Except not one hundred percent aware. It's almost like we're hanging onto the real world, but only by a thread. So, we're way far down in the well, unable to really experience the world above us."

My chest grows heavy with compassion as she talks. It does sound very much like torture, being aware but having no control over anything. Even oneself. The *volshebnitsya* sure did a number on this kingdom.

"It sounds different than a curse that turns someone into a beast. That really is the only information he's ever given me. And that came mostly from my papa. But maybe your curse is not entirely his curse."

"We never thought of looking at the curses as separate entities. We've always simply assumed they were connected," Yevgenii says.

"I think they are connected, but maybe they're not entirely attached? Something like a puzzle piece that fits into another but hasn't been fully pushed in?" I say, shrugging. "I'm very new to the magic world, and I have absolutely no idea how everything works, but maybe that's what's helpful here. I can think outside the box. And this is pretty outside the box."

"It's a very good observation," a new voice comments. I twist around to watch a woman step inside the study. She's beautiful in that way that I see in paintings, sharp features and clean jawline. Her blonde hair is twisted up on top of her head, and she wears a golden tiara. The dress she has on is a deep pink, a ballgown with a full skirt, and long sleeves that start at her shoulders, leaving her collarbones exposed. She carries herself with a dignified pose. I can instantly tell she's someone of high social status.

"*Princessa* Larisa." Dina and Yevgenii bow immediately while I continue to stare. Belatedly, I do a half curtsey, which earns me a very regal chuckle.

"No need for formalities, Nikita. Not when you are wearing my clothes."

I glance down at the simple green dress I have on. It's nothing like her glittery gown, but it's beautiful in its simplicity. It has a wide neckline with sleeves that go down to my elbows and a skirt that swishes softly around my ankles. That's when it hits me. Of course he didn't find clothes just for me. I'm using someone else's wardrobe.

"I'm sorry, I didn't know."

"Of course you did not. My brother is even more tight-lipped about his affairs than he used to be."

This makes sense. She's the other part of the creature's inner circle that comes alive. She's royalty. I can tell that even without all the pretty clothes; it's in the way she carries herself. But for some reason, after the initial shock, I don't find her as intimidating as I thought I'd be if I met a royal. I suppose I have met one in the form of the creature, but I don't think he counts until he meets me face to face.

"He really is being most difficult," I say, shrugging. *Princessa's* laugh rings out around us as she winks at the soldiers. Dina and Yevgenii smile. They seem comfortable with each other, even with the status of birth between them. That makes me like them even more.

"He is. But from what I've heard, you are handling him wonderfully."

"Well, I wouldn't go that far. But I haven't tried stabbing him yet, so that is a big deal to me."

This time, all three of them laugh, and it hits me just how much I have missed such a simple sound. Or just the sound of other people talking. I think I may have forgotten those types of noises exist. It's just been me with my thoughts, and the drafts within the castle walls that keep me company. Now, I will have to get used to the quiet all over again.

"You are a rare breed, Nikita," *Princessa* Larisa says with a smile. I realize then that she's a little older than the rest of us, maybe in her late twenties, early thirties. That makes me wonder, once again, how old the creature is. I don't ask because I don't think they want to talk about him right now. Not when I gave them this whole new aspect of their predicament to focus on.

"I was wondering about something," I begin. I know they think I want to know about him, but I do go in that direction. "If the curse was cast by this person—"

"*Volshebnitsya*," Dina supplies.

"Yes." I point at her, and she smiles. "Shouldn't she have given you a way to earn a way back? Isn't that how these types of curses work? From what I've read, the curser always provides a way for redemption, depending on the type of curse it is. You have to work for your life, to put it in simple terms."

"You are correct on the type of curse this is," *Princessa* Larisa says, taking a seat on the love seat. "But even though the type of curse is a redemption one, she casted it in punishment and decided not to provide a way out."

"But I thought it's part of the curse makeup to provide an answer to that question if it were asked?"

"Yes, but no one has had a chance to ask."

"Why not? Why can't we find her now? Isn't there a tracking spell we can perform or something?" I'm getting a bit eager, but I'm finally feeling as if there's tangible action I can do about this whole mess. And not because it might mean my freedom. I truly want to help these people. I've spent twenty minutes in their presence, and I can tell their characters right away. I guess the syndicate is good for something, because it has taught me how to be a judge of character based on one simple interaction. Here, I've received a few, I know they're not bad people. They didn't ask for the curse. They were just at the wrong place at the wrong time. I can't imagine how that would feel. Well, maybe I can.

"No one has been able to track her for years. There was a rumor going around Skazka that she was defeated by the queen of the *Zelenoye Korolevstvo* and stripped of her powers."

"Stripped? That's possible?"

"In a way." Yevgenii picks up where *Princessa* Larisa leaves off. "Because of the type of an ancient creature she is, the stripping of powers is not forever. Her powers are rejuvenating even as we speak. But in the meantime, we cannot track her, for in this space and time, her magic only exists within these castle grounds."

We grow quiet then as I mull over the information. Clearly, they too have spent time in this study looking for answers. If we can't find her, that means we have to do it the old-fashioned trial and error way. I have no idea how that works when it comes to magic. We might do something that makes it worse. From what I've gathered from my readings, there is a time limit, or a countdown, with these types of curses. But the creature hasn't provided me with that information. I can only assume he's getting desperate, if me being here is any indication of that. The only thing I can do is try.

I suppose it's not up to me to make the decision anyway. It's up to them. They have to decide for themselves if they're willing to risk it all. I'm about to ask that question when another one pops up, my curiosity peaking.

"This *Volshebnitsya* that you speak off, who is she?"

The three of them exchange a long look, as if stilling themselves against the answer. Then, it is Dina who answers.

"Her name is Baba Yaga."

"You mean to tell me that the crazy old witch who eats children and lives in a house that moves around on chicken legs is a real creature?" I ask when I finally find my voice. I'm not sure why that thought terrifies me so much, but out of all the creatures I've read about, she's the one who stuck with me. I walk over to the table and pick up a book I've been reading, flipping it open to a full-page drawing. "Her?"

The woman on the page looks like a walking corpse. Her skin is old and rotting, her teeth black and pointed. Her hair hangs like limp noodles around her face. She's dressed in rags, and she's riding in a barrel. Right beside her is her hut, on two chicken legs. According to the story, the hut moves around, so no one can ever find it. Baba Yaga is the original bargainer of these lands. She lures children into her yard so she can feast on their flesh.

"That is a very interesting representation of her," Dina says, looking over the page. "In all honesty, Baba Yaga is a stunningly beautiful and ageless woman. She entices you with her beauty and charm, and when she cooks you for dinner, that's when she shows this side of herself."

I glance between the three people in the room, wondering if they're joking. But there's no merriment on their faces as they stare at the page I'm holding open. There's sadness and regret. I slam the book shut, making them jump.

"Well, if we can't find her, let's see if we can find something that might unbind you to whatever curse was put on your royal prince." I turn back to the table and my notes.

"You really don't like him, do you?" *Princessa* asks from the couch. She too has a book open on her lap now, but she's watching me curiously.

"I don't know him enough to make a valid judgement, just an educated guess. So far, he's holding me against my will to pay off a bargain that shouldn't have been made in the first place. But he hasn't done anything to hurt me since I've been here, and he has provided for my normal human needs such as food and sleep. That makes him a contradiction."

"And if we tell you he's not as bad as his father?"

"I would say I need to be able to see that for myself. I don't take other people's words for anything. Plus, I don't know his father. I don't know what he's done on a personal level. If we were all to pay for the sins of our fathers, well —" I stop, before I go down that rabbit hole. After clearing my throat, I continue. "I make my own judgments, and so far, he has taken my freedom and hasn't given me much in return. The scales are not tipped in his favor."

No one says anything to that, and that's when I hear it.

There's a whisper of a noise, right beyond the hidden door leading to the piano room. My eyes zero in on the sliver of light peeking through the tiny opening, and I see the shadow move. Without hesitation, I race for the door, pulling it open and running into the piano room. He's there, right beyond the shadows.

I'm breathing heavily, my body alive with anticipation. I take a step closer, no longer cautious in my movements. So much information has been thrown at me at once, but what I said stands. I need to be able to judge for myself.

"Show yourself to me," I whisper, knowing full well he can hear me. We're close enough now that if I wanted to, I could throw myself at him, and he'd have to catch me. He doesn't reply at first, but I can hear him breathing. The sound mingles with that of my own beating heart. I don't understand why this is so important to me, but it is.

"Why does it matter?" His voice is gruff, as if it's full of the emotions I'm feeling as well. I don't know if the others followed me in here because my full attention is on him.

"Because you brought me here to help, and I want to know who I'm helping."

The words echo around us, as if I've shouted them into the wind. In fact, I spoke them so softly, they're but a whisper. I know in my heart that what he looks like doesn't actually matter to me. Hideous or not, it's the glimpses of his kindness and the way his people care about him that intrigues me. But if he shows himself to me? That's important. Because it's all about trust.

If he steps into the light, then he trusts me.

"You have already created an image of me in your head." The words startle me with their venom. "Does it truly matter for you to see the monster I've become? I'm already a monster in your mind."

Then, before I can say or do anything else, he leaps right at me. The shadow of his large body is all I see as I jump out of the way. I land on my hands and side. When I turn, he's already in the secret passage and disappearing into the pitch black.

I stay on the floor, every positive thought of him gone. I don't know why I keep trying to humanize him. He's nothing but a monster.

"Nikita." Dina is by my side in two strides, pulling me to my feet. "Are you alright?"

"I'm not hurt, if that's what you're asking." I know it's not. She wants to know what my opinion of her boss is. The question is obvious in her eyes as she leads me back into the light study.

"He's just trying—"

"No, please don't try to justify his actions." I interrupt her, pulling gently out of her grasp. "You may see him as something other than a beast, but that's all he's been to me. He can do whatever he wants in his solitude. I don't care. Let's focus on helping you."

They all want to say something in his defense, I can see it on their faces. Yevgenii glances at Dina and *Princessa* Larisa before he walks out of the room. They keep trying to make the creature seem like something other than a monster, but even a villain shows a soft side to those who are important to them. It's how they are with the rest of the world that matters.

Clearly, I don't matter at all.

❧ 15 ❧

We spend the next few hours in the study, making lists of curse-breaking rituals and spells to try. Apparently, anyone can perform these, with the proper ingredients. Finding those will be the real challenge. Especially since we're on borrowed time here, which they all but proved to me. I still don't have an exact time frame, and that's a little more than frustrating.

"So, every full moon you reanimate for twelve hours? But what about in between?" I ask Dina and Larisa—she said I shouldn't stand on formality—hours later. Yevgenii hasn't returned since he left to go with the creature. At this point I am absolutely refusing to think of him as anything but. I hope Yevgenii tells him a thing or two about his behavior. But I'm not hopeful. That creature is as stubborn as they come.

"In between," Dina replies, "we wait for the full moon."

"You said earlier that you're conscious? But is it more like putting something on pause?"

"Somewhat conscious," Larisa replies. "We have heard you play the piano."

"What? How?"

"The sound really carries when the world is silent." She's not looking at me as she speaks, her eyes in a faraway land. I can't imagine what they're going through, being suspended like that. I keep thinking about it. To be aware but not able to do anything about it. My heart goes out to them, and my need to fix things burns even hotter. There has to be a way I can help them. There has to be.

"How do you know it was me who played?" Suddenly, I realize what Larisa said.

"My brother hasn't touched the piano since this whole ordeal has begun."

So, it was he who played. It makes sense, I suppose. He was very defensive when I first found the instrument. It seems like a lifetime ago that I put the ring on and ended up in Skazka. I glance down at it now, where I still wear it on my pointer finger. Maybe I shouldn't bring attention to it, but I'm going to anyway.

"Do you know how this works?" I ask, raising my hand and wiggling my fingers. Dina and Larisa look up, they're eyes zeroing in on the ring.

"Where did you get that?"

"He gave it to my papa as part of the bargain. It's how I got here."

They're silent as they let that sink in. I'm confused on why this is such a big deal. It's only a portal ring, right? Or maybe, once again, I'm missing something.

"What are you not telling me? Besides, a lot." I train my eyes on them, and they smile.

"It's complicated, Nikita."

"Isn't everything, Larisa?"

She inclines her head in agreement, but of course, she won't explain further. This family sure loves their secrets. I'll chalk this up to another mystery I need to solve. I have so many of those, I don't even know where to start.

"Well, if you're not going to tell me all about the history of this ring, then what are we doing next?"

We have created a list full of ingredients I need to get, we just haven't come up with where I'm supposed to get them from.

"I think we should have dinner."

"What?" I turn toward Larisa, a little surprised. I haven't even thought of food.

"Do you guys eat? Get hungry? Wait, how does that work?" Now, another million questions are spinning in my mind.

"Thankfully, we don't get hungry while we're in that statue form. Have to be thankful for small favors I suppose," Dina replies, but she has already put the books down and is heading to the door. "But I am hungry now, so shall we?"

Larisa and I don't hesitate to follow. The candles are lit once more, guiding us toward the kitchens. Not that any of us need any help at this point. I have learned my way around this part of the castle.

"Sit, sit. Let me cook us something." Larisa motions to the counter, and I glance at Dina.

"Don't even argue with her. She loves this."

Taking my seat beside Dina at the counter, I watch as Larisa moves effortlessly around the kitchens, opening cupboards I haven't even touched. There are so many little nooks and crannies, I'm a little overwhelmed.

"Does she do this often?" I ask as Larisa opens a drawer in the fridge I've never seen before. Pushing myself up on the stool, I watch where she pushes it in before sitting down.

"Oh yes, *Princessa* is an amazing cook. It's one of her favorite pastimes. She will always make a feast, even if it's just a few of us eating."

"Does he eat with you as well?"

Dina doesn't have to ask who he is. It always comes back around to the creature. No matter what we do, it always will. I'd be lying if I said a part of me hasn't been staring into the shadows trying to see if he's there. Lurking, like he does.

"Sometimes. Lately, we've had to drag him to stay with us."

"Dina."

"What?" The soldier glances at Larisa. "I know he doesn't want us to talk about him, but I'm not saying anything she doesn't really know already. He hasn't been all that forthcoming with his company lately."

"Ain't that the truth," I mumble.

Larisa gives me a look but doesn't comment further. She continues to move around the kitchen, like she was born to do only this. I've never been a good cook, nor were my sisters. Mama was a fantastic one though. I've always wanted to be like her, but I burn more dishes than not. It's why I've stuck to the absolute basics since being here.

The way Larisa moves reminds me of my mama. She could always anticipate what a dish needs, without having to look at a recipe. It's a sweet memory, and I'm kind of thankful Larisa forces it out of me. I've been trying not to think of my parents while I'm here, because thinking about them only brings grief.

As Dina and Larisa chat, I realize that even when I was home with my sisters, we didn't have this. A simple time together where we discussed the most mundane of things, like why Larisa is using the pan she's using instead of the first one she pulled out. Larisa is explaining to Dina that this one feels better in her hand when she grips the handle.

These people have been cursed for who knows how long, they live in a constant state of suspension, but they still take the time to talk to each other and spend time together. It's beautiful and sad at the same time. But I soak it all in. It seems, I need this as much as they do.

❧ 16 ❧

When Larisa is finally finished, we have a feast in front of us. There's a salad, potatoes, and grilled chicken. Apparently, all those items were hiding in the kitchen. I thought it was just eggs and bread. Not that I could cook any of this on my own, but it is curious.

"How can this food be here?" I ask after I swallow a bite of the delicious mashed potatoes. It's been so long since I've had them made creamy like this with milk and butter and garlic, it makes me forget all my worries. For just a moment. Comfort food is its own breed of magic.

"It's part of how the curse works," Yevgenii answers, coming into the kitchen. Involuntarily, my eyes search the space behind him, wondering if the creature will make an appearance. But of course, he's doesn't. That stubborn creature loves to make everything more difficult.

"It smells amazing, as usual, *Princessa* Larisa," the captain of the guard continues, giving her a grateful smile and a small bow. Larisa sets a steaming plate of food in front of him with her own smile.

"Eat up, soldier. There's more where that came from."

Yevgenii digs in, and for a few moments, we eat in silence. But I can't switch my mind off things as easily as they can. I'm sure they've practiced in this art, since they only have small amounts of semi-freedom. I'm still on Yevgenii's comment.

"What do you mean it's part of the curse?" I finally ask, leaning forward so I can see his face. His hand freezes on the way to his mouth, and he gives me a look before he grins.

"You really are relentless, just like he said."

My skin warms up at those words because they mean the creature was talking about me and I—well, I don't know how I feel about that. Yevgenii takes a spoonful of food, and I narrow my eyes.

"Thank you for the compliment, but don't try to distract me, *Capitan*. I *am* relentless. So, you really should just give in now."

Both Larisa and Dina chuckle at that, probably glad I'm turning my attention on Yevgenii and not them so at least they can eat in peace.

"Okay," Yevgenii finally says, putting his spoon down. "The whole point of this curse is to punish, *da*? Well, the best way to punish someone is to take away the things they love most. In Gavriil's case, that thing is freedom. The curse provides for itself. So he can live here for as long as his body will allow it, and the food will replenish, and the milk won't go bad. The clothes will stay clean and fresh.

It's those basics necessities of life, and it's simply part of the torture."

"Something went bad in here," I point out, because when I first got here, there was definitely something in the kitchen. The smell is gone now, so I'm not sure what it was or what happened.

"That might've been the aftereffects of one of the useless spells we've tried." Dina says. That perks me up.

"Wait, so you have tried various spells?"

"Not in the same way we will with you. We've tried breaking his curse, but since we're only here periodically, it's difficult to work on different options. And now that our time—anyway, the curse is—"

"What he's trying to say..." Larisa interrupts flawlessly, but I don't miss the effortless way she commands the room. Yevgenii gives her a grateful smile as I look between the two of them. "Is that we appreciate you helping us. Regardless of how you came to be here, for which we are extremely sorry."

She gives me a kind smile, and I shake my head in return.

"It's not you who needs to apologize," I say, all thought of food fleeing. I'm getting antsy again. The need to do something, to have some kind of control at least over an aspect of this situation, rises within me.

"We need a plan," I announce. "On how I can find the ingredients."

Just then, a bell resounds in the castle, echoing through the near empty hallways. It makes me jump. Now I know they're not exactly empty, not with the statues residing all over the castle grounds. That somehow makes this all the more terrible.

"What in the world is that?" I ask.

"I'm afraid that's our cue," Dina says, jumping off the stool. I watch as they grab their dishes and carry them over to the sink before they turn to me.

"It's time for us to take our places. We will see you again in a few months, on the night of the full moon."

"Places?" I follow them out into the hallways.

"Yes. We must return to where we were standing, or we'll experience pain until we're there."

"Wait, what if you don't return? What if you stay here, even in pain, won't that be better?"

"No, Nikita, it would not be. One day, you will have the answers you seek, and you will understand," Larisa says before she reaches over to give me a hug. Her arms come around me, holding me to her as if we've been friends for ages instead of half a day. It's been so long since I've been touched, I nearly start crying.

"Do not be too hard on him," she whispers in my ear. "Try to find common ground. You will be surprised at how much the two of you actually have in common."

She releases me then and rushes after Dina and Yevgenii. I watch as the soldiers hold hands, giving the other a quick squeeze and then go their separate ways. I follow Larisa to a room in the opposite direction of my bedroom. Or I suppose, her bedroom. She turns to give me one last smile, stopping in front of the window, and then she's a statue once more. There's no sound, no flash of light. One moment she's alive, and the next, she's something other.

My hand reaches toward her, but I can't bring myself to touch her now. Thinking back to how many times I've brushed against them, or wished they weren't in the way, makes me feel guilty.

I glance at the other statues up and down the hallways, and my heart goes out to them. I have two and half months to figure out a way to help them. Or at least a place to start. I have a lot of work to do.

❧ 17 ❧

Two days later, I hear him outside the study. It
sounds like pacing. It's officially my birthday,
and I am in a foul mood. He's been hiding from
me for days, and now he shows up, on a day that was
supposed to be special to me. Except now, it'll be the day I
will try and forget.

I'm supposed to be home. I'm supposed to be cele-
brating this huge milestone with my papa. I'm sure my
sisters would've made an appearance as well. It's the first
birthday I've truly cared about. It's the point in my life
where I was going to be taken seriously. Well, it would've
been a start, an open door I could've walked through. I
never expect anything to be easy, but at least, legally I
would have a say. Finally.

Yet here I am, combing through more useless information. Okay, now I'm just being nasty to myself. No information is truly useless. I'm just extra salty today. Given the
circumstances, I think I'm allowed.

But now, my already bad day is about to get worse because he's back. Mr. Broody himself. I'm fed up with his shadow play.

"Are you coming in or are you going to sulk in the hallway?" I call out, loud enough for him to hear. The noise stops, as if he was pacing before and now, he's focused on me.

"Coming in would be pointless. I cannot help."

Oh, he's back to his formal tone. Well, fine. Two can play that game.

"That is very unfortunate, Mr. Princely Beast. Maybe you can try sharing some information with your prisoner as to why that is?"

There's a moment of silence, then a small growl, and that brings a smile to my face. I'm getting to him. Good.

"Don't call me that."

"*Nyet?* You don't like Princely Beast? I thought it was fitting. My other choice is Broody Pants, but I don't even know if you're wearing pants. Maybe you prefer robes? Or kilts?"

"I wear pants."

"Look at that, learn something new every day."

He growls again, and this time it's unmistakable. I'm pushing all his buttons. It's interesting how I don't have to do much. He reminds me so much of the boys I used to know in the organization. Their need to be the smartest or the coolest in the room outweighed everything else. In the creature's case, I think it's a combination, but it's also what he's used to. He's royal. That means I should be falling all over myself trying to please him.

Tough luck, *malchik*.

"You are being difficult again," he comments. For a second, he sounds almost tired. That makes me grin even bigger.

"I told you it's my best quality." I shrug, even though I can't tell if he can see me. Since he's been so distant lately, I can't begin to guess what kind of mood he's in, but this is as good a time as any for me to bring up my proposition. I thought about it all day yesterday, and I think it'll work.

"I found some old maps in the desk," I begin, raising my eyes so I'm speaking directly to the doorway. "There's a village, not far from here. I assume that's where a lot of your servants lived."

"It's not close."

"Anyway," I hurry on before he starts spewing facts. "There are vendors there, at least according to your catalogues, that might be able to retrieve or even already possess the needed ingredients."

"You are absolutely not leaving the castle!" The creature's voice is sharp and strong. I know he's expecting me to cower, but that's not how I play. Placing my hands on my hips, I walk around the desk and stare at the doorway.

"This is our only option, unless you can scour up any of these herbs or containers. They have to be very specific, in order for the spell to work. I assume your people gave you a rundown of what I'm trying to accomplish. I need these ingredients."

"Absolutely not."

"You can't just keep saying no without an explanation."

"I can."

Groaning, I throw my hands up in the air.

"You are insufferable!" I say, taking another step toward

the door. "Your people are in trouble and there's a possibility that I may be able to do something about that. Isn't it worth trying?"

At first, he doesn't reply. For a second, I think he left, but no. I can hear his breathing as he mulls my words over.

"It's too dangerous."

"I can take care of myself."

"Can you?" It's his turn to let out a little anger. "You know nothing of these woods, of the dangers they hold. It is not a stroll in the park but a treacherous path. It is out of the question."

He gets significantly quieter when he talks, and I find the stillness in his words a lot more intimidating than the shouting. If he was anyone else, I'd think a part of him is concerned about me. But I know better. He needs to protect his investment.

So, I try another tactic.

"Am I bound to the castle grounds as you are?"

He pauses for a second. "*Nyet*."

"Will the village be able to provide the ingredients I seek?"

Another pause. "*Da*."

"Can you get the needed ingredients any other way?"

"*Nyet*."

"Do you care about Yevgenii, Dina, and *Princessa* Larisa?"

There's no hesitation in his answer now. "I do."

"Then let me try. What's the worst thing that can happen?"

This time the pause is long enough that I don't think he'll answer, but then he does.

"You could die."

There's something in his voice I have not heard before, and it makes me want to close the distance between us and reach out. Instead, I curl my hand into a fist by my side, chiding myself for such a foolish emotion. I am not here to comfort this creature.

"And I could die eating a piece of bread if it goes down the wrong way," I say instead. I think I've stopped him for a second.

"Nikita—"

"Please," I interrupt, because I can't deal with hearing him say my name like that. Like we're more than just a prison guard and a prisoner. There has to be a line drawn between us, and neither one of us can cross it.

"I am more than capable, and I need to do this. You need to let me do this."

I really think he won't, but then, "You leave tomorrow, at first light."

❦ 18 ❦

I'm up before the shadows have a chance to dissipate outside. That's something I've learned since coming here; there is no morning sunrise. The shadows simply pull back for the day before claiming the castle grounds every night. The moon is the only celestial body that makes an appearance. The rest of the time, it gets lighter and darker when it's supposed to, but it's always gloomy, as if there is continuous cloud cover that surrounds us. And that fog. That insufferable fog. It leaves me cold and damp, and I hate it.

This morning, I'm dressed and ready to go in nearly no time at all. Just like I used to do for important meetings, I picked out the clothes I would wear last night and had my toiletries laid out for use. Papa was always impressed by how little time it took for me to get ready and how put together I looked. It reminded him of Mama.

Pausing, I give myself thirty seconds to feel her absence. A part of me yearns to see her face, for even only a moment, and hear her say that everything will be okay. I miss my parents. Maybe that might sound strange to others, but to me, my parents have always been my closest confidants. With my mama when I was a little girl, and with my papa for the years since. I can't imagine what he must be thinking right now. I've been gone for over a month with no way of contacting each other. Or returning home.

But then the thirty seconds have passed, and I push all those thoughts away as I square my shoulders and reach for my clothes. Opting for one of the less flashy dresses, I shrug it on, wishing for my pants something fierce. The dark blue of the dress compliments my complexion. The sleeves cover my arms all the way to the wrists, for extra protection against the elements. The cut is simple with a full skirt that goes all the way to the floor. It's not my outfit of choice, but it's necessary.

I know what it means to fit in, to work with what you've been given. Since I now live in a magical realm with very specific wardrobe requirements, I have no choice in the matter. Not that I mind the dress. It's just easier to protect myself if I'm wearing pants. I've never fought in a dress before.

This is simply how my mind works. It creates scenarios and outcomes, projecting the options in front of me. It's why I've always been good at handling papa's business. It's why he started taking me to the meetings with him. I could see the whole picture, not simply the parts others wanted to present. This skill is going to help me now.

Brushing my long hair out, I make quick work of the strands as I braid them. All of this takes less than ten minutes. Once done, I give myself a quick study in the mirror. My eyes roam over the braid, the dark blue dress, and my boots hidden beneath my skirts. Plus, I wear a cross body bag I found in the closet.

I look like my mama. A ting of pain comes again, the longing for home nearly pushing through my sturdy walls. But as much as I am my mama's daughter, I am also my papa's. He taught me how to work through those waves of feelings and not give them a place to control me.

There's no use in letting my emotions rule my actions. If I let them, I can spend days on the bed, crying myself to sleep. But that won't do anyone any good. That is why it's important for me to stay proactive. That means doing what I can to break this stupid curse so that the bargain can be fulfilled, and I can be free. My desire to kill the creature has dwindled down, but it rises back up every now and then, especially when he's being particularly stubborn.

Leaving my room behind, I power walk down the stairs and to the study. The list of ingredients I will need is waiting for me on top of my books, but I don't reach for it yet. I did this when I first came here, but I want to do another quick search.

"What are you doing?" The voice comes from the shadows in the direction of the piano room. One of these days, I swear I will find the blueprints to this castle and then I'll be the one sneaking up on him.

"Good morning to you too."

There's a low growl, which only causes me to smile. I pull out another drawer, giving it a quick scan.

"I'm looking for a weapon, if you must know." I reply, and there's an almost stunned moment of silence.

"A weapon?"

"Don't worry. This time, it's not for you. I need a knife, at least, when I head to the woods." The kitchen knife I keep in my room isn't going to do much if I come across anyone.

There's another pause filled with silence.

"You are still determined to go." It's not a question, but I stop what I'm doing and turn toward the direction of his voice anyway.

"Don't I look ready? I got Larisa's best non-royal dress on, and my hair is braided."

"Does the hair have a special meaning?" He sounds incredibly curious, and I try to suppress my smile.

"But of course. Every hairstyle has a meaning. The braid is the one that gets me through long tough days. Ponytails are for business meetings."

"And when it's down?" I'm surprised by the question and the tone. His voice is suddenly softer and more— gentle somehow. It's as if my answer means something. I don't understand why that makes me want to answer him, but I do so. Honestly.

"Down is strictly for people that I care about."

There's that silent pause again, but this time, it's filled with something else I can't identify. He feels closer, even though the half-open door hides him from me. I get that urge again, to see if he'll step into the light and let me see him. But I squash it before it can take root.

Today is not about him. He's still a pain in my side. Today is about helping his people, who I like much better than him. Focusing on the task at hand, I pull out another drawer, even though I already know what I'll find in there.

"So, are you going to find me a knife? Or a gun. I know people can't bring them here, but do you have any? Because that would be very helpful."

When he doesn't reply right away, I turn back to stare at the doorway. It's so frustrating, having to gauge his moods when I can't even see his face.

"Have you looked on the desk?" he asks, making me narrow my eyes.

"On?"

"Yes, on."

If I didn't know any better, I'd say that's a smile I hear in his voice. But obviously, I know better. Except, I kind of want it to be a smile. What is going on with me today? I'm all over the place. This is not how Nikita Arturovna handles herself. Living here, away from the organization, is making me soft.

Shaking my head—at myself—I glance at the top of the desk. My list of items is still there, but now I see there are items underneath it I didn't notice before. Picking the list up, I find a map, a bag of coins, and a dagger. Grinning, I reach for the weapon that is about the size of my forearm. It's sheathed. The blade is shiny when I pull it out, situated against a hilt that's more beautiful than any dagger I've ever seen.

Intricate vines grow around the handle. When I wrap my hand around it, it feels secure and sure. It feels like it was made just for me.

"Thank you," I whisper, completely mesmerized.

"You are welcome."

His gentle whisper carries over to me like a breeze, sending goosebumps over my skin. These tiny glimpses into the kind of man he could be are doing something to my insides. I have no idea how to handle it.

Growing up in the organization, I have always known how to handle the male gender. And the female for that matter. But the syndicate is a boy's club, and I've done my best to learn how to play their game. But with him—my shadow captor—the rules don't apply. I don't like that.

Rules are there to keep everything running smoothly. Rules are helpful and good.

Now, I'm living a life with no rules and it's making everything in me unbalanced. Closing my eyes briefly, I take a deep breath to try and center myself. My mind is flighty, and now I realize it's because I'm nervous. Of course I am. Any sane person would be. Just because I'm strong, doesn't mean I'm not still human. I'm about to walk into a magical forest all by myself.

"Nikita?" The soft whisper snaps me out of my metal freak out. I glance up toward the doorway. There was real concern in his voice just now, and that makes me even more unbalanced than I already am.

"A map?" I pick up the parchment, holding it tilted in his direction. It's better if I stay on track.

"Yes." He clears his voice. "If you follow it east right out of the gardens and north at the first fork, you will reach the closest trading village in a few hours. I would offer you a horse, but they are all in the same predicament as the rest of the castle."

Makes sense. I study the map, realizing it seems to be inked by hand.

"Are you sure I can take this with me? It looks to be one of a kind."

"It is. But I want you to have it. Even if you get turned around, there are markings for you to follow."

I look closer at the drawings, realizing that's true. Folding it carefully, I place it in one of the two pockets in my bag, along with the list of ingredients. The dagger straps around my waist and then I'm ready.

"What about the ring?" I ask suddenly, remembering the heirloom I still wear on my finger. There's a small pause, as if he's finding the words before he replies.

"It won't work." There's a catch in his voice, and I'm definitely missing something.

"You can have it back. I—"

"No!" The protest comes fast. I pause in the process of removing the ring. "Please, keep it. It's important to me, and it is safer with you."

There's definitely something else there, but now is not the time or place to discover it. I keep the ring on though, making a mental note to dig into this later.

Turning toward where the creature is hiding, I give him a confident smile.

"You will not change your mind." It's not a question, but I answer anyway.

"Of course not."

The air fills with tension, the same type of tension he and I seem to carry with us whenever we're in the same room or close to it. If I could see his face, I'd bet his eyes are on me, roaming over me in a slow perusal, as if he's trying to figure me out. He knows I'm doing the same to him. But he can see me, and that gives him an unfair advantage. I grow bolder, the nervous energy inside me coming out with the next few words.

"How about a kiss on a cheek for good luck?"

I think I've shocked both of us into the very statues that occupy the majority of the space in this castle. My extremities are completely frozen as I try to process the words that I've spoken. The only thing I hear is my heartbeat, filling up the room around me. I can't tell if he left, or if he's still there, wondering if I've completely lost my mind.

"*Udachi*, Nikita."

His softly spoken words shatter the silence, and then there's a sound of movement, and I know he's left. Leaning against the desk, I give myself a moment to calm my racing heart. My emotions are running too hot. I need to get a grip on them before they get me into trouble.

Squaring my shoulders, I raise my chin and head for the door. I have a whole castle full of people to save. That's what I need to focus on.

❧ 19 ❧

As I make my way out the front door and down the castle's steps, I keep thinking this is a trap, and the creature will spring on me, laughing hysterically. Before he drags me off into a dungeon.

It's so much easier to paint him as the villain here. He's not innocent by any means. He's selfish and spoiled and ill mannered. But I don't think he's a villain anymore, and that's new for me. Not sure it's a wise road to take, but I've always been a good judge of character. I can see the kind of man he is underneath all that self-created armor.

He doesn't come after me.

Just like everything else in the castle, the garden is frozen in time. The one time I came out here, I didn't even stop to realize how surreal it looks. The trees are tall and green, but when I look closer, I see that they're petrified and solid. They're almost living but not quite, like the rest of this place.

I pass by the only area of the garden still alive. The hidden garden, the flowers that started this whole thing. Simply another piece to the puzzle that is this place. Why do the flowers there grow, while everything else remains in this state of suspension?

But really, should I be thinking about that right now? Of course not. I have an important journey in front of me, and I'm not quite sure I am ready for it.

I come to the edge of the gardens, farther than I've ever been before. Turning, I glance over my shoulder at the castle rising at my back. Taking it in, I realize I've never seen it as a whole before. It's a gorgeous structure with many turrets rising and falling around the circular layout. And so many windows. It makes it seem as if the castle itself is a living breathing entity, and it's watching me, waiting to see what I will do.

For a second, I think I see a shadow in the big window near the front doors. Somehow, I know it's the creature, studying me in the same way I study the castle. Wondering what kinds of secrets it—and he—hold behind their strategically erected walls.

Strangely enough, at this exact moment, it doesn't matter. All that matters is that there are innocent people inside those walls, cursed into a life of not living, and I have something to say about that.

It doesn't matter that I know nothing about the magical world. It doesn't matter that I've been brought here because of a bargain struck with my papa. I am here now, and I am my parents' daughter. If there is an injustice in the world, I will do my best to do something about it.

Turning back around, I face the forest.

A magical forest.

The trees seem taller than before, more foreboding. They rise high into the sky, getting lost in the dark blue of it. There isn't a wall here, not a physical one at least. Still, I can tell a barrier is there. I wonder if it's the curse's magic, created to keep the creature trapped here. It's funny I never thought of it this way, but he's just as much of a prisoner as I am. My heart pangs at the thought.

I will not feel sorry for him. Or for myself for that matter.

That is not who I was raised to be.

My heart feels like it will jump out of my chest at any moment. Even walking into a room full of syndicate leaders hasn't given me this much anxiety before. It's as if I'm standing at the edge of a cliff with only my will to keep me from falling into the abyss. Truth be told, that's how I've felt since I stepped foot inside the castle.

A part of me—the part that misses my family—would love nothing more than to return to a time when the only concern I had was making sure the men of the organization saw me as an equal. What a simple thing, but the most difficult to achieve. I've had to fight tooth and nail my whole life to be seen as capable.

Well, now I get to prove to myself just how capable I've become.

Inhaling deeply, I take a second to focus myself. Exhaling, I step over the invisible barrier and into the woods.

The trees stand at least 400 feet tall, and they're so big in circumference, I think I could live inside of them. There are probably creatures here who do. The only information I have about this place is what I've learned from the books in the study. Older than time itself, the forest is a living, breathing entity, full of secrets even the historians can't discover. Or put into words. There's magic all around me, but it's so new and unexplored, it's nearly intoxicating.

Creatures, such as *Leshy*, are a constant threat, so I listen for any unusual noises or voices. Old-looking trolls love to lure innocents into their traps by throwing their voice and pretending to be their loved ones. According to the books I've read, they snare innocents into their traps and then boil them alive for food. Definitely not a pleasant way to die.

I make my way through the trees, staying in as much of a straight line as I can. There's a bit of a path here, but it's been overgrown with time. According to the map the creature gave me, I will come to a fork in the road when it's time to turn.

There is a film of darkness that hangs low over the forest. Even though I know the sun is there, I can't see it through the thick branches. And yet, I know whatever barrier surrounds the castle isn't here, and therefore, the sun is. It's a knowledge that I don't understand, but I can feel deep in my gut.

Maybe I'm simply romanticizing the journey to keep myself from noticing all the noises the forest brings with it. I didn't realize how used to the silence of the castle I've grown until I can hear every leaf rustle in the gentle breeze. I stay attuned to my surroundings, just like my papa taught me. My hand is wrapped securely around the dagger's handle, sitting comfortably at my side.

The feel of it, at least, makes me think I'm prepared.

Not that I'm naïve enough to think I'm truly prepared for anything this forest, or this realm, has to offer. I haven't given myself nearly enough time to deal with the fact that I'm living in a magical castle with a cursed prince. For the first time since I stepped foot inside of this magical world, I'm alone, so I give myself a full minute to think about this. I'm a different person than I was a month ago, and that is something else I'll have to come to terms with. But that's it. Because this isn't a frolic in the woods for my own enjoyment. It's a mission.

I'm lost in my thoughts, and then I'm not. Something catches my attention. I stop, giving my surroundings a three-sixty, seeing nothing. The movement of the forest propels me forward as I hurry my steps. Nature dances around me, but there's also something just beyond my sight.

I'm not stopping again. If there is something out there stalking me, I'm not going to give it an advantage. Keeping my head held high, I walk on, making sure I'm constantly watching for traps or snares. It would be my luck to fall into one of those and be left for dead. A forest such as this is bound to have a few tricks up its sleeve besides just the creatures who live here. I don't want to get on the bad side of this forest, not if it's truly alive.

There's a small part of me that wants to get lost in the magic. When I was a little girl, I still believed in the glam of the fairytales. In good versus evil. In love conquering all. But life rarely works out that way. Especially in the Bratva. The syndicate isn't for the faint of heart, and it's definitely not for anyone who has their head in the clouds.

I keep pushing forward. The longer I walk, the louder the forest grows around me. When it seems that I'll be stuck in between these trees forever, I see it. A small clearing and a fork in the road.

It's time to go north.

❧ 20 ❦

The first thing I notice here is the sun. It's high in the sky, presiding over the trees. It stops me for a moment as I raise my face toward its warmth for the first time in weeks. Taking a few minutes, I simply soak up the light coming through the trees before I resume walking again.

The forest seems quieter here. I'm not sure if it's because I'm closer to the road. It looks well-worn, like many travelers have come through here. The creatures probably don't hang out right on the outskirts, although, I'm just guessing. I meet no one on my walk. The road is empty, yet I still stay as close to the trees as possible. I don't want to give anyone any ideas in case I do come across a traveler.

If I'm to estimate, I think I walk for another hour before the sound of people reaches toward me. I'm not quite to the town yet, but there are a few houses here and there, peeking through the trees. It's the only indication that the forest doesn't stretch for an eternity.

There isn't as much information about the land in the books I've been reading as I would like, but I do know that villages such as the one I'm about to visit are common. There are no large metropolitan cities in Skazka. There are only villages clustered together within the kingdom. It reminds me of how things are in Ukraine, my mama's birthplace. I only went there twice as a child, but I remember the smell of the town not polluted by the cars and other various fumes.

I'm sweaty and tired, and it's difficult not having a watch to keep time. It makes me feel unbalanced. But then, everything about my current situation is unbalancing.

The hum of people's voices and everyday hustle and bustle reaches me in the next half hour. The village comes into view, as if curtains are being drawn open, and suddenly, the whole stage is lit. There's a slight bend in the road. When I round it, I'm greeted with buildings and crowds.

A few people move past me, not giving me a second thought. I was in the forest, and now I'm in the village. There's almost no transition between the two.

I'm not sure what I was expecting, but it isn't a mesh of past and present that I see spread out in front of me. Many of the people wear the same type of clothing as me. It's something out of 15th century Russia. A woman passes me adorned in *sarafan* over her *rubashka*—a standard multi-colored dress with open shoulders, over a shirt. During traditional events, some of the wives of the syndicate members adorn the silk and velvet type of these dresses, as a way to show social status and preserve the heritage.

But it's been a while since I've seen them as an everyday outfit.

However, that's not as surprising as the pieces of modern clothing I see throughout. The village itself looks like it materialized from one of the old fairytale books. The buildings are mismatched and wooden for the most part. They stand close together as one continuous line, and if I'm to assume, I'd say most streets look like this.

But the people. They look like they could be from any point of time. Some are dressed in jeans, others are wearing more traditional celebration dresses from the 1700s. If someone were to ask me to describe what I'm seeing, the word "confusion" comes to mind. It's like the village couldn't pick one time to exist, so it picked all of them.

The only reasoning I can come up with is the fact that Skazka isn't a secret realm anymore. After all, my own papa travels here on business. I assume pieces of my world have simply ended up here. Just like I have. I'm not quite sure how much this world knows about my own. I wish there was someone I could ask. I have such a small amount of knowledge about this land.

There is a forest that spans across the whole of Skazka, a forest that's magical and alive and filled with wonders and walking nightmares. The kingdoms, including the creature's, carve themselves a spot between the trees, and the villages are situated throughout. There is a river that turns into an ocean, but I haven't found much information regarding that. I'm desperate for more, but I doubt anyone here will be forthcoming with information, and I don't want to push my luck in case they don't know about the human realm. Or have very limited information about it.

No one pays me any attention as I make my way with the flow of traffic. The hum of dozens of people talking is white noise that brings a plethora of memories. Even as a little girl, I accompanied papa on his travels, back when he still traveled in our realm. I remember him walking me through the crowds, my hand firmly in his, as languages I didn't speak twirled around me. Now, I'm walking all alone on my own mission. I wonder what my parents would think if they saw me now.

I really can't keep letting myself fall into these bits of despair. I miss them, yes, but that doesn't accomplish anything. Once again, I square my shoulders and raise my chin just a tiny bit, giving everyone—and myself—a visual cue. I'm not here to play games.

The narrow street takes me to the center of this small village. Since it's a trading post, it makes sense to have so many people present. But when I step into the center of town, I'm slightly overwhelmed. An outdoor bazaar stretches in front of me, with so many bodies moving through it, I can hardly see the stalls.

Gripping the hilt of the dagger in one hand, and the coin bag in the other, I push myself through the crowd. The going is slow, the bodies squishing me on every side. I may be outside, but the air is stiffer than when I was within the walls of the castle. The sounds of the *balalaika* mix with the noise of people talking. I glance over to the left to find a group of musicians. I smile automatically, the music so familiar to my ears. It makes me feel slightly better.

It takes me a good amount of time, but I finally spot a stall that could be useful.

The woman behind the table looks like every *babushka* I have ever met. My own had passed before I could meet her, but plenty of syndicate members still honored their elders, so I've seen them at the main events.

"*Dobrii den.*" I greet the woman with a smile. She's dressed much like the women I first encountered at the edges of the village, in a *sarafan* over her white shirt. Except even with the table between us, I can tell her *sarafan* is of the expensive kind, all velvet and ribbon and hand stitched designs. A beautifully patterned multicolored headscarf is tied around her hair and under her chin. She greets me with her own smile, putting me at ease somehow.

"*Zdrastvui, devochka.* What has caught your eye?" she waves her hand over the table in front of her, and I glance down, wondering what did. My gaze finds jars, neatly stacked at one end.

"I am in need of herbal glass jars. I see you also have lavender."

She moves to grab the items for me before I even finish speaking. Laying them out in front of me, she smiles.

"What you seek is not for the faint of heart. Are you truly ready for the sacrifice?"

For a second, I think she's speaking to someone else. But her kind eyes are trained on me, waiting for an answer. I'm not quite sure what to say, considering I don't truly know what she means.

"What do you mean by sacrifice?"

She smiles again, and somehow, there's even more kindness in the way her lips curl up. She seems to be looking inside of me somehow. I don't know how to react. There's wisdom of the years in her eyes. Maybe I can risk asking a question or two. It's not like the creature said anything about keeping him a secret. That's something I was planning on doing myself because I don't like to give away tactical advantage when it comes to enemies. In my situation, everyone is an enemy right now.

Except this woman. Somehow, I don't think she means me any harm, and I decided a long time ago to listen to my gut.

"*Pozhalusta*, if you—" I have to phrase this the right way. Leaving closer to her, over the table, I run through scenarios. I can't outright ask her, can I? But maybe there's something on my face that clues her in because she reaches over, giving my hand a gentle squeeze.

"You are of a good heart, and you have done a noble deed. But the journey has only begun, *devochka*. Much is still required of you."

"You mean—the curse?"

"A harsh and terrible magic." She *tsk tsks* a few times, leaning back. Her hands fold over her middle, and she keeps my gaze. "But there is a stronger magic still. You will find it when the time comes. Take these, and they will be of service to you. They will help you see." She pushes lavender and two more pouches toward me, along with a jar. There's a loud commotion at my back, and I twist around to see two men arguing. When I turn back to the woman, she's gone. It's as if she was never there at all. The ingredients wait for me on the table, and I pick them up without hesitation. Looking closely, I see the pouches contain the crystals and the herbs I need for the spell.

Grabbing my bag, I place the items inside, along with

the glass jars, before moving away from the stall. For some reason, it feels like the eyes of everyone at the bazaar are on me, but I don't dare stop and look around. By some magic, I have everything I need. It's time to head back.

❧ 21 ❧

Leaving is not in the cards just yet. I'm only pretending to do so. It's a trick I learned from papa, in case someone becomes too interested in me. It's the easiest way to figure it out because they will break away from the crowd.

I walk quickly, keeping the cross-body bag close to me as the throng of people becomes overwhelming. My mind races with questions about the woman, and how exactly she knew what I needed. Especially since she disappeared right after. This place simply doesn't make sense. I have questions, with no way of getting any answers, and it's the most frustrating thing in the world.

A sign over a door catches my eye, and I pivot toward it. Stepping inside, my senses are instantly assaulted by the smell of bodies and alcohol. This looks like any bar I would imagine from the olden days. Wooden decor, cigarette smoke, stale whiskey, and a piano in the corner included. At the back of my mind, I wonder if my realm was the one to inspire this setup, or if it's the other way around. The lines between these two realms have been blurring for so long, I'm not sure I can tell the difference anymore. It truly is amazing that I spent so much of my life not knowing this place existed, and now this is all I know.

Walking over to the bar, I give the bartender a smile and ask for a glass of water. He doesn't bat an eye, handing me a glass before going back to his other customers. I take a seat in the corner, my back against the wall, my eyes facing toward the front entrance. This is also a trick papa taught me at a young age, and I use it constantly. Getting caught unawares is the worst thing that can happen. I'm not about to give anyone that advantage. There are maybe a dozen men in the room and one female server, walking around the tables, handing out drinks. She's wearing a simple brown dress with a white apron tied around her waist. It's not the barmaid's outfit I would associate with such an establishment.

I do take the time to catch my breath though. I should probably also eat something, but I'm not that trusting of the people around me. Water will have to suffice until I get back to the castle. I make sure to sniff it and taste it with my finger before I take a sip. Nothing seems to taste amiss.

While I rest, I take survey of my journey. Yes, I seem to have all the ingredients needed for the spells, but the whole situation is making me suspicious. I am not about to trust some random village woman who appeared out of nowhere and went right back there. I need to find more ingredients. It's never a bad idea to be extra prepared. Plus, there is something that I want to see if I can find.

When I was reading over the dozens of books in the

study, I've come across many spells that might be helpful in my situation. None very specific to the curse but to other areas of life, maybe? Possibly? It's hard to say considering the whole magic aspect is brand new to me. But nothing I'm thinking about will make things worse. I hope.

There's a cleansing spell I think could be beneficial to the castle grounds. And to *him*. The lavender and sage the woman left me should be enough, but what I'm missing—if I'm going to try a cleansing ritual—is a feather and black tourmaline. Both of those items seem like they would be pretty easy to find, so I finish off my water and leave for the bazar.

Now that I've put some distance between me and the outdoor market, I walk back into it with fresh eyes. Scanning over my surroundings, I double check the area for that woman, but also to see if anyone is paying attention to me. No one seems to be, but I still feel like I need to move fast. I certainly do not want to be walking back to the castle in the dark. That might already be the case as it is.

Leaving the bar behind, I step back out into the sunshine. That's something else I'll have to say goodbye to when I reach the castle grounds again. Giving myself a moment to soak it in, I head back toward the outdoor market.

Moving through the throngs of people, I search the tables for any sign of the materials I need. There are a few vendors selling items like herbs and crystals, but as I walk through, I don't see what I need. A prickle at the back of my neck alerts me, but I don't do the typical looking around me right away response it brings. I take my time to walk over to a stand, picking up one of the items to study it, while I discreetly turn my body to where I think the danger is coming from. Flicking my gaze up, I do a quick once over before my eyes are back on the bobble in my hands. I do so a few more times, but I don't see anyone or anything that sets off my inner alarms.

Placing the item back on the table, I give the vendor a smile before moving away. It takes me what I assume is ten minutes—but it might be longer—to find what I'm looking for. It's another table set up with crystals and herbs much like the old woman had. This time, a young man is behind the table. There are a few people before him listening to him explain how to charge a crystal in the moonlight. When he turns his eyes to me, I smile.

"Three feathers and three tourmalines please. Oh, and some rosemary," I say, pointing to the items at the corner of his table.

"A lady who knows what she wants," he replies. His accent isn't like what I'm used to hearing. I wonder where he hails from. It's similar to a Moscow accent, but slightly harsher. Maybe he's from the southern part of Russia. Or maybe it's simply the Skazka accent. Although the creature, nor his people, sound like this.

"That she does," I say, keeping the smile in place. His eyes crinkle at the sides, evidence of years of laughter. Just the opening I need. "Do you know of anyone else who sells crystals and herbs? I thought there was an older woman here earlier, *nyet?*"

He shakes his head as he packs the items up for me.

"As far as I know, I'm the only vendor here today. I like to have a specialty. It brings in all kinds of clientele." There's that smile again, and I wear one of my own.

Learning how to flirt was not something I wanted to do but did anyway. It's way more effective than not. It's the old saying, you bring in more bees with honey, instead of vinegar. So, I watched my sisters, and I took notes.

"And what exactly is your specialty? Are you a magic dealer or enabler?" I ask, keeping my voice low and sweet, as I lean slightly toward him.

"Maybe a little bit of both." The way he winks at me, and his drawl, solidifies my initial thought—he's not from around here. I'm not sure why, but it gives me a moment of comfort. The borders between the realms are clearly still open. Or maybe I'm reading into things, and he's stuck here just like I am. I decide to test my theory.

"Traveling between realms might make others call you a dealer."

"Ah, beautiful and smart." He grins, handing over the items. "I can't say I'm disappointed in finding out magic isn't just some fairytale. What about you?"

"The jury is still out on that one," I reply, handing over some coins. He takes them with a smile before leaning in.

"If you ever find yourself in these parts again, I'd love to buy you a drink."

"If it's meant to be, it'll be." I use the line I've heard my oldest sister utter a dozen times. The men really seem to like it, especially if I follow it up with a quick up and down look and a smile. He seems to be no different.

With a tiny wave, I leave the stall behind, grateful I found everything I needed. And maybe, even some peace of mind. Simply seeing another person from the human realm helped calm my heart somehow, and even though I had to use Masha's famous flirting tricks, I don't mind it as much.

There really isn't any more time to waste. I have to get back to the castle before it's too dark to see. The creature didn't exactly provide me with a flashlight. I can already tell the sun is too high in the sky, and I'll be cutting it close.

The feeling of being watched intensifies suddenly as I walk. I can't tell if it's my paranoia or if someone is actually tracking me. Keeping my gait steady, but firm, I make my way out of the outdoor market and back the way I came. No one seems to pay me any attention, but the feeling of being watched doesn't go away. I pause at the corner, acting like I need to fix my shoe, as I study the area. I'm trying to compare the people I saw at the market to those around me now, but no one looks similar.

I have to keep moving though. It's not as if I have any other choice. I can't keep waiting around. I need to get back. It already feels like I've been gone for too long. Standing up, I fix my dress, making sure my bag is secured over my shoulder, before I turn the dagger closer to my front, for ease of access.

With that, I step back out into the main road and toward the outskirts of the village.

❧ 22 ❧

I t doesn't take me long to reach the crossroads. My memory is quite good when it comes to directions, and I'm glad I don't have to take the map out to look at it. I'm afraid I'll ruin it. It's too beautiful, and I still can't believe he let me take it with me.

When I turn off the main road and into the forest, the darkness reaches out to me immediately. There's definitely a divide between the rest of this land and where the castle sits. Even though I'm still a ways away from it, the trees here are already more dense. The noises of the forest surround me, keeping pace with my walk. I'm tired and hungry, and I probably should've planned better for this, taken a snack or something. But it's too late to be thinking about this now.

I know what I'm doing—I'm distracting myself with random thoughts because even though I'm nowhere near the village, I still feel that prickle at the back of my neck. Even now, in the middle of the forest, all by myself, I can feel an imprint on my skin. It might be the creatures living in these woods or my own exhaustion, but I swear I can almost hear footsteps tracking behind me.

Discreetly, I place my hand near my waist, ready to grab the dagger if the situation calls for it. I'm not an amateur when it comes to the blade, by any means, but I've also never fought another person when it wasn't on purpose. Mostly, it's an intimidation tactic. The men in the syndicate would never look at me with any kind of respect if I wasn't at least a little bit as ruthless as them. When in fact, I'm more so, but that would simply scare them. It's all about finding that balance.

When a twig snaps, I know it's not a creature of the forest. There's a specific way the sound falls, as if someone didn't realize what they did until it was too late and stopped themselves before making more mistakes. That just proves someone is there. An animal would keep walking.

As I rearrange my bag to the other side of my body, I slip the dagger from the sheath. My hand, holding the blade, slides into the pocket of my dress to keep it hidden. It's one of the reasons I picked this one. All dresses should have pockets—it should be a law. In my case, I knew it would come in handy.

There's another noise to the left of me, and then, a body steps out from behind the tree in my line of sight. I'm not even slightly surprised. Mildly scared, my heartbeat picking up its pace. But also, slightly thankful. It means my instincts were right on par, and it wasn't paranoia. My papa taught me well.

"Fancy meeting you here," the man says. I cock my

head to the side, trying to place him. He looks slightly familiar. When another man steps out from a tree on my right, it clicks. The men at the bar that the bartender was serving when I came in. Which means...there should be at least one more.

Before I can finish my thought, he steps out behind me. That leaves the area to my left unprotected. If I went in that direction, it would take me off path and farther away from the main road.

There aren't many options. And I'm running out of daylight.

The prickle of fear is at the back of my neck, causing sweat to pool. But even though I'm scared, I'm also ready to do whatever I need to do to cause them the most damage. While I can't show my cards all at once, I also know I can't cower. Not completely, at least. It's that whole balance thing again.

"I'm sorry, I don't know who you are. Or what you want. But I have to go." I give my voice enough tremor to sound slightly helpless. I see the ringleader glance to the right with a smirk.

"Oh, darling. We haven't met officially. But we're about to be best of friends."

All three of them take a step toward me at once. This is a practiced routine for them, I can see it clearly. There is even a possibility these were the same men who attacked my papa. This fuels my already solid resolve to not let them escape unscathed. Granted, I doubt they think they're the ones in danger here. But I haven't spent my whole life in the organization not to have a few tricks up my sleeve.

I turn, keeping my back open to the left, so I can see

the three of them without having to spin. My free hand grips the strap of my bag, as I open my eyes wider to appear more scared than I am.

I won't lie to myself and say I'm not scared at all. Fear is natural and healthy when faced with these types of situations. But it's my mama's voice in my head that says I can't let fear rule me or my actions, or I won't come out of this alive.

Even though I've only seen them for two minutes, I can tell there's murder in those eyes of theirs. Murder and greed.

They're here for my coin.

"How about you hand over that bag of yours, and you can be on your way?" The leader asks, taking another step toward me. One of the other men chuckles. That just proves the fact that they're not letting me go. At least, not whole.

"I don't have anything of value. Please, just let me pass. My family will be worried."

"A family, huh? A rich one at that?"

"Not rich—"

"Don't lie, girl. I can see the golden thread on your dress even from here."

The others laugh as I dare a glance at my dress. I chose it because it was the simplest looking, and functional, but I didn't even think that it might still be a little too flashy for the village. That's on me.

"It was a gift. And it took everything we had."

"Such an expensive gift. It's a shame to let it go to waste."

They move closer still, and they're almost where I want

them. As far as I can see, there are no weapons in their hands. They probably don't think someone like me will put up much of a fight. Not when there's three of them.

I can't wait to prove them wrong.

Another three feet, and they'll be where I need them.

"No, please—" I whine again, and then, they've reached the spot I designated for them in my mind. The man that came from behind walks over to me, grabbing my upper arm. My grip on the hilt of the blade tightens as he yanks me toward his leader.

I'm face to face with him now, and I can see his sagging skin and greedy eyes. I can also smell alcohol on their breaths. But even intoxicated, they're much bigger and stronger than I am, so I have to be quick.

The leader reaches over and grabs my chin, raising it up.

"I bet we can get a pretty penny for you too," he says, spit flying out of his mouth and onto my cheek. When the man holding my arm moves behind me, I act.

My knee comes up, slamming into the leader's groin. In the same movement, I step out of the circle, spinning to slash at the one behind me. He jumps back, but he's not fast enough. I nick his arm. The third man rushes at me, but I'm ready for him. I drop to my knee, using his momentum against him, as I throw him over my shoulder.

The leader has recovered enough and grabs my braid before I can get up. He yanks it hard, sending tears into my eyes as he pulls me backward. I twist with the movement, landing on my knees right in front of him. Without a moment's hesitation, I slam the blade right into the space where his leg meets his torso. He screams as I yank the blade out, blood splattering out like a firework lighting up the sky. Learning where the femoral artery is was my mama's idea. He'll bleed out fast.

But there are still two more men to take care of. I jump to my feet just as one of them grabs me from behind. He pins my arms to my sides, dragging me off the ground. I wiggle with all I have to try to get free. When that doesn't work, I relax my body completely, taking him by surprise. We stumble to the ground. When my feet touch the dirt I throw my body forward. He moves with me. I twist my body, but I'm not quick enough and we land on our sides.

The wind is knocked out of me when the other man slams his foot into my stomach. He goes to do it again, but I grab his leg, dragging him down to the ground with me. Leaving nothing to chance, I scramble up to all fours, climbing on top of him as I grab his head and slam it against the ground.

I'm not strong enough the first time, and his arms fight me, smacking me across my arms and face. Pushing away the pain, I punch him in the face. I lunge forward as something slams into my back, pain radiating across my body. The other man wraps his arms around me, yanking me off his companion. I think this is it. My head is spinning too fast. I can't focus enough to breathe. Sadness and regret fill me as I realize I will never be able to help anyone. I will never be able to see my papa again. I slap at my attackers' hands as they grab my hair and pull. Then, his arms wind around me from behind. Before I can do anything, his arms are torn away.

A roar shatters the forest, echoing through the trees. I push to my feet unsteadily and turn just in time to see the other man fly through the air before he slams against a tree and goes limp.

The last man tries to crawl, but the large shadow of a beast is upon him. Somehow my attacker has found his way to my dagger. When he stabs my rescuer in the arm, the scream is louder than the roar. The man manages to swipe the blade across the other's stomach, and then my rescuer grabs the man by his leg and tosses him away.

There's a scream, a crunch, and then silence.

My savior turns slowly, towering over me as I lean back against a tree, his eyes pinning me in place.

His gaze is as dark as the midnight sky and just as fathomless. The hair around his head is in disarray, and there's more of it growing out from around his cheeks. His features are sharp, but distorted somehow, as if they couldn't decide between two options. He's easily over seven feet tall with broad shoulders and a steady gait as he comes toward me. As I let my eyes run over every part of him, I notice his hands are covered in what appears to be fur.

But his clothes are royal.

"Are you hurt?"

His voice. I'd know that voice anywhere. That's when I realize who he is.

"Gavriil."

❧ 23 ❧

S tanding there, leaning against the tree, I'm unable to look away from him. It's difficult to take him all in at once. He's bigger than I imagined, even when I was picturing—I'm not sure what I was picturing. Some grotesque monster, maybe. But he doesn't look like a monster. Still, he doesn't look all the way human either.

The fur—because I have no other name for the patches of hair that cover him in random places—looks blue, almost black, but not quite. The shirt he's wearing is more of a tunic, but even I can tell it's made from the best material. Gold stitching runs down the arms and around the wrists. He's bulky inside the shirt, probably because of the hair. His hands have it the worst and almost don't look human anymore.

"You called me by name."

It takes me a second to realize he's spoken. Tearing my gaze away from his body, I meet his eyes. My heart skips a beat as we hold the gaze, something otherworldly passing between us. He seems to be breathing heavily, as if he ran all the way here.

"What?"

"You called me by name. I have not heard you use it...before."

I realize he's right. Until this very moment, he's been the creature and nothing else. It was another wall I put between him and me to keep myself protected. The others—Dina, Larisa, and Yevgenii—were different. I don't have to keep the same walls around them. And calling him by his name was going to change everything for me. It's like a protective mechanism, but now it's been shattered into a million pieces. Because I don't think I'll ever go back to thinking of him as just 'the creature.'

Not when he's bleeding on my behalf.

That doesn't mean I'm going to make things easy for him. Now that the initial shock of seeing him is wearing off, it's being replaced by annoyance. And a little bit of anger.

"This is why you've been hiding from me?" I wave my hand up and down, staring at him incredulously. He's taken back by my sudden mood shift but recovers quickly.

"I thought you'd hate me on sight."

The truth, so simply spoken, surprises the both of us. His eyes flash, as if he's confused at why he uttered those words. I try not to let them matter. I have to hang on to the annoyance at least. He's put me through so much, for nothing.

The rational part of my brain knows that it's not nothing to him. He's valid in feeling and thinking whatever it is he does about this situation. But it's stupid of him to think that what he looks like matters to me.

"Well, you didn't need to worry about that. I hated you anyway." I turn away, ready to get back to the castle. I'm tired, covered in someone else's blood and my own bruises, and I want my bed. That thought stops me. I'm not thinking about the bed back at my papa's house. I'm thinking of the one at the castle. Not sure how to take that but—

"Past tense?" Gavriil's voice stops me. Glancing over my shoulder, I find him still standing there, his eyes focused on me.

"What?"

"You said "hated." Do you—do you no longer feel that way?"

"I'm not thrilled with you," I reply honestly, shrugging. "But no, I don't hate you."

And I realize I mean it. Sometime in the last month, things have shifted between us. I can't pinpoint what it was, or when it happened. Maybe it was the simple way he cared about his people, or maybe it was his people's opinion of him. But I've learned that while he may need a few lessons on treating people with respect and not making bargains with unsuspecting and desperate travelers, I don't hate him.

Glancing up at him I find his eyes on me, but I can't read the emotions brewing in there. I need to refocus. I don't like the emotions brewing inside of me either.

"Hey. How did you even find me anyway?" He doesn't answer right away, and I stop walking to look over my shoulder. "Well, now is definitely not the time for secrets."

I still think he's not going to answer, but then he does. "The ring."

I glance down at the small piece of jewelry he insisted I keep.

"You put a tracking device on me?" I nearly yell.

"Kind of."

"Unbelievable."

Maybe I should rethink the not hating him part.

"Is that why you're able to leave the castle's grounds?"

"Kind of. I'm tethered to you..."

Okay, definitely rethinking the not hating him part. I march over to him, ready to rip the ring off my finger. When I notice just how sweaty he is. Giving him a quick once over I realize the dark shirt he's wearing is becoming darker by the minute.

"You're bleeding. Why didn't you say something?" I reach for his arm to take a look, but he flinches back. "Don't tell me you're afraid of me." His eyes flash at that, having the desired effect. He lets me grab his arm. The moment I touch the material, my hands are stained.

"Larisa is going to hate me for this," I mumble. Moving away, I find where the man dropped my dagger before I slash it through the end of my dress. Ripping off a piece of fabric, I march back over to Gavriil. I can't move his shirt away from the wound, so I place the string of material over it and wind it tightly. There's a hiss of pain, but he doesn't move away until I'm done.

"That should hold until we get back. We should go now because there's no way I'll be able to carry you if you pass out." I start walking, now even more eager to get back. My own head feels heavy, but at least I can breathe somewhat normally now. I don't think I cracked any ribs. I'll have to check myself out when we get back.

"You wouldn't just leave me in the woods?" His voice comes from behind me, and not looking directly at him, I let it wash over me as I catch my breath. What happened? It shook me more than I thought, but I can't give into that now. My emotions are going to have to stay in their boxes until I have a moment to myself. But there's comfort in knowing he's at my back, and I'm not alone in these woods any longer.

"That's always an option," I reply, not turning back around. The faster we get back to the castle, the faster I can untangle the web of emotions I'm currently experiencing. Until then, I'll do what I do best and put on a brave face.

❦ 24 ❧

It doesn't take us long to get back to the castle. It was a lot closer than I thought. Gavriil moves like a snail behind me. I'm staying as close as possible to make sure he doesn't fall over and impale himself on one of the many branches littering this forest.

Once inside, I lead him to the sitting room right next to the kitchen. It's the closest room, and he collapses into the love seat as if his legs can't hold him up anymore. Placing my bag on the table, I hurry into the kitchen to grab some water, rags, and gauze. I found the miniature first aid kit when I looked through the kitchen before, and it's about to come handy.

I catch a glimpse of myself in the glass of the cabinet, nearly dropping everything I'm holding. I look like I've been through a battle. My face is smeared with blood. There is a bruise forming on my left cheek, and there's dirt on my face and in my hair. I've definitely earned myself a bath and a ten-hour nap. But first, I have to make sure my captor turned savior doesn't bleed to death. I have no idea how the rest of the castle will be affected by that. Or I, for that matter. Since that stupid blood bargain has us tethered apparently.

Walking back into the sitting room, I pull up a chair and get to work.

"Stop being such a baby," I say as he pulls his arm away again. The cut is mostly superficial, but it is close to an artery, and therefore, bleeding a little too much for my liking. I give him a quick once over before I stand and take a step back. "Strip."

His eyes fly up to meet mine, a mask of shock falling over his features. He seems almost—scandalized. Placing my hands on my hips, I stare him down.

"What? I thought you magical beings weren't squeamish about that sort of thing. Have you let yourself go? Is that it?"

Fire blazes in his eyes as I deliver my digs, and he looks just as dangerous as I suppose he thinks he is. The look ignites all kinds of sensations in my body, running from hot to cold, but I don't back down. It feels like if I to look away now, he'll win. And I play to be the victor.

"Well?"

"I thought you human girls had a thing about modesty."

"We also have a thing about not bleeding to death." I raise an eyebrow as his eyes flash. Not sure where he's been reading about the modesty thing, but he's clearly never been to a syndicate party. They're all about flashy outfits and exposed skin. My sisters are a prime example of that.

"I'm not going to bleed to death."

"If you bleed enough to pass out, I'm leaving you on the

floor." With that, I turn back to the gauze and water, starting to pack it up. I feel, more than see, him rip the shirt over his shoulders. There's an undeniable hiss of pain, and my lips curl up in a hidden smile. That's what he gets for arguing with me.

When I face him, I'm not prepared for it. His chest is large and toned and there is nothing hideous about it. I can't take my eyes off it. Upon further inspection, I notice signs of the curse. Hair seems to grow out of random areas on his skin. It's that same mid-shift that's on his arms but a little more subtle here. I'm not sure why I expected it to be worse. Well, he did make a big deal about it, so that's probably why.

"You're not turning into a statue, are you?" I nearly whisper.

"I'm turning into a wolf."

Tearing my gaze away, I look up and find his eyes on me. The temperature in the room blazes surface-of-the-sun hot as his deep eyes find mine. There's that cliche of holding one's breath, but I feel like there is too much oxygen in the space around me, and my head is spinning. A million emotions are in his eyes, the storm assaulting me where I stand. My chest feels heavy, my skin hot. It takes some serious willpower for me to take that step toward him.

When I do, his eyes flash again, and this time, it's not a trick of the light. It's pure male hunger. My stomach turns in knots when I realize I don't dislike it. Immediately, my gates slam down, putting the walls back up to full protection mode. This is not why I'm here. Whatever is happening between us, I have a job to do. Right now, that involves me binding his wound.

Picking up the gauze, I close the remaining distance between us, careful not to look into his eyes. That whole interaction probably took less than fifteen seconds, but it feels like it's added a year of life to me. I can still feel his eyes as an imprint on my skin, and that's when I touch him.

A spark of electricity makes me jump back. I would've hit myself against the table if his other arm didn't snake out and wind around my waist. With him sitting, we're eye to eye, our faces much closer than they've ever been. I can't seem to make the tension dissipate.

"Easy does it," he whispers.

Maybe it's the wholly human phrase that snaps me out of whatever spell he has me under, but I blink, breaking eye contact.

"Must be some serious imbalance in the air around here. The static electricity is off the charts," I mumble, reaching for him once more. This time, when I place my fingers against his skin, the spark is there, but I choose to ignore it. Making quick work of the rags, I mop up the blood and give the wound a more thorough study. I've bandaged syndicate members multiple times. Even Ilya. It's never felt this...heavy before.

Heavy with unsaid words, with unshared emotions.

I work in silence, seeking the comfort it brings. Because trying to put into words the confusion that's running through me right now would be near overwhelming. But it's he who breaks the silence.

"Did you really mean what you said back there?" he

asks. I glance up at that. The fire is still in his eyes, but it's tamed. I can tell he wants an honest answer to his question, and I don't need to ask what he's referring to.

"I did. I don't hate you."

"Why?"

If my brain was working properly, I would've predicted that question. But it's not, so it takes me off guard. I give myself time to think it over as I finish binding the wound before I take a step back and glance up at him again. He's waiting for me, patiently it seems, and that sends another wave of confusion over me.

"Hate is a strong emotion for someone I don't truly know," I finally reply. "I hated the position I was put into, choosing to protect my family by taking my papa's place. But—I've learned that you didn't have much say in this either. I can't really hate that, can I?"

"You can," Gavriil says, reaching for his shirt. He's no longer meeting my eyes. I wish he would. They're way more expressive than he thinks they are. I like having a chance at being able to read him.

"Why do you say that?"

"Because I am not an innocent in this. If you only knew what I've done..." He trails off, but that just makes me laugh. He turns his head sharply at the sound, confusion plain on his features.

"Gavriil, you are not the only person here who has done things he is not proud of."

"You don't know—"

"And you don't either," I interrupt, because I hate him feeling sorry for himself. Living in the past, focused on those mistakes, is a dangerous place to be, especially if he's not doing anything about them. Even according to his people, he's not the same as he was. And it's annoying to me for him to dwell on it. Or not realize how far he's come. Even in the last few months that I've been here. "The worst thing you can do is never change. If you're at least working toward being a better version of yourself, then you are on the right path. Your past mistakes, you may have to work on making up for them, but they don't define who you are. Not if you're doing better now."

He stares at me as I finish my tiny speech, not sure where all that raw emotion has come from. I think a part of it has to be my own experience. I've been defined by the Bratva syndicate before I was even old enough to make my own choices. Gavriil's father was the main reason he's here today, just like my own family choosing who I was for me. Making the best of that situation is what pushed me to take matters into my own hands and work at becoming a powerful member of the organization. I knew I could never survive on the legacy of my papa or my grandpapa before him. I had to make my own way in the world, even if that world was chosen for me.

"You really don't think we're predestined to follow in our family's footsteps?"

I meet his gaze, unwavering, when I answer. "The only destiny that matters is the one we make for ourselves."

✵ 25 ✵

I leave him resting in the sitting room and then I take the stairs two at a time. Food and drink are forgotten as I make a beeline for the bedroom and the promise of a bath that's waiting for me there. My body is sore and dirty and bruised, and the water sounds as inviting as a hug after a long day.

Making a beeline for the bathroom, I immediately turn the water on in the sink, ignoring the mirror above it. But the moment I see my hands stained with blood, the floodgates open up. Tears come uninvited as the events of the day assault me. I can't control them as they come. I stumble out of the bathroom, back into my bedroom, trying to hold myself together. Too weak to stand, I drop down to my knees, right there in the middle of the room.

I killed a man.

Someone who was going to rob me, take advantage of me, and sell me to the highest bidder, yes. But a person, nonetheless.

And I took his life.

In all the training, in all the time I've spent becoming the ruthless daughter of a mafia boss, I have never been a killer before. I'm not naïve enough to think there's no blood on my papa's hands. But I also know—from overhearing my parents' conversations—that he has only done so in self-defense.

It's what I've done now.

I suppose this makes me like papa, like daughter.

But I still can't stop the emotions from overwhelming me. The blood is still on my hands, mingled with that of Gavriil's. He could've died too.

Rationally, I know going to the village was the right decision. The people of this castle need me. But the emotional side keeps screaming at me that if I had only stayed within these walls, I would've been safe. Even from myself. From knowing what I'm capable of.

A slight noise catches my attention, and I whip around to find Gavriil right behind me. I should be embarrassed of being caught in such a vulnerable position. No one has seen me cry but my parents. But I don't hide, and I don't turn away.

He doesn't ask any questions or utter any words of comfort. As I watch him through the tears, he sits down beside me, my side pressed into his front. It's me who leans into him and only when I do, does he wind his arms around me. As if he was waiting for permission.

I let myself cry, grieving for the girl I was and the innocence that I will never get back.

Gavriil holds me against his chest, giving me all the time I need to come to terms with myself and who I am now. My body, full of exhaustion and emotions, is too heavy for me to even stay upright. It is only his strong arms that keep me from slipping.

He smells of the forest and roses, and I want to crawl inside of his arms entirely and never leave. In this moment, he is my safe anchor, and that is exactly what I need.

After a while, my tears subside, and the sobs stop shaking my shoulders. Gavriil's arm moves up and down my back as my head is tucked under his chin. I know I need to get up, to get cleaned up, but I can't seem to make my body move. Turning my head just slightly, I stare into the bathroom and the tub that waits for me there. Sighing a little, and feeling spent, I wonder how I'm going to find enough strength to move.

Just then, Gavriil pulls back gently before leaning me against the end of the bed. Confused, I watch as he gets up and walks over to the bathroom. Turning the water on, he lets it fill the tub as he disappears from view. In the next moment, he's back beside me, a damp washcloth in his hands.

I stare up at him, completely baffled by this gesture. When I don't move away, he reaches over and begins wiping dirt and blood off my skin.

My eyes are on his face. I'm unable to look away, and I watch his brow furrow a little as he runs the cloth over the bruised side of my face. There's concentration there, but also real concern, and so I make my lips move.

"I'm okay."

His eyes fly up to meet mine. The intensity there nearly burns me on the spot. It feels like I shouted the words as they echo around us. But he still doesn't say anything.

Once satisfied that the majority of the blood and dirt are off me, he stands up, heading to the bathroom once more. He returns with a new rug before kneeling down before me and reaching for my hands. His movements are careful and meticulous. My hand looks tiny compared to his large one. My skin burns at every point where it touches his, sending tiny sparks of pleasure up my arm. He refuses to meet my gaze again, concentrating solely on cleaning my hands.

Satisfied, he stands, glancing down at me. I take that as my cue to stand as well, but my legs don't seem to be working. There's a slight hesitation and then Gavriil moves again. This time, he swoops me off the floor and into his arms.

I grab onto his neck to keep myself balanced as he cradles me to him and heads for my bathroom. Sitting me down gently on the toilet, he bends down, unlacing my boots and pulling them off my feet. One by one.

Once done, he sits back, looking up at me with a question in his eyes. I know what he's asking, and I suddenly have no idea how to answer. There's so much here in this tiny moment between us, it nearly overwhelms every small space inside of me.

I take a deep breath and then I reach for my dress. My limbs feel heavy and uncooperative. After a few tries, I know I can't get it off without help.

I meet Gavriil's eyes once more and give him the slightest of nods. He steps forward, lifting me to a standing position and placing my hands on his shoulders to hold onto. Then, with very precise moves, he grabs the side of the skirt and slowly pulls the dress up and forward over my arms. His eyes do not leave my own. When the dress is freed from my body, he keeps it in front of me, assisting me to a sitting position.

Then, he takes a step back, looks down at the floor and turns to walk out the room. On the way, he makes sure to turn the tub water off. The door shuts behind him as I stay where I am, holding the dress to me. He may have left the room, but I know he's just on the other side of the door.

I exhale, my body fully alive from his nearness, and then I whisper, "Thank you."

❧ 26 ❧

T hankfully, I don't pass out in the tub. That has always been a fear of mine, even as a little kid. I soak until the water turns cool, and I have no option but to get out. I do feel tired enough that I might pass out on the floor though. It's only the knowledge that Gavriil would be the one to find me that pushes me to get out of the tub and dry off, keeping myself upright. I've unbraided my hair and finger combed it as best as I can. My arms are too heavy to lift so I simply leave the hair down as I reach for the robe hanging by the mirror.

Catching a look at myself, I'm taken back by how bruised the left side of my face has become. There are also marks on my body where the men grabbed me, and my stomach is sensitive after being kicked. I didn't think I was as hurt as I am. But I suppose I'm not surprised. They didn't pull any punches.

Tying the robe securely around me, I push the door open and step out. A movement catches my eyes, and I turn in time to see my bedroom door closing. Gavriil has been here, watching over me, but now he's back to hiding. I almost go after him until I smell the food. He left a tray on my bed.

Walking over, I see boiled potatoes with butter, pepper, and sour cream. I didn't even know we had sour cream in the castle. There's also a cup of tea, and I don't hesitate to reach for it. I've been craving it for weeks, and apparently, we do have it. The first sip centers me a little bit, and then I dig into the food.

Potatoes have always been a comfort food for me. I think it's the Russian in my blood. Mama always made the best potatoes, no matter the form they were in. She always said there's nothing better than a bowl of soup, except if it's a bowl filled with potatoes. I've never been able to replicate her recipes. Papa does the cooking most of the time. At least when he's home.

As I eat, I think of them. My family. The people I left behind.

I can't say that I regret making the choice that I did. In the beginning, I resented this place and the creature that caused all of this. But now I think this was just a path on my journey to becoming who I need to be. There's no use in crying over spilled milk. So why beat myself up about a choice I made? It's not like I would've chosen differently. I will always choose to protect my family.

The best thing I can do for myself is to take what I've been given and make the best of it.

Is that what I've done here? Maybe not at first. But deciding to help the people of this castle? Yes. That is the best use of my time.

But I really shouldn't lie to myself. Not tonight.

I want to save him too.

If I'm to be honest, I've been leaning in that direction for days now. Maybe longer. There's just something particularly appealing about a man caring about his people. He's given me glimpses of who can be, and now I can't see anything else. From everything I've learned since coming here, Gavriil could be completely on track to becoming just like his father. But he's not. This curse is a punishment, but it's also an opportunity.

And I intend to help Gavriil make the best of it.

According to the rules of the syndicate, we would be bonded by blood now. An individual risking his or her life for another is a brotherhood bond. But I'm not in the syndicate, and this place doesn't play by the same rules.

I get to make my own.

Without even realizing it, I eat all the food and drink the tea. My limbs feel heavier than before, so I push the tray to the side and climb under the covers. My mind drifts over to the whole reason today happened and the ingredients that are now waiting to be used. I know there is no way I can do so now. There are also questions I would like to ask Gavriil first.

As if I conjured him up, I hear a noise on the other side of the door, and I smile to myself. He's there. I can feel him, just as if he was in the room with me.

"Good night, Gavriil," I mumble, turning over into the pillow. I almost swear I can hear him respond before sleep claims me.

"Good night, Nikita."

The story unfolds,
A scroll full of words.
The curse is foretold,
A life torn apart.

The countdown has begun,
The stage is all set.
The heartbreak and pain,
Simmer, grow, wait.

But hope springs forth,
Like the first flower blooms.
The bond is in place,
The connection is forged.

True feelings ignite,
Burn deep, hot, and strong,
With no end in sight,
The first chords of a song.

Beyond the horizon,
Beyond the despair,

The first ray of light,
The rainbow after the rain.

❧ 27 ❧

I wake up refreshed, but sore and slightly hurting. The tray of food is gone, letting me know Gavriil has at least checked up on me. Something has definitely shifted between us. I'll have to figure it out as we go along because today, we need to try the spell. Glancing out the window, I see that I've slept the day away. The moon is a sliver in the sky.

Getting out of bed, I brush through my hair and put it in a ponytail before I get dressed. A simple blue dress that feels more like a comfy sweater than formal attire is what I choose. It's only when I'm walking out that I realize I picked the color of Gavriil's eyes.

Pausing, I give myself a stern talking to. *Nyet*, that's clearly not what I did, and I have no idea why my brain is doing that to me.

Instead of changing, I walk out of the room.

I head toward the kitchen first, grabbing a slice of toast

and some jam. After downing a glass of water, I walk toward the sitting room. My bag is where I left it, so I carry it with me back to the study.

I spread out the jars, and the herbs in front of me on the table. Taking a survey, I pull out the book with the spells to read over the ingredients one more time. And then the instructions. They're as clear as mud, but they're also the only option I have.

Taking out the bundle of lavender first, I separate it into three parts, keeping some of it on the side. The rosemary comes next. I'm thankful that at least I'm familiar enough with the herbs to distinguish which are which.

Even as I work, my mind drifts to Gavriil. I wonder if he's back to hiding from me. It shouldn't matter. I have already decided I'm going to help him. I owe him for saving my life, that's all it is. But I also can't get the feel of his hand on my back out of my mind, and I have a million questions to ask him. The more I find out about him, the more intrigued I become.

Then, I feel him.

His presence fills the room even before he steps inside, sending butterflies tumbling over themselves in my stomach. It takes some of my self-control not to immediately react to him being there. I wait for him to speak first.

"*Dobroye noche.*" His voice reaches out to me, and I smile at his attempt at a normal greeting.

"Good evening to you too," I reply. "Glad you could join me."

He does that grunt thing at the back of his throat. It's a good thing my back is to him because I have to smile. He seems just as unsure of us as I am, which makes me feel better.

Glancing over at the book, I pick up the salt I grabbed from the kitchen and measure out the indicated amount. Gavriil doesn't speak again, but after a moment, he steps farther into the room. As if testing the waters. I don't react, giving him whatever time he needs to adjust to this new dynamic. When he starts picking up the jars and the papers on the side of the table, I can't stand it anymore.

"Can you please not touch?" I ask.

"What do you mean? I thought I was helping," he replies.

"Yeah, it's way more helpful when you don't touch things."

He puts the jar down but doesn't move too far away—only back to the doorway. I can feel his eyes on me and finally look up. He looks concerned, but not for me. This is a deep kind of a concern, and I realize it's for his people.

"Do you think it'll work?" he asks, his voice low. I wish I could offer him some kind of reassurance, but I'm flying blind here. This is my first time doing anything of the sort and I can't fake bravado here. Not when it comes to this.

"We have to try, right?" I ask, glancing up to where Gavriil is leaning against the doorway. He's still keeping to the shadows, but at least he's close enough that I can meet his eyes. As shrouded as they are by the near darkness in the room, they're full of emotion—fear for his people. The shadows make him seem so much more menacing than the person I've come to know in the last day. But I can see past his expertly put together armor. After all, I wear one as well.

"We do."

But there's no hope in his voice, and no matter how much I want to, I can't give him that. However, it does make me pause. He's been supportive of me trying this, but I can't tell if he actually believes it's possible.

Then, something occurs to me.

"Have you tried it before?"

The long silence is answer enough already. I wait him out anyway, giving him the time he needs to figure out how to say whatever he's thinking.

"In the beginning, I tried many things," he finally says. His voice is sad, giving me a slight glimpse into his heart. "Before I couldn't anymore."

"So, when you said you couldn't read, you meant because the curse took that from you?"

"It was just insurance for the witch, to make sure I couldn't find a way out."

"No, you simply found a way around."

There's a smile on my face as I say so because there's no malice in my words. Somehow, I can joke about being here, in this way, and it feels right. How twisted is that? But I'm learning to accept myself, and this is another aspect of that I suppose.

"I never meant—"

"We should—"

We both stop, waiting for the other to continue, but the walls are back up. He retreats.

"It would be best to perform it in the ballroom. It has the biggest windows."

Narrowing my eyes, I focus on him. "A ballroom?"

I really haven't explored as much of the castle as I

should've. Every time I want to, I keep thinking about the frozen people filling the hallways and various rooms. It's too creepy and unsettling. Even for me. I've even kept my runs to a very small area of the foyer because it's the only place not consumed by people.

But he's correct. I need a full view of the moon but without wind or rain or anything else that might disturb me. That means I still have to be inside.

Picking up the ingredients and the book, I put them into my bag. I turn toward Gavriil.

"Lead the way."

He gives me one searing look before he turns and walks out of the study. I hurry behind him.

Walking through the castle this evening I notice he left the candles burning to light the way. They seem to burn without losing wax. I wonder if that's another side effect of the curse. This whole castle is a self-sustained world. The isolation of it would be punishment enough if Baba Yaga wasn't such a cold-hearted witch. I've read about her plenty, and that's one magical being I don't need any explanation about.

We walk to the complete opposite side of the castle, still on the lower floor. I realize it's much bigger than I anticipated at first. The castle seems to be built in a circular pattern, with areas growing out of the center. It's much like flower petals.

We come to such a spot, and when Gavriil pushes the double doors open, I take a second to catch my breath. The room is circular in the way that most ballrooms are. The large windows cover one third of the room and are the only source of light.

Slowly, my feet carry me toward the windows. I stop in front of the middle one, unable to keep my eyes off the sky. While the shadows are perpetual in this place, the sky comes out to play at night. Tonight, it's filled with stars. It feels almost like I am standing inside of them.

A shadow dances across me. I turn to see Gavriil making his way around the room, slowly lighting the candles. There seem to be hundreds of them here, but he lights them one at a time.

As the room comes to life, I see that the walls are painted and so is the ceiling. It's not the normal way a room such as this is usually decorated. The ballrooms I've been in are adorned in gold and carry some of the most beautiful paintings there are. While the gold trim encompasses the room near the top, it's the only familiar architectural decor that matches the rest of the castle. I can't see much more of it because Gavriil only lights the lower candles, but the space feels grand. And this room?

This one is filled with flowers.

Green vines twine around the room, seemingly growing out of the floor and into the sky. Even in the dim light, I can tell that whoever painted these is skilled beyond anything I've seen. The lifelike quality is breathtaking. The flowers that adorn the vines aren't just any flowers either.

"The scarlet roses?" I whisper, turning to where Gavriil has stopped to watch me study the room. It's as if he was waiting for me to realize what I'm seeing.

"They are," he replies, that intensity that burns me on the inside is back in his eyes. There isn't enough oxygen left in the room, and I can't tear my gaze away from him.

"They're beautiful," I finally say, but my eyes are still on him. That gaze shifts, filling with an intensity that's nearly overwhelming. It's like he's the hunter he always makes himself out to be, and I can feel the imprint of that look in every part of my being.

It takes everything in me to look away, turning my attention back to the walls. It's only self-preservation that keeps me from him now, which isn't something I was expecting. Now, I don't know what to do with that knowledge.

"Larisa painted them for me." He continues moving through the room, lighting the rest of the lower candles as he speaks. "She's always been a great artist, and when these roses became my only thread to the living, she took it upon herself to bring them to life. In here."

"That must've taken her a long time." It seems near impossible that she painted all of these. It would've taken a hundred years doing it by hand. That makes me pause as I spin toward Gavriil. "How long?"

"Not as long as you think," he says. I think there's a hint of a smile on his face. But I can't tell because of all the shadows. "She carries a bit of magic with her."

"She does?" That's news to me, and I would've never been able to tell. She carries herself as someone who doesn't. But I guess I don't know much about magic, so what do I know? I'm only used to people with power throwing it in other's faces. I could never imagine Larisa doing something like that.

"It's an enchanted paintbrush. She simply has to touch a place she wants the picture to show up, and then draw the actual picture. She painted this wall by hand, and the rest of it painted itself at the same time."

I step closer to the wall he indicates. The details stand out to me, making them look almost as the real as the ones in the garden. The beauty of the art, the way Gavriil speaks of his sister, it makes me want to help them even more. I turn to him, giving him a small smile.

"Let's get started."

❧ 28 ❧

I place my bag on the floor in front of the middle window before settling in front of it. The book goes beside me as I open it to the page I marked earlier. This is a pretty standard unbinding spell, but I want to do something different. Something I'm sure Gavriil didn't try.

"What's this?" He points to a bottle I took from the kitchen earlier.

"Water."

"Why do you need that?"

"Because I'm going to do a cleansing ritual before the actual spell."

I glance up at him and his confused face. "You can sit, or you can leave. Please don't hover."

He sits down beside me almost immediately, and I try to suppress my smile. He's eager, that much I can see. I can't blame him. If this works, his friends will be free from the constant bondage being frozen brings with it. They'll still be tied to this place, I don't think the spell takes care of the actual curse, but it can help.

Maybe.

I hope.

"What does the cleansing ritual entail?"

This time I do smile. "From what I've been able to gather, it's a simple ritual to cleanse negative energy in a space. I assume with a curse such as yours, there is a lot of negative energy floating around. My readings tell me that such energy can be a hindrance to other magic, which is why I want to cleanse the space before we try the main spell."

Gavriil simply nods, watching me as I begin preparing the items.

When I said it's a simple ritual, I meant it. Many books talk about herbs and crystals being used for cleansing. I've seen that in my realm as well. Some of the syndicate members believe that bringing a piece of green jade to a business meeting will yield wealth and abundance. Now that I'm learning more about this magic, I wonder if they were onto something.

"Would it help if I explained what I'm doing?" I ask, because Gavriil hasn't taken his eyes off me. He looks up and nods eagerly. "Okay. This is the part of the ritual that requires us being near windows, and moonlight. Could we possibly get some fresh air in here?"

Gavriil doesn't hesitate to jump to his feet and rush to the window. There are doors on each side, leading out to the balcony. He pushes them open before rejoining me on the floor.

"Thank you."

He nods in response.

"Now, I'm going to take this sage bundle and light it. After I do so, I will wave the feather through the smoke, asking for cleansing. Then comes the tourmaline. It will need to be immersed in the smoke before I set an intention and speak the words out loud. After the intention is set, the stone will be placed inside this jar." I pick up one of the jars the woman gave me. "The jar will also be filled with water and salt. The jar is to be kept inside the home from them on."

As I explain the ritual to him, I fill the jar up with water and add a few pinches of salt. Then, taking the matches I found in the kitchen, I light the sage bundle before blowing on it to create smoke. The air fills with the aroma of the plant, and my eyes find Gavriil's. He's watching me with complete concentration, without holding back the waves of emotions he's going through. I can see it there, in the midnight color of his gaze.

Hope. Fear. Guilt. Trust.

They go through him, one after the other. And I think I recognize them all because I'm feeling them too. This is a huge moment in both of our lives—at least it feels like it. The fact that Gavriil is still here and isn't hiding in the shadows means that last one—trust—he's finally building it. And maybe, so am I.

Picking up one of the feathers, I move it in a circular motion over the smoke, guiding it away from the sage and into the air. The world is silent around us. The only sound is the movement of the material of my dress against my skin as I wave the feather around.

Once I'm satisfied there is plenty of smoke around, I hand the sage to Gavriil and he takes it without hesitation.

"Hold it steady," I say. He does as I place the black tourmaline over the smoke, holding it between two hands. The smoke builds up, completely covering the stone before I uncup it and let it escape into the air. Now comes the hardest part.

There are only pieces of information on what kind of intention works the best. The only thing I know for sure is that whoever sets an intention must be of a strong mind. Their will is the driving force behind the words they speak. So, I choose the words that come to me.

"I ask for the unwanted energy to leave this place. I ask —" I pause for a moment, rethinking. "I command the crystal to hold the intention, the magic to purify and cleanse. *Pozhalusta* and *spasibo*."

Then, I look over at Gavriil. "Say it with me. I command this crystal to hold the intention." His voice joins mine as his eyes lock onto me. "The magic to purify and cleanse. *Pozhalusta* and *spasibo*."

The sound of our voices vibrates around us, and I can't seem to tear my gaze away from him. We sit like that for a few tense minutes as the air from outside softly dances around the ballroom, making the smoke twirl. Finally, I remember where and who we are. I look away, refocusing on the task at hand.

Reaching for the prepared jar, I place the stone inside carefully and seal it. The wind settles and the room becomes colder the moment I do.

"Will you place it near the front doors for me?" I ask Gavriil, and just like before, he doesn't hesitate. He takes the jar from my extended hands before he walks out of the room.

Exhaling, I give myself a moment to simply sit here, quietly. The night sky stretches out over me. These windows make it seem like I'm surrounded by the stars. I think this might be my favorite place in the whole castle. Or at least, it is from what I've seen so far. A melody my mama used to play with me as a duet comes into my mind, and I hum it softly, looking up. A sense of peace washes over me, for the first time since I stepped foot into Skazka. I can't tell the exact source of it. I hope it's the spell, but I also hope it's something deeper.

Shaking myself out of the moment, I focus back on the job. Taking out the lavender and the rosemary, I wind them together and prepare to light them. Both will help with the purification and the protection. The spell is simple. I burn the herbs, sprinkle them on the people, and read the spell. I also need to hold a carnelian crystal in my left hand as I sprinkle the herbs with my right. Somehow, the old woman at the bazaar knew all that.

When Gavriil returns, the bundle is about halfway burnt. He settles down beside me to watch me work. I suppose now is as good a time as any to ask him about the woman. Since I like to tackle situations head on, I don't beat around the bush.

"At the bazaar, in the village, I met someone. An older woman, a *babushka* it seemed, who handed me the exact ingredients I needed for the spell. What do you say about that?"

Gavriil is clearly taken back by my bluntness but only

for a moment. I think I keep surprising him, but he's getting used to my antics.

"There are talks, rumors more than anything, of magical beings helping the land heal. There was a time when Skazka was under constant assault from the Shadowlands."

"Shadowlands?"

"A brotherhood of dark magic wanting power and control. No matter the cost."

Well, doesn't that sound like the organization I grew up in?

"Since they were pushed back by the queen of *Zelonovo Korolevstva* the land has been healing itself. These magical beings are kind of like ambassadors to the people, blessing them with gifts or helpful direction."

"Sounds like a fairy godmother." I chuckle, but Gavriil nods.

"I suppose they are. Maybe—" He stops, taking a deep breath. "Maybe the land has seen something in me, in this place, that is worth saving."

There's a joke here, and I could say it, but I don't. I think for the first time, Gavriil is realizing that he has a say in all of this. Especially in the kind of a person—and later ruler—he's going to be. I don't know why, but I kind of like having a front row seat to that discovery.

We grow quiet for a moment and then the bundle has burned and only ashes are left.

I stand, taking the ashes and the crystal with me.

"Can you take me to Larisa please?"

We don't talk as Gavriil leads me out of the room. I suppose we could've started with any of the people hiding in the shadows of the hallways, but I can't get the roses out of my head. Gavriil leads us upstairs, but instead of turning toward my room, we go in the opposite direction. He steps into another room and walks to the window. There, turned to look out of the window, stands Larisa.

She's completely stone, but I can still see some of her features. She looks as kind and regal as when I met her. Gavriil studies her for a long moment, then moves back to give me room. Having read over the spell a dozen times, I have the words memorized. Reaching over, I sprinkle a few pinches of the burnt rosemary and lavender on Larisa's shoulders, crown of the head, and feet. Standing right in front of her, I hold a pinch of the mixture in my right hand and the crystal in my left as I begin to speak.

"Fire destroys and fire heals.
The world turns and the world sleeps.
Pieces of the land,
Pieces of the heart,
Magic of the soul,
Wishes from the mind.

Asking for a gift,
Asking for a debt.
Willing to repay,
Willing to fight back.

Severing the hold,
Severing the string.
Pushing, learning, growing,

Giving power to complete.
Now it's time to heal,
Now it's time to burn.

Fire.
Air.
Earth.
And water.
Now, please,
Restore."

THE WORDS SEEM TO SPIN AROUND AND AROUND ME, twining Larisa and I in a cocoon of magic. I stand as still as possible, willing for it to work. Wishing it with all my heart. My mind tumbles over itself, as if overwhelmed by the magic. I dare not breathe.

But then, the feeling dissipates and there's nothing left. Larisa doesn't move.

❧ 29 ❧

We try the spell three more times on others, but there is no response. After Yevgenii didn't reanimate, Gavriil walked out of the room, leaving me alone. I cleaned up the supplies and took them back to the study before I went and got something to eat. The spells took most of the night, so I went to bed, with my heart heavy.

And I dreamt for the first time since coming here.

I saw glimpses of my old life, but in a new light somehow. Papa didn't look like himself, sitting at a desk, pouring over papers. In the dream, I walked toward him, ready to say something, when I was ripped away.

I woke up confused and with an aching in my heart. I miss Papa terribly.

The events of yesterday return the moment I'm dressed and walking toward the piano room. That's when I find Gavriil in the study.

He doesn't move from his spot in the chair when I

come in, but I know he can tell I'm there. He's just as aware of me as I am of him. I have no idea when that started, or if that's always been there, but I feel it now. Anytime he's near.

He's staring at a book on the desk in front of him. There's pure frustration and anger on his face. I almost turn around and leave, but something stops me. It's probably my stubbornness. I don't want to give up so easily. Also, seeing him like this is doing something to my insides.

"I thought the whole point of me being here is because you couldn't read. Am I out of a job now?" I keep my tone light, but just like always, my words have the desired effect. His eyes fly up to meet mine and narrow. "What? Are you losing your ability to talk too?"

He slams the book shut, standing up to his full height in one swift move. It takes him two strides to come around the desk and then he's in my face. It takes everything within me not to flinch, but I hold my ground. I haven't flinched in front of him yet. I'm not about to do so now.

"Is this a joke to you?" he roars, rattling the books on the shelves around us. "My friends—my family—are frozen in stone statues. I am losing my mind, my abilities, and my humanity, and you have the audacity to joke about it?"

"There he is." I keep my voice steady and low. The level of my tone is such a contrast to his that he immediately takes a step back.

"What?"

"This angry beast of a man is my preferred version of you, compared to the poor prince who keeps feeling sorry for himself."

"You don't understand—"

"I swear if you're about to tell me I don't understand what it feels like to be trapped in a life you didn't pick for yourself or some other crap like that, I will scream. Poor little princeling, got cursed to turn into a beast because he was a bad boy." Now, I am getting riled up. This whole situation is messed up. Me being here is messed up, but I'm not going to sit around and baby this man.

"I'm not going to feel sorry for you, *Gavriil*." I narrow my eyes at him, standing my ground.

"I liked it better when you didn't use my name as a curse," he replies.

"I liked it better when you stopped being such a spoiled brat." I smirk as his eyes flash. It really is much easier to argue with him when I can see him.

"I'm not allowed to be sad about my situation?"

"Of course you're allowed. But how long are you planning on being sad? Because I don't know about your lifespan, but the average for a human is about eighty years, and I don't want to spend all of my years dealing with a mopey prince."

I cross my arms in front of me, staring up at him. He stares at me like he's never seen me before. Then a laugh escapes. He seems just as surprised by it as I am, but then he laughs again. I kind of want him to keep going because the sound is near otherworldly. It travels up my spine, leaving pleasant tingles along the way.

"I really have become a mopey prince, haven't I?" He manages to say between the chuckles. I smile.

"I know you're hurting, but feeling sorry for yourself isn't going to help anyone. You really can't read anything?"

The last question is gentle. When he raises his eyes, they're full of pain.

"I'm losing pieces of myself, Nikita." He barely whispers my name, and I hear it echo inside my head. "Reading went first. Sometimes I forget words, sometimes I forget that I'm a human."

He folds into himself then, sitting in the chair, head buried in his hands. What do I say to someone who's losing pieces of himself daily? How do I make it better? A part of me wants to reach over and hold him. But I stop. I don't think it's my place to comfort him, even though he's done it for me. But maybe, just maybe I can help heal his soul. Just a little bit.

Moving swiftly, I push open the secret door, keeping it ajar as I walk to the piano. The melody my mama taught me has been with me all day. When I sit down in front of the piano, my fingers find the keys automatically. The music spills around me, reaching to the darkest corner. I pour my heart into every gentle touch, getting lost in the feel of the piano and the sound coming from it.

The feeling that I attribute specifically to him touches me, and I know he's in the room. He doesn't speak, doesn't move any closer. He simply listens as I pour my heart out through my fingers.

When the last note hangs in the air, neither one of us moves. Then, it's gone. I turn, just slightly to find his eyes on mine. There's a moment of tension, fire filled tension, and then, two words.

"Thank you."

We continue to watch each other, our breaths finding a

rhythm until we're in sync. So many words spring to mind, but then he's the one to break the moment,

"Can I show you something?"

❦

WE LEAVE THE LOWER FLOOR OF THE CASTLE BEHIND AND climb the stairs. Moving past the corridor leading to my room, we turn the corner to another room. Gavriil pushes the door open, taking a candle off the wall to guide the way. I stay close at his back, the shadows reaching out to me. It's much darker here. I can't even make out the furniture.

Gavriil comes to a stop, and I see that we've reached the opposite wall. He places his hand on it and pushes. To my surprise, the wall shudders and moves.

"This is how you sneak around?" I ask, keeping my voice low.

"I do not 'sneak around,'" he replies instantly, a little offended. I can't help but chuckle.

"What would you call it?"

He grunts but doesn't reply because I got him there. Instead, he turns back to the passage and ducks to step inside. Without hesitation, I follow.

"The stairs lead up, and they are steep."

"I can handle myself."

There's a pause, as if he's going to say something else or was expecting a different response, but then he leads the way with only a candle for a companion.

We ascend to another floor, going straight up until we reach the top. There's a hard right, and Gavriil is pushing another door open. A sliver of light shines through the open doorway. Stepping out into the room, I see that the room is square shaped with absolutely no furniture. On the left is a huge floor to ceiling window that leads out onto a balcony. That's where the light is coming through because the stars are out again tonight.

"You asked me once about my father," Gavriil says. I turn to face him where he stands, blocking my view of the room.

"I did."

"Well, I thought it was time you finally meet him."

Confusion clouds my vision and then Gavriil steps out of the way. At first, I have no idea what I'm looking at as my eyes adjust to the darkness.

When the face of a man in pain materializes in front of me, I nearly step back. The statue is large, about the size of Gavriil. He has broad shoulders adorned in a royal mantle, which falls all around his body. Even though it's made of stone, I can see the wide variety of braids woven out of thread, sewn into the garment as evidence of regality and military status. He was clearly a king and a conqueror. An orb and a scepter are also etched into the sash he wears across his body, under the mantle. The crown on his brow, heavy and expertly adorned in jewels and pearls, has a large stone at the tip of it. But it's his face that captures my attention.

He's in agony, screaming a silent scream for an eternity. The sight of it is forever in my mind now. I don't think I will ever forget the feeling it evokes. Fear and horror and dread.

Even though he looks like the other statues, he's different. He's crumbling to pieces, while the others stay in pristine condition.

"The king—" I stop, because what can I say? Almost automatically I raise my hand. That's when Gavriil moves.

"Don't touch him." He blocks me from the statue immediately, and I have no choice but to take a step back.

"What's happening to him?" I barely whisper. An emotion crosses over Gavriil's face, but it's too fleeting to identify. His voice is hard when he replies.

"He's the countdown."

"The countdown?"

"*Da*. Like an hourglass keeping time. When he crumbles, the curse is complete. And I—" He's looking at everything but me. I will him to meet my gaze. I take the tiniest steps toward him, capturing his attention.

"You what?"

"I won't be human anymore."

The words echo in the empty room as his gaze latches onto mine. My heart beats out of control. A barely suppressed shudder rushes over me as I try to wrap my mind around what he said.

The curse has taken everything from him, and now, it's going to take his humanity.

Up until this exact moment, I truly did not realize what him turning into a wolf meant. But as I watch his eyes hold mine, he lets his walls down, and the pain there nearly takes my breath away.

Pain and fear.

He's losing himself before he even has a chance to discover who he truly is. There's nothing I can say to make this better, so I do the only thing I can. Reaching out, I wrap my fingers around his hand. He jerks back at the contact, as if he's unused to any kind of touch. Maybe he isn't. But he doesn't pull away; he doesn't run. After a moment of hesitation, he holds my hand a little tighter, taking the small comfort I provide.

Then, hand in hand, we walk back to the secret passage and leave the dying king behind.

❧ 30 ❧

Two days later, I'm in the kitchen making myself a sandwich when I feel him. I don't have to turn around to know that he's creeping in through the shadows just like he always does.

"Are you just going to stand there?" I ask, continuing with my food prep. At first, he doesn't say anything. But there's tension in the air that tells me he hasn't left and that he's trying to figure out what to say.

Finally, he simply says, "Yes?"

"Wait, are you asking me or telling me?" I say, turning to where his voice is coming from just beyond the shadows. He's still hidden by the darkness, and I squint to try to see him better.

I don't see the point of him hiding anymore. But then, maybe it's not his physical form that he's hiding from me. We've been walking on eggshells around each other for days. Everything between us has changed since my trip to the village, and it's like we're both trying to figure out the new rules, especially after he took me to see the king. I can't even call him Gavriil's father, he doesn't deserve the title. I think it's the real reason Gavriil has been avoiding me. It would be nice if he simply talked to me instead.

"Come on. Seriously, why can't you just have a meal with me?" I say, motioning to the sandwich I'm making.

"A meal?"

"Yes, you know, food that is digested three times a day."

I reach over for more bread, cutting off a couple more pieces and begin making him a sandwich. I know he eats. I've seen the evidence of it in the kitchen. Just never with me. Until now. He doesn't say anything else as I make quick work with the condiments. After I'm done, I turn, placing a plate in front of me. Then I place one on the counter near him.

"Now, we sit and eat this together." I point to the food as if I'm speaking to a child. "And we can even make polite conversation, but only when we're not chewing our food. Because that's gross, and no one should talk when they're chewing or chew with their mouth open." I smile, teasing. He's so still I expect him to leave. I don't know why. Maybe because I've just come to expect him to do that.

But he doesn't. Stepping into the light, he makes his way toward me. For a second, I think I need to prepare myself for the way he looks. Even the size of him alone is intimidating. When coupled with the random hair growth and skin changes, he can present an intimidating figure. His face has elongated so much since I saw him for the first time. The long nose of a wolf takes shape with human features still holding on.

Yet, I don't see the curse on him the way he expects me to see it.

He's just a person to me, who put himself in danger to come save me from the bandits, who's given me glimpses of his broken heart. A misunderstood prince who is cursed to become something that he's not by nature.

It's kind of interesting for me to analyze myself and my feelings as an outsider. Gavriil started to change in my eyes the moment his people spoke highly of him. And when he showed the kind of loyalty people only dream about.

But I've seen it for myself too. I think the bargain he made with my papa was to save himself, yes. But it was also to save his people, and I can't fault him for that. I've had to make plenty of tough decisions in my life as well. Maybe not to this extent, but magical or not, we're not so different after all. Every day, I see that a little more.

"See, this isn't so bad," I say before reaching for my sandwich and taking a bite. I chew it slowly, savoring it as much as I can while I watch him.

The hair around his face is a little longer and more matted. I feel like he's been taking a knife to it just to keep it at bay.

But his eyes.

His eyes are still the same, deep, dark blue. They're watching me with intensity as I eat my food. There's another moment where he hesitates, thinking if he should stay or go, and then he's sitting down in front of me, reaching for the food.

I take another bite as well as I celebrate the small victory he's just given me.

But then I freeze as I watch his hands shift into paws and back to human hands to paws and to hands again.

"Gavriil? I say his name like a question, and he sighs.

"It's just what the curse does." he says. "I can't really control it. I...wait for it to pass. Like a seizure." His quiet words squeeze at my heart. I don't have to be a doctor to know he's clearly in pain. His hands shift again, and I see a vein throbbing at his temple.

For just a second, I want to reach out and touch his hand to offer him some kind of solace, some kind of comfort in knowing he's not alone. I think he's been alone for a very long time, even before the curse. When someone is like that...the feeling doesn't just go away, even when they're with another person. It makes me want to help him even more.

"Does it do it more often? Now since—" I stop, not sure I want to bring the king into this, but we both saw the crumbling statue. There was more of the king on the floor than still standing upright. Time is clearly running out.

"*Da.*"

"And the others? What happens to them when time runs out?"

There's so much pain when his eyes meet mine. "They stay statues forever. Only statues."

I understand what he says—they die. My heart squeezes. I don't know what words to offer. But Gavriil isn't done.

"The curse," he says. "It's taking parts of me in a way I never imagined. But...I've found that something helps—" He looks almost sheepish as he glances up at me. "Music. Music helps."

He doesn't say anything else as he reaches for his food and takes a bite. Yet, I replay the words in my head because they speak volumes. The last few days, I've played every day. I give myself over to the melodies after spending hours combing the books for answers. He's been there every time.

I watch as he eats his food. His hands seem to have ceased their shifting. He's such royalty, even in this state. I can't imagine what he was like before this began.

We fall into a comfortable silence as we eat, and I soak in this small sense of normalcy. Not that eating dinner with a cursed prince in a magical land is any shred of normal. But the mundane act brings me comfort.

I keep thinking how he said my music helps. The small act of playing the piano, of letting my fingers dance across the keys, helps. That knowledge makes me want to do more.

Although, I don't know if there is anything more to be done. I've exhausted the texts. I've tried the spell two more times with no results. Maybe me being here isn't the best thing that has happened to him. Maybe I'm not meant to save him.

The thought brings a sharp pain to my chest, and I push it away. I can't think like that.

I simply can't give up hope.

❧

EATING TOGETHER HAS BECOME SOMETHING WE DO every day. He comes and finds me in the kitchen and some- times he even suggests different types of meals. Mostly though, we have very generic eggs and bread. And potatoes.

But we talk, and that's something we didn't have before.

He is a very well read royal. My desire for traveling is slightly clenched as he tells me stories of Skazka and the lands that are in this realm. He makes me want to see all of them for myself.

He says that the green forest is the most beautiful place ever, and the queen there is probably the kindest person I could ever meet. Coming from him, that feels like a huge compliment.

He's changed in the days that I've been here. But then, I can't tell if it's true change or if he's simply more comfortable being himself around me.

If I am to believe his friends and family, he's never been cruel, not like his father. And now I'm seeing that too.

It makes my heart all kinds of confused.

"I have something to show you," he announces as soon as we're done eating breakfast.

"To show me?" I'm a little nervous because last time it wasn't the greatest thing ever. Well, in a way it was because it showed his trust in me. As I look at him, he seems eager in a good way, instead of sullen like last time.

"Yes."

"Okay." I place the plates in the sink, rinsing them off and then turn to him. He motions for me to follow. He doesn't disappear into the shadows like he used to do but walks in front of me and a little to the right as we make our way through the hallways. The candles are now lit constantly, making the castle look almost inviting. As inviting as a gloomy, statue filled, slightly haunted by a curse castle can be.

We take the stairs to the upper levels, but instead of turning toward my chambers, we go the opposite direction.

Even though I still haven't explored much of the castle, I no longer have any desire to poke around. Not when the statues of people who live here still stand around every single hallway and room. It's kind of like I'm in their space. And I don't want to do that to them.

"Okay, where are you taking me?" I ask when we continue down the hallways without any indication of stopping. "You know you already kidnapped me. You don't have to take me to your dungeon and chain me up. I'm a willing prisoner."

There's my sarcasm again, but this time, he isn't offended or angry. Actually, he might be laughing with me.

"Wait, was that the start of a chuckle?" I ask and receive a grunt in response. My lips curl up in a smile, but I don't say anything else as I hurry after him. I don't think I'll ever get tired of riling him up.

We come to a set of double doors before he stops me. There's an intensity on his face as he turns to me.

"This is something that is important to me," he says before pausing. He takes a deep breath, as if preparing himself for whatever is on the other side. My curiosity is more than piqued. Suddenly, I have the desire to reach out and offer a physical representation of how I'm feeling inside. I want to offer a touch on the arm, because if he's truly sharing something important, I'm touched. But I don't reach out. Instead, I link my fingers in front of me and wait in anticipation.

He pushes the doors open, and we step inside. Immediately, my breath catches in a way that it has never done before. Walking fully into the room, I stop in the middle, spinning slowly to take it all in.

"Is this what I think this is?" I ask, my eyes still on the shelves in front of me.

"Yes." His answer is but a whisper, but it reaches me anyway. I feel it in every part of my being.

"How many are there?" I ask, finally taking a step toward the shelves and reaching for one of the items there.

"I'm not sure. I've tried to collect as many as I could."

I smile at that as I pull out a piece of sheet music. So many songs, so many melodies, fill this room. The biggest room I've ever seen, and it's full of sheet music. Before playing a note off the pages, I can hear the music twirling around me. I think I could stay here forever—in this place, this moment. Slowly, I spin around again, trying not to feel overwhelmed. That's when I notice there's a grand piano in the corner.

Without hesitating, I walk toward it, still holding the piece of music I pulled off the shelf. I sit down at the piano. It's dusty from years of misuse, so I wipe it slightly before I place the music on the stand. Unlike the piano I found downstairs, this one has sat idle. Gavriil probably hasn't opened this room in ages. But now, he's opening it up to me.

The thought brings a smile to my lips as my eyes read the notes on the page. Then, I let my fingers play the melody sketched out in front of me on the piece of paper. It's not a long one, but it's the sort of melody that soothes and comforts and brings with it millions of memories. It's a song that dances in the wind on a summer day, ruffling the leaves and bending the branches just a tad. It's the melody that compliments the sound of morning rain, wrapping itself around you in a cozy hug.

I play without saying a word, needing to finish it—to understand what it's trying to say. Because that's what music is to me. It's a language, and it's the one that I want to be fluent in no matter who's speaking it.

When I'm done, Gavriil is in the middle of the room staring at me. His face is full of intensity and emotion that I'm sure mirrors my own. My skin buzzes with the feeling the melody ignited. I want to play it over and over again until I have it memorized.

"Thank you for showing this to me," I say, my voice barely above a whisper, because suddenly, I can't seem to catch my breath. As if it was I, and not my fingers, that danced across the black and white keys.

"Thank you for playing," Gavriil replies, his voice breaking a little. We stare at each other—as has become our custom—until I feel like my heart is going to burst out of my chest.

"I should've guessed you were the musician." I smile gently, still unable to tear my eyes from his.

"It was frowned upon by my father, but I can't turn off the music inside of me anymore than you can. I can see it on your face. You feel it as intensely as I do. It's—" He stops abruptly, and I nearly lean forward to demand an answer.

"It's what?"

"Nothing. Just...it's nice to hear it played again. This place has been missing music." I can see in the way his gaze roams over the piano wistfully that it means a lot to him. He glances at his hands, and I almost offer to stand so he can take my spot. But then I realize that's something the curse has taken from him as well, just like the reading. His words from the other day come back, about my music helping him to keep his humanity. It makes me want to play nonstop.

"Will you let me stay here?" I ask. Gavriil grins, shaking himself out of his melancholy.

"Only if you keep playing."

❧ 3 1 ❧

I hear them before I see them. Dina doesn't bother knocking on the door as she pushes it open. Larisa is right behind her.

"Sure, come right in." I chuckle right before Dina launches herself at me. She hugs me tight, holding on for dear life. I hug her back just as tightly, knowing that she needs this more than I do. I'm not the one deprived of physical touch here.

That small thought brings an image to mind of my fingers on Gavriil's skin, but I push it aside immediately. This is really not the time nor place. Actually, there's never a time nor place. Ever since I've started dreaming again, I keep thinking he'll show up in one of them, but it's only been my papa and my family back home. No happy dreams regarding a certain prince, which is—

Yo Mayo, Nikita. I need to make my brain behave.

"How are you?" Larisa asks from over Dina's shoulder. She looks just as poised as if she just came from the throne room. She's always put together, and always asking about others. I'm assuming Yevgenii went straight for Gavriil.

"I'm hanging in there," I reply as Dina pulls back. "But more importantly, how are you?"

I study the two young women, my heart hurting with the knowledge that they're still stuck in this loop of freezing and unfreezing. Sure, I only spent half a day with them the last time they were animated, but it doesn't take long to see a good thing when it's in front of you. And these? These are good people.

"We're okay, Nikita," Larisa answers, a small smile on her face. She simply can't turn it off—the poise and royalty she carries within her.

"I'm sorry I couldn't help. We tried the spells, and we'll try more. I just, I'm sorry," I say, glancing between the two of them. "Whatever this curse is, it's—"

"But you did help." Larisa's soft words make me freeze in place. I glance over at Dina, then back to Larisa, confused.

"What do you mean?"

"Remember how we said we can hear your music?" Dina asks, taking a seat beside me. "Since you performed the spell, it's been clearer. Like it was in the beginning. It's as if you cleared the airways and we are tuned in more fully again. It takes some of our loneliness away to hear you play. It's like a thread to reality."

Her words bring tears to my eyes as I let them sink in.

"Oh, Nikita." Larisa takes a seat beside me on the other side and takes my hand in one of hers. "You gave us a gift. We are very grateful."

"I wanted to do more. I really thought it would be

possible—maybe if I knew more about the magic. If I had any of my own."

"I don't think even the strongest *volshebnytsia* would be able to stand up to Baba Yaga's magic. You gave us something we didn't have before. Peace."

I swallow the tears that are rising up, and I don't think I can hold them in any longer.

"I want to save you," I whisper.

"That's not your burden to carry," Larisa replies, giving my hand a gentle squeeze.

"No, that's mine."

The three of us glance up as Gavriil fills the doorway, Yevgenii at his side. The captain of the guard is always near the prince, and I don't think it's simply out of duty. The friendship between this group is precious and real. Anyone can see that.

But just like in recent days, the rest of the world disappears. I'm not looking at anyone but Gavriil. He stands right inside my room, taking up all the oxygen, as if the space is too small to contain him. The last few days, since Gavriil has given me the gift of that piano room, the dynamic between us has become charged. He no longer hides from me, physically or emotionally. That fact is underlined now as his eyes give away just how much that burden weighs on him.

There's pain and guilt, a storm of regret brewing. For a second, I want to go to him, to offer some kind of comfort. Instead, I push the impulse away, curling my fingers into Larisa's. She doesn't miss the movement. Neither does he. His eyes flicker down before coming to rest on mine again. It's almost like he can read my mind.

Yevgenii clears his throat behind Gavriil, shattering the stare down. Gavriil glances over his shoulder as Yevgenii does his best to keep the smile off his face. My cheeks heat up as I feel Larisa and Dina's eyes on me.

"I've missed you, *sistra*," Gavriil says, stepping up to Larisa as the young woman stands. He reaches for her, taking her into his arms. They hug for a long moment before stepping apart. Dina is immediately on her feet, back straight as Gavriil walks over to give her shoulder a squeeze.

"It is good to see you, my friends."

"It's good to be seen," Larisa replies. "We have enjoyed the recent developments, but it's nice to be able to experience them a little more fully."

Gavriil refuses to meet my eye as Dina sends a wink my way. I'm probably as scarlet as those roses, and I'm waiting for the floor to swallow me up. Please and thank you.

"I've been thinking," Larisa continues, oblivious or simply ignoring my embarrassment. "It's been ages since I've seen the garden."

"Oh yes! We should definitely go visit. Come with us, Yevgenii."

I glance between the two girls, who are clearly up to something, but they don't meet my eye. Yevgenii also seems confused, but he doesn't get a chance to comment as Dina loops her arm through his and pulls him out of the room.

"They're not very subtle, are they?" Gavriil asks, his lips curling up on one side as he looks at me. I raise my eyebrows, waiting for him to say whatever it is he came to say. Because he clearly came prepared with something.

"Gavriil, are you nervous?" I finally ask as he shifts from one foot to the other. His eyes roam around the room. "Wait, no. You're scared. A big bad prince, shaking in his boots?"

That gets a rise out of him, like I knew it would, as his eyes zero in on mine. I let my lips curl with a smirk as his deepen in color. But he picks up the challenge I put in front of him.

"I would like to invite you to dinner. Will you accept?"

That is definitely not what I'm expecting.

"A dinner? Don't we eat dinner together every night now?"

"This is more of a formal affair, how things used to be. A bit different. You wear a pretty dress, I'll be a complete gentleman."

"Oh yes, that's very different." I smile. "Will there be desert?"

His eyes heat up, fully intense on mine. "Absolutely."

"Then I accept."

"Perfect!" The voice comes from the hallway, and Gavriil and I both turn in that direction as we hear Larisa admonish Dina. I turn back to Gavriil smiling. His eyes are still intense on mine. When he looks at me like that, I see nothing else.

The magnitude of his gaze, the full focus on my face, makes my cheeks burn red again. My skin is on fire, but I can't look away. I can't even make words form on my tongue. I think I might faint from lack of oxygen, until his lips curl up again. That small movement breaks the spell.

He grins, a full-blown display of happiness. It blinds me for a moment. His face is mostly overgrown with hair now, and a lot of his features are lost. But that smile is all him. I like the way his eyes sparkle in the process.

There's more noise at the door, and Gavriil and I both freeze as we listen. There's another thud, and then Gavriil chuckles.

"Come back in here. You clearly heard she said yes."

The door opens back up, and all three of his friends stand there. The surprise is evident on my face as Dina rushes back in with Larisa following her at a slower pace.

"That's your cue to leave." Larisa squeezes Gavriil's arm as she passes him, and he doesn't hesitate to walk to the doors. With one last look at me, he shuts the doors behind him. I turn to the girls.

"What is this?"

"This is us getting you ready for a royal dinner."

32

The moment the boys are out of the room, the girls descend on me.

"Larisa, you have to pull out your official 'royal business' dresses. There's one in particular—"

"I know exactly the one you mean." The other woman smiles as they circle me.

"We'll curl the hair, maybe? With a half updo? Oh, and the shimmering powder you have," Dina says, sounding nothing like the tough soldier I met in the beginning.

"Can you please slow down for a second and explain to me what's going on? Dinner?"

"He's just trying to do a good thing, Nikita. A thank you for all the effort you've put into trying to help us. He knows he didn't go about it the right way in the beginning."

I'm not sure what to say to that, but it doesn't matter because Larisa is already moving toward my closet. Well, her closet. Dina motions for me to follow. When we step inside, Larisa beelines for the opposite wall, pushing clothes out of the way. There, behind all the hangers, is one of those double doors.

"You didn't know about this?" Dina asks as I gape at Larisa pushing the doors open to another room and more clothes.

"I certainly did not."

"Of course not. It's not as if my brother did a tour of the place, right?" Larisa glances over her shoulder. I shake my head as I follow her into the mini closet. This one is long, with dresses only on one side, but they're more breathtaking than anything I've ever seen.

"What are these?" My hand reaches out of its own accord, but I drop it before I can touch the fabric.

"These are the official business dresses, as Dina calls them," Larisa replies. "You probably don't know this, but I have another half sibling. My sister. She's an incredible seamstress, and these are her pride and joy. She created each one for me, and they're one of a kind."

"I can't wear these." Not when they're clearly so precious to her. The sadness in her voice isn't to be missed. I wonder how long it's been since she's seen her sister.

"You can, and you will." Larisa turns to me, the royalty coming off her like perfume. "I want you to."

There's no arguing with that. Larisa pushes more clothes aside before reaching for one of the dresses. My breath catches as I stare at the scarlet fabric. It's the same color of those roses that I love so much. The skirt is covered in tulle, and there are a million diamonds sparkling up at me.

"I—" I have no words as I stare at it.

"It's perfect for you, Nikita," Dina says from her spot beside me. I glance up at the ladies, completely overwhelmed. They're showing me so much kindness and why? Because their prince kidnapped me? That's not a good enough reason, and yet. Here we are.

The girls lead me back out into the room and sit me in front of the vanity. Dina spreads out the dress on the bed, and I keep glancing at it in the mirror. I know it'll fit me because Larisa and I are nearly the same size. But I don't think I've ever worn anything close to how magical the dress is.

"Let's do your makeup, shall we?" *Princessa* asks, so I turn my eyes to her. "Not that you need much. We'll just add a little shimmer to your skin, to match the dress."

She opens one of the drawers on the vanity and pulls out a brush and a small container. I went through the desk when I first came here, looking for a weapon, but I haven't touched anything in there. My sisters never taught me anything about makeup, so I only picked up what was necessary. And that is to look well groomed. Hair slicked back, eyebrows brushed, one coat of mascara. But this? Getting my makeup and hair done—it seems fun.

Larisa begins working on my skin, moving the brush gently over it. I close my eyes, and a thought suddenly occurs to me.

"How did you know what he would ask? You came straight here, no?"

They do that whole look between them again before Dina is the one to reply. "Gavriil told us."

"How?" That makes no sense, since he said hello to his sister as if he was seeing her for the first time in weeks. I wait for them to reply. Larisa steps back from my face, looking down to meet my eye.

"We can hear your music, but we hear his voice too."

I'm not sure why I didn't think of that. He talks to me now, but he's spent all this time here alone, with his family on the other side of a curse.

"You can't hear me?"

"No, only your music."

I wonder why that is. But honestly, that's not even what shocks me the most.

"He's been talking about me?"

"You've helped him, Nikita," Larisa says, reaching over and giving my shoulder a squeeze. "This whole situation may be unorthodox, and you came here under terrible circumstances, but he needed you. Even if he'll never say it out loud. He's still a prideful man."

I let her words sink in, letting them take root in my heart. The warmth of the knowledge that I've done something right fills me. Right then and there, I do wish things were different. If only because then Gavriil and I would have a chance—no.

These thoughts, they have no place in my current situation. We've become friends, and I want to hold onto that. I close my eyes again as the girls brush the mascara over the lashes and add more color to the corners.

"There you go." Larisa catches my eye in the mirror. I see the way my skins glitters, even in this light. My eyes seem bigger somehow and full of emotions I won't speak out loud.

"Thank you," is all I can manage.

"Dina will take care of the hair," Larisa says, meeting

my eyes in the mirror, her lips curling up at the sides. "I have a dinner to cook."

She leaves then, without waiting for a response. Dina and I both watch her go. When the door closes behind her, the soldier turns to me.

"You might not think I have a lot of skill in this, since I sport my signature braids, but I actually used to do hair all the time."

"I'm not worried." I smile at her as she begins brushing out my locks. It's been so long since someone has brushed my hair, tears come into my eyes uninvited.

"Oh, am I being too rough?" Dina pauses immediately, and I shake my head.

"No, it's just been a while since I've been pampered."

There's a look of understanding in Dina's eyes, as well as sympathy, which makes me want to cry harder. That will ruin all the work Larisa put into my face, so I squash the desire with all I've got.

"You know, you guys don't have to do this. You should be spending time on yourself and the people who are important to you." I smile, and she knows exactly where I'm going with this.

"You mean like Yevgenii?" Dina's face takes on a dream-like quality, a soft smile on her face. "We love each other, *da*, but we also love who we are, Nikita. He's the captain of the guard, and I'm his second in command."

"A power couple," I say, and she grins.

"I like that." Dina goes back to brushing my hair as she continues. "Being of service, helping a friend, that's what we do. And it's been a long time since we could. We don't have many choices in front of us, but we chose to be here."

They really do seem to care about Gavriil, and their hearts are in the right place. It's interesting how different it is within these walls. Even though Gavriil has been a cruel master, making mistakes when he was younger, they still show loyalty to him. But they do it in a way that reminds everyone they remember the person he can be. The syndicate does not evoke that kind of devotion. You stay with the Bratva because you want to survive.

"Thank you, Dina," I say, and the other girl smiles.

"Let's get you ready."

✣ 33 ✣

I look like a princess. That's the only thing that comes to my mind as I stare at myself in the full-length mirror. My hair is curled and falling softly over my shoulders. Dina wanted to take it up halfway, but I wanted to leave it down. So, we compromised by pinning one side of it away from my ear with a clip shaped like a crescent moon. A matching necklace hangs round my neck. My skin is glowing and shimmering in the light, all the way down to my fingers. My lips are painted a dark red that matches the dress exactly.

The dress.

It fits like it was made for me. The bodice wraps around my body, the neckline below my collarbone. My shoulders are naked as the sleeves fall halfway down my upper arms—almost like a gentle loop of material. The skirt is full, a proper ball gown. I can't stop touching the top layer. It looks like I'm touching stars, sprinkled on a scarlet sky instead of a blue one.

Underneath the skirt, my boots are hidden from sight. I could've worn heels, in fact Dina picked some out for me. But I'm not a heels person and never will be. The wedges on my boots provide me with height, but the comfort of shoes I love makes me feel less like an imposter.

I've never been one to spend time in front of a mirror, but I look so—right somehow that I'm entirely too confused. I've spent my life in clothes that I knew would make me look like a proper businesswoman in the sight of the Bratva. Now, I just look like a girl in a pretty dress and it's not weird. Not weird at all.

"It's time."

Turning to where Dina waits by the door, I give the dress another pat down, as if making sure I'm still wearing it. Everything seems so surreal. Dina looks proud of her work, and I give her a warm smile.

"Are you sure you're second in command in the king's army? You could have your own salon." I'm happy to announce my voice did not come out breathless at all, and I know I said the right thing. Dina grins with pride.

"I wouldn't give up my service for anything, but I do love makeovers. Maybe one day—" She stops herself, and the sadness is instant. I'm too far from her to offer comfort before she shuts it down and smiles again. This time, a little of the spark is missing. "Let's get you down to dinner. Prince Gavriil is going to have a heart attack when he sees you."

"Oh, I don't know about that," I say, but she simply grins.

If I'm being honest with myself, there is a part of me that's excited to see his reaction. That also annoys me because I was just telling myself how we're friends. No matter this shift between our dynamic, that's all we'll ever be. As Dina and I leave my room, I keep up with admonishing myself. There's no use for me to be affected by whether he likes or dislikes my outfit. I look good in it. It doesn't matter what he thinks. At all.

But then, he steps out of the shadows at the top of the stairs, and all my thoughts disappear.

The absolute pure appreciation in his gaze as he looks at me sends my heart soaring. My hands fist over my dress, and I have to remind myself to breathe. It's such a simple thing, so why is it so hard to force air into my lungs? I know Dina is still here, but she disappears into another world as Gavriil and I stare at each other.

He's even more of a beast than he was the last time I saw him. His hair is in disarray and long. His skin is nearly covered in it now. He looks bulkier in his dark turquoise suit coat. But his eyes hold me prisoner.

Deep and blue and filled with everything I can't say and all the things I imagine. His guard is down, maybe for the first time ever, and I can see his wants as clearly as I see my own. He moves then, breaking the spell as he reaches his hand toward me.

Without a second thought, I place mine in it. He turns us toward the stairs. My dress fans out around me as we descend, neither one of us speaking. This moment feels too electrified, and I'm afraid no word is good enough to fill it.

When we reach the bottom, we don't turn toward the kitchens or the dining room. Glancing up at him in confusion, he simply gives me a small smile and then steers me in the opposite direction. It isn't until we're there that I realize he'd led us to the ballroom. The doors are already open. The candles are lit. The room with the painted roses and the thousands of flickering flames is otherworldly.

"Everything is set, Your Majesty." Yevgenii appears out of the shadows, inclining forward at the waist.

"Thank you, my friend," Gavriil answers, receiving a smile from his captain of the guard before the man walks out of the room and shuts the door behind him. My eyes zero in on the table setup in front of the middle window, nearly in the exact spot where I sat to perform the spell.

"Shall we?"

I nod, unable to make my mouth form the words. I allow Gavriil to lead me to my side of the table. My eyes scan the ballroom, seeing it for the first time in fuller light. I notice that roses are painted on the ceiling as well, gold trim circling it at the top. He pulls out a chair, I sit, and everything is fine and normal and too much all at once. I can't find my footing. I feel off balance.

"Where are Larisa, Dina, and Yevgenii?" I ask as Gavriil takes his place at the table. I'm not sure why, but I expected them to eat with us. Maybe because their time as live people is so precious.

"Yevgenii and Dina are having their own dinner. And Larisa," his gaze shadows with sadness for a moment, "she wanted some time in the garden."

My heart thuds in awareness at the knowledge. I wish there was something I could do.

"Can we invite her to dine with us?" I ask and receive another one of Gavriil's soft smiles.

"I already have. She wanted time to herself, but maybe we can go find her later."

I nod at that, satisfied for the moment. In the few times I have spent with her, I already think of her as someone I care about. The same goes for Dina and Yevgenii. I don't meet many genuinely good people in my life, and these three—four—are. It's funny how I put Gavriil in that category now. He's not at all like I thought him to be. He wears his family's legacy as a shield, just like I do. It's an interesting thing we have in common.

"She really prepared all of this?" It seemed like it only took Dina and I a few hours to finish getting me ready, but there's a feast in front of us. Potatoes and *katleti*—one of my favorite meat dishes—with a traditional layered salad with fish and potatoes and carrots.

"Yevgenii helped."

We share another smile, and it's like we're incapable of anything else. I glance down at the food in front of me, thrilled at the prospect of eating something other than bread and eggs. I can't find a way to understand how Larisa finds all the ingredients she needs when I can only find two. I might have to do an extra run tomorrow morning to make up for all this good food.

There's a comfortable silence between the two of us as we eat, one I don't feel the need to fill. Gavriil seems to think so too. Periodically, our eyes meet across the table and hold, saying whatever our lips aren't. We're halfway through dinner before we feel like we can talk. I'm not sure if we both were working ourselves up to it.

"Have you always wanted to follow in your father's footsteps?" Gavriil asks as I put my silverware down and reach for my drink. The question takes me by surprise for a minute because I haven't thought of it in a while. But then I take a sip and answer.

"*Nyet.* When I was little, I wanted to be a musician. Mama worked with me on the piano day and night, it seemed. My sisters never wanted anything out of life but to marry rich, but for me, music was everything."

"What happened?"

"Mama died. And Papa needed me more than my music did."

"And what did you need?"

It's such a simple question, but it holds so much weight. For a long time now, I haven't thought about what I needed. All I knew is that I would do whatever it took to stay powerful. There is no room for anything else if you want to survive in the Bratva. But Gavriil isn't asking about any of that. He's asking me—Nikita—what it was that I needed. And the answer to that has always been simple.

"I need to not feel afraid. Or alone."

We lock eyes as I answer and then we stay there, frozen in this moment. I've never admitted that to anyone before, but for the first time, I think I found someone who would understand that kind of need. I can see in his eyes that he does.

"You are a brave young woman, Nikita Arturovna."

It is the use of the patronymic name that gets me. So often, I've had to fight for people to see me for who I am. Those in power in the organization make sure to only call me by my first name, because it is a sign that I am nothing but a child to them. But Gavriil sees me as an equal. Not only that, he's shown me a sign of respect by calling me by my first and my father's name. It is more than I have ever been given from those who say they care about me.

And now, the man who has held me prisoner is giving me that gift. What a strange life I live.

"Would you like to dance?" Gavriil asks suddenly, pushing to his feet. I don't hesitate to follow.

"Yes."

He walks over to a table near the wall, where someone —I'm assuming Yevgenii—has set up an old *magnitofon*, except without the records. Instead, it holds a small tube where a needle runs over it to create music. It's the type that has only a few songs stored, and to hear the music, one has to wind the lever. Gavriil turns it until it won't turn anymore. When he lets go, a beautiful melody fills the air.

Gavriil walks over to me slowly, his eyes locked on mine. When he's only two feet away, he stops, putting out his hand for me—giving me a last chance to retreat. But I don't. I step into his arms, one hand on his shoulder, the other holding onto his. He brings his free hand around my waist, molding our bodies together and then we begin to move.

The melody is soft, almost like a lullaby. It moves with us as we spin around the room. It's been a long time since I've danced, but it doesn't seem to matter. Gavriil and I move as if we've been doing this our whole lives. Two broken pieces, finally making a whole, spinning in sync in a room full of flowers.

I can't take my eyes off his. I don't want to.

The pressure on my back intensifies as he lifts me with one arm, spinning me around before gently placing me on the floor once again. We don't skip a step as I twirl out of his arms and then back into them. The simple touch of his skin against mine intoxicates me, as if I'm breathing in the fumes of a hundred big cities. Along with his smell—roses and dark forest—I think every possible dream I've ever had is coming true right here in front of my eyes.

We spin and spin until the world is just him and I, lost in our own magical realm.

When the music finally stops and we come to stand-still, my head is spinning. Whatever shift I felt between us before, it has become so much more.

"Thank you for tonight," I whisper, refusing to make myself move out of his arms. Not that he's in any hurry. He continues to hold me, my front to his, with not a sliver of air between our bodies.

"It was long overdue," he replies. I think he's out of breath. There are a lot of things I can say here, but one question remains unanswered.

"Why now?" My question is but a whisper, but it nearly echoes across the ballroom. He doesn't answer right away, but I can feel the way he tenses under my touch. And I know. "You don't have much time left."

His eyes meet mine, full of pain and regret and the truth he doesn't want to speak out loud. My hand curls over his shoulder of its own accord. I want to pull him into my arms and never let go.

But then he does. Abruptly, he takes a step back.

"I should go find the others. We have plenty of food left over."

He doesn't wait for a response, turning and walking out of the room, leaving me feeling cold in the night air.

❧ 34 ❧

Dina and Yevgenii arrive first and find me leaning against the doorway to the balcony, looking out into the garden.

"His Majesty has insisted we come keep you company!" Dina announces as Yevgenii looks on. He really is such a quiet man and seems much older than his years. Probably because he's the calm beside the storm that is Dina.

"We have plenty of food, and we wanted to spend time with you before—" I don't finish as Larisa and Gavriil walk in as well. My eyes find his immediately. I can tell, even from this distance, that his are filled with regret. Running away from me probably wasn't the way he wanted to finish off the evening. But I won't call him out on it right now. I'll do it later when we're alone. That's what I've decided while I watched the stars come shining through the clouds. He gave me a perfect moment and then he ran. I have heard that's a typical response when it comes to males in general. So, I'm not about to let it ruin the rest of my evening.

"Larisa, you have outdone yourself." I walk over to the princess, reaching out to take her hands in mine and give them a squeeze. "It was delicious."

"Thank you, Nikita. I see you're not the only one who thinks so." She nods toward the table, and I turn to find Dina and Yevgenii already eating.

"There are not enough chairs here," I say. "Should we take it to the dining room?"

"Or we can have a picnic," Larisa replies. She glances over at her brother. He nods before walking out of the ball-room. "Are you alright?" Larisa asks, turning her eyes on me.

"Sure, of course."

She gives me a knowing look. "He's not really good with emotion. His father didn't teach him about that."

I furrow my brow at her words, but before I can comment, he's back. And he's carrying some blankets. Yevgenii rushes over immediately, taking the items from him and spreading them out in front of the floor to ceiling window. I smile at Larisa as we grab the plates off the table and place them in the middle of the blankets. Once everything has been transferred, the group settles in a circle. I take my place between Larisa and Dina. Somehow, I sit opposite Gavriil, and it's like we're back to our dinner, saying things with our eyes. I give him a simple smile. He seems to relax, if only slightly.

I'll have to explore that whole 'bad with emotion' comment Larisa brought up. I didn't think about that before, but communication is a learned skill. Especially when it comes to one's emotions. If it hasn't been properly taught, it ends up being a hindrance. Suddenly, I can't help but feel like this may be my next project. I simply want to help all of them. Gavriil is on that short list, if not at the top of it.

"When we were kids, we used to do this every time I visited," Larisa says as she takes a bite of her potatoes. Gavriil and I aren't hungry since we ate already, but I grab my glass and take a sip as I settle more comfortably onto the floor. My dress pools around me as I cross my legs, leaning slightly forward on my elbows.

"You didn't grow up here?"

"Oh, no. I grew up with my mother and half sister in her kingdom. It's north of here, near one of the biggest trading passages between the western kingdoms and the eastern ones."

"I really know nothing about Skazka," I say, shrugging. "I thought it was one big kingdom, to be honest."

"There are several kingdoms. The forest spans across all of them," Dina comments, reaching for more food.

"Have you visited them all?"

"Not for a long time. The king did not like to travel," Yevgenii says. The rest of them pause for a second, as if mention of the king affects them physically, which I suppose it does.

"It was my plan to visit our allies and those who are no longer such and to rebuild relationships," Gavriil says, looking at me in that intense way of his. "Father didn't think it was necessary. His main concern was to remain in power. So, as I got older, that became my number one goal as well."

"It's a good thing that you can make your own decisions now," I comment and hold his gaze for a long moment before he smirks and looks away. No one here is saying anything about the curse. It's as if it doesn't exist for the next however many hours the rest of them are animated.

But I'm not forgetting the way Gavriil reacted when I said he's running out of time. Because it means they are also.

"I would love to visit *Holodnoye Tsarstvo*," Larisa says. "It's a frozen paradise."

"Frozen?"

"Well, it's mostly in perpetual winter. But it's so beautiful there. Everything is white and blinding and sitting by the fire is the best past time." Larisa sounds dreamy as she speaks, and that makes me smile.

"My mama always thought I was crazy for liking the cold, but I simply like the variety."

"Our kingdom has the best Autumn," Yevgenii says. There's a tone of wistfulness in those words too. They're all thinking it, but no one wants to say it out loud. This place may never see another normal season, and neither will they. It's a thought—no matter how hard we try to push it out of our minds—that simply won't leave.

We spend the rest of the night talking about everything and anything. We laugh and we eat and we give this moment of time the reverence it deserves. Because in a few hours, they will go back to being statues and Gavriil and I will be left on our own. With very little hope left.

I came here wanting to protect my papa, not knowing what I was getting myself into. But now, I want to protect these people who feel more like family than my own ever did since Mama passed.

Back when she was around, she held us together. But

when she was gone, Papa threw himself into work, and I threw myself into being in control. My sisters have long stopped trying to understand my ambitions or why I hated the Bratva, even as I tried my best to become a powerful entity within it. It never mattered to me to be understood.

But now, as I sit surrounded by new friends, I realize I was simply not around people who were made of the same stuff as me. You have to find those who fit, and this group fits. It breaks my heart to know that soon, they'll be gone, and I'll be right where I started.

❀ 35 ❀

A dream comes like a lightning strike. One minute I'm sleeping, and the next, images assault me on every side. Sitting up in bed, I gasp, my head spinning.

It felt so real.

My papa was on his knees in front of Ilya as the syndicate watched. He told Papa to beg for his life, but Papa wouldn't do it. He stares right into Ilya's face as the man holds a gun over him.

I've seen the scene before, when I snuck into a meeting I wasn't supposed to be near. It haunted me for years. But it's not even close to what I'm feeling now. The dreams I've been having for the last week, including this one, make me feel like everything is falling apart back home.

Wiping at the tears running down my cheeks, I hug my arms around myself as I focus on my breathing. My heart is racing a mile a second, my skin is clammy from the nightmare.

I miss him so much. I miss our nightly talks and quiet morning breakfasts. But I wouldn't change my decision to come here for anything.

Getting out of bed, I put on my shoes and grab a blanket, wrapping it tightly around myself before I leave the room. Larisa, Dina, and Yevgenii are gone, back to their suspended stasis. I didn't watch them return to it. We hugged and said a quick goodbye before I shut my bedroom door and went to bed. I didn't want to think about what was happening to them. Or what's happening between Gavriil and I.

I simply wanted to escape.

And I did. For a few hours. Right up until the dream neatly took the wind out of my sails.

Wandering through the castle, the only sounds that follow me are my own footsteps. I have no idea where Gavriil is or if he's even sleeping. I don't know what he does at night. I have never asked.

I make my way to the kitchen and pour myself a glass of water. Images from my dream refuse to dissipate, and I push away the tears that keep pooling in my eyes.

Maybe it's the time I spent with everyone that has me so emotional. Maybe it's my own heart breaking for these people that is letting in every other worry I may ever have. My papa is fine and safe. He has to be. The Bratva would never hurt him.

I'm making my way back to the staircase when I see a light through the window. It's coming from the secret garden, and somehow, I know that's where I'll find Gavriil. It would probably be wiser if I simply went to bed, but I'm pushing the front doors open before I can even think about it.

The air is much cooler than I'm used to. I wrap the blanket tighter around me as I walk down the path. When I reach the garden, I push inside without hesitation.

Gavriil is sitting on the ground in front of one of the rose bushes, checking the leaves one by one. I've never seen him actually work in the garden before. The care he's taking with every leaf brings a smile to my face, even though my heart is heavy. There's something about seeing a man being gentle that changes everything.

"Couldn't sleep?" he asks even before he turns, as if he felt me there. I shake my head as I meet his eye. But he must be able to read something in my face because he's on his feet instantly. "What is it, Nikita?"

A single tear escapes, and he catches it as it runs down my cheek. My breath hitches at his nearness. I open my mouth to speak, except I can't. He raises his arms on either side of me, as if he wants to hug me but is waiting for permission. I don't hesitate. I step inside immediately. When his arms wrap around me, all I can do is cling to his shirt with my hands.

I expect myself to cry, but I don't. I simply breathe him in and let his touch calm my racing mind and hurting heart. If only for a moment. He's given me comfort before, and maybe that's what I was looking for when I came out here. Maybe I am—I don't know what I am anymore. I only let him hold me close as I try to hold myself together.

"Talk to me, Nikita," he whispers into my hair. Even though I wasn't going to, I tell him everything.

"I had a dream about Papa."

There's a slight pause. "What did you see in your dream?"

"Him begging for his life. I've seen the scenario before in real life, and I think I just miss him and—" I don't finish because Gavriil's body shudders beneath mine and then he drops his arms from around me. Stepping back, he bends in two, a growl emitting from him.

"Gavriil?" I take a step toward him, but he moves away.

"Stay back."

His voice is low and dark and dangerous, but I don't back away.

"No, what's happening?" I reach for him, and he jerks his head up. I see the shift between man and beast, the illusion trick his hands have been doing. His body morphs into that of a wolf before he bends over again, grunting. His body shakes in obvious pain.

When I move toward him this time, I don't hesitate. He drops to the ground, and I drop with him, landing on my knees.

"Focus on me, Gavriil," I command, placing my hands on either side of his face and raising it to look me in the eye. Our faces are inches apart. I hold him there, breathing in and out. "Come on, focus on me. Breathe."

He shudders under my touch, but he doesn't look away. His midnight eyes pierce me straight to my soul. His breathing mirrors mine, and we become one and the same. Breathing the same air, our heartbeats in sync.

"There you go. Come back to yourself. Breathe."

We stay like that until his face stops shifting, until

sweat collects on his brow. I came out here to seek comfort, and yet I'm the one to give it. I didn't even have to think about it.

"I'm dangerous," he finally says as I run my hand over his forehead and brow.

"That makes two of us." I try for a smile, but his doesn't come. He continues to stare at me intensely, and that's when I realize I'm still touching him. I sit back on my heels as he watches me, one hand on his knee. I've dropped my blanket, but under that gaze, I don't feel cold anymore. Not when he's burning me from the inside. When he speaks, his words don't register at first.

"What?"

"I said you need to go to your father."

"I don't understand."

"The ring you have, it can take you back."

"You said it didn't work."

"It only has three uses and one left. One use is full travel, of going there and back. I wanted to use—it doesn't matter. I give the ring permission to be used by you as you see fit."

The moment he says the words, the ring glows. I realize that's why it didn't work before. He has to allow for the magic to work. I've read about such artifacts in all those books in his study. But I don't speak up right away. I think I know what he wanted to use it for, and if I'm correct, he's giving up something for me—something huge.

"You wanted to use it to leave, right? To protect your people."

He doesn't even try to deny it. Which is progress for us.

"When I'm a beast, I'll have no control over who I hurt. Even now, I forget my name sometimes." He inhales deeply, such pain in his eyes that I want to reach for him again. "Sending myself into the ocean is the only way I can protect them. Maybe then, somehow, they can find a way out of this."

"That's not an answer," I whisper, because now I can't imagine a world where he doesn't exist. But I can't say that, can I? "They're tied to you. What if that makes it worse?"

"Worse than death? They're dying because of me anyway. At least this way, it won't be because I tear them to shreds."

I know he's trying to scare me with his words, but I don't budge that easily.

"There has to be something else."

"It doesn't matter, Nikita. You need to see your father."

"But I thought the blood bargain—" It always speaks of death when the two people in the contract are separated.

"There are stipulations. If you don't come back—well, that also doesn't matter anymore. I'm releasing you from the bargain in the only way I can."

"Is that possible?"

"It is if the bargainer deems it so."

I want to believe him, but there's something here that he's not saying.

"Gavriil." I reach over, placing my hand on his upper arm. He shudders under my touch, but this time it's not from the shift. It's a different kind of feeling, and it makes me hold on that much tighter. I come to a decision. "I'll come back. In three days. I'll come back."

He looks up at me, his eyes full of hope for the first time since I've met him.

"Are you sure?" he whispers.

"I promise."

❦ 36 ❧

I don't wait until morning. There's no use since I have no idea how time works between this realm and the next. Plus, there is no way I can sleep anyway. Gavriil doesn't follow me as I make my way back to the castle. On the steps, I turn and look back down to the garden, but I can't see him.

What I said is true; I am coming back. There's no way I can simply walk away from what's happening here, not when there are still areas left to explore, a shred of hope left to hold onto. I have no idea what they are, I just know I haven't read every book in that study or tried every spell.

But in order for me to focus on Gavriil, I need to make sure my papa is safe and that he knows I'm okay. It's been nearly five months since I first left. I have no idea what's waiting for me back home.

I dress in my own clothes quickly, feeling slightly strange, as if they don't quite fit me anymore. It's true I'm not the same girl I was when I left, but I didn't think I was going to miss the feel of dresses around my ankles or the comfort of this room. Turning toward the mirror, I give myself a quick study. I wear pants, a button up shirt, and my trusty booties. I look like I did before, except there's a sort of maturity around my eyes that's new.

Glancing around the room, I smile to myself before reaching for the ring I've been wearing since the beginning. It makes sense now, why Gavriil said it's important to him. And he's giving me his one use—there and back again—because he knows this is important to me. But I am coming back.

I made a promise, and around these parts, that's just as much of a bargain as anything.

Taking the ring off my pointer finger, I think of my family's home. Then I place the ring on my ring finger. Just like that, one room dissipates around me and another materializes.

A scream comes first. I open my eyes to find my middle sister, Olga, on the floor. She stares up at me as if she's seen a ghost. She screams again, this time with Papa's name on her lips.

"Nice to see you too, Olga." I smirk, discreetly moving the ring back to my pointer finger. Then, my eyes are on the doorway as Papa and Masha rush in. They freeze on the threshold, their eyes as big as saucers.

"*Zdrastvui*, Papa," I say, unable to take my eyes off him. My simple greeting breaks the spell, and he rushes toward me. His arms wrap around me, holding me to him as his body shakes with sobs.

"I thought I lost you forever, *dochenka*. I thought I lost you."

I cling to him, soaking in the comfort and feel of him, my own eyes filling up with tears. We stand like that for a while until Masha's voice breaks through.

"How in the world did you get away?" she asks. I pull away from Papa to glance to where she stands on the other side of the couch that Olga is now sitting on. Olga looks slightly indifferent about me being back, but Masha looks near hostile. She's always had a particular hate toward me that I never understood. But she was more subtle about it before.

"I didn't. He let me go."

"What?" Olga exclaims. "That hideous creature let you go?"

"He's not hideous." I'm immediately on the defensive, and I feel everyone's eyes on me. "There's more to him than meets the eye," I finish, glancing back at Papa. He hasn't taken his eyes off me, his hand wrapped tightly around my own.

"What matters is you're safe now. I tried for months to reach you, but the passage to that kingdom has been cut off. Most of Skazka is shut down as they search for some sorceress."

"A sorceress?"

"Baba Yaga if you can believe it," Masha says, and this time, I do glance at her. "There's some manhunt. Or whatever."

I know better than to show any more interest in the situation. Thankfully, my face is practiced in all the different masks I can wear.

"I'm sorry I couldn't contact you sooner," I say instead, turning to my papa. He gives me a smile, and I notice then just how tired he looks. He seems to have aged a few years since I've been gone.

"What is that around your neck?" Masha is next to us then, reaching for my necklace. I realize I never took the crescent moon off. I push it back into my shirt, but it's too late. She's seen it. I can already see her eyes sparkling with curiosity. "So, this 'not hideous' kidnapper. He's got a castle, right?"

"I told you, Masha, the castle is huge. He's a royal no doubt." My papa beats me to a response, sounding tired. But she doesn't turn to him. Her eyes are on me. I can tell she's taking stock of how I look. My hair is still curled from dinner, my skin shining. I'm clearly well nourished. Her lips curl up in a smile, and she turns away. But my heart fills with dread because my sister is dangerous when she's scheming.

"Well, I'm sure everyone will be thrilled to see you. We were just leaving."

"Papa?" I turn to him, a question in my eyes.

"Balakins are hosting a family dinner," he replies. It makes sense why he's dressed in a suit then. I glance over at my sisters and both of them are in evening wear. Masha is dressed in a dark green number with slits on both sides and barely-there spaghetti straps. She walks over to a mirror, expertly putting on makeup as she talks.

"You have a few minutes if you'd like to put on something a little more...appropriate." She turns, giving my outfit a quick look. "We wouldn't want to be late."

I glance back at Papa, and he gives me a small smile and a nod. There's no way he can miss appearing at Balakins. Family dinners are a façade. I've known that since I was old enough to understand what kind of organization the Bratva is. The Balakin family has always been on top, and the dinners are their way of making sure they exhibit that control. The fancy parties are for outsiders. The family dinners are for the elite.

"What aren't you telling me?" I ask, lowering my voice. Papa's eyes find mine, a glimmer of pride in them.

"Always the smartest one in the room," he whispers before he raises his voice a little. "There has been some shifting of power. We must go and present a united front. I'm sure everyone will be happy to see you."

"Oh yes. She'll be the belle of the ball." Masha smirks, and my heart sinks further.

My papa's position in the organization is in trouble. Even without all the facts, I can see it. I've spent enough years learning the ins and outs of how the organization works. If Papa says there's a shifting in power, it means the power is shifting away from him.

"Why are you in trouble?" I ask, keeping my voice low, but Olga is close enough to hear it.

"Because of you, dear sister." She gets off the couch, grabbing a glass of wine on the way. "He's been putting all his focus on finding you. Neglected some duties. You know." She downs the glass before refilling it. I see Olga has been taking lessons from Masha on how to behave. At least when I was around, there was a filter. Since I've been gone, Masha has clearly sunk her teeth into our middle sister. I turn to my oldest as she smiles at me.

"Things change."

"I'm sure you had nothing to do with it."

"Nikita, don't," Papa says, squeezing my hand. "You're home. It will all be fine."

I don't have it in my heart to tell him right now that I'm not staying. Instead, I stare at my sister, coming to a decision. If she wants to go up against me, then so be it. Clearly in my absence, she has decided to make a power play. Interesting that she had to wait until her baby sister was out of the picture. But I know one card that I can play right off the top, and it will not make her happy.

"Give me five minutes to change," I say before I give Papa a kiss on the cheek and walk toward my room. Dina and Larisa's handiwork on my hair and makeup is about to be put to use once more.

❧ 37 ❧

My room is just as I left it. That probably means my sisters have been in here looking for something and everything. I have no doubt they've been through here like a hurricane. They just made sure to keep everything in place because it would've undoubtedly upset Papa.

Maybe I should be more affected by what transpired downstairs, but honestly, I was preparing myself for that kind of reception. My sisters have always hated me, whatever the reason. Personally, I think it's as basic as competition. Masha wants it all—most of all power. She had none while I was around. And then I wasn't. Olga is a sponge, always picking up whatever Masha puts out. We're so close in age, but realms apart in every other way. They care very little about me, so I don't feel bad about my plan at all.

After spending months learning for myself what is important and what I will stand for, I'm not about to pull any punches. Gavriil and his kingdom need me, but so does my papa. So, I'll start with one problem at a time.

Walking over to my closet, I push aside the typical outfits I would wear for these events and reach for the dresses. I have a few. Most of them I haven't worn. But I always like to be prepared, and that's about to really score me some points with the Balakins, and lose me some points with my sisters.

I rip my clothes off quickly, my hands on the red dress I picked out. The color is bright, nowhere near the beautiful scarlet I wore for the royal dinner. But the cut leaves my collarbone and shoulders exposed, and it hugs my figure nicely, all the way down to the floor. The slit goes high, right over my right leg, which is kind of perfect since I'm wearing my black boots underneath. It also provides easy access for the knife I strap to my other thigh.

A girl must be prepared at all times.

Next, I make sure to run my hands through my hair, fluffing it up and rearranging it to one side, much like I had at the castle. My skin is still covered with the illuminating powder, and my eye makeup hasn't smudged. It might be magical since I cried some, but I double check that it's in place anyway. Opening up my own vanity, I search through the items until I come to a three pack of lipsticks. These are the ones I never use, the bright colors that are nothing like the usual me. I pick out the red that matches my dress and put it on.

When I step back and look at myself in the mirror, I look dangerous.

This is perfect because I'm about to stir some things up.

When I descend the stairs, the look on my sisters' faces is priceless.

"What are you wearing?" Masha exclaims as my papa tries to hide his proud smile beside her.

"A dress. You should know what it is. You're wearing one."

"But you don't. Ever."

"Correction. Didn't. And now I do. Shall we?"

My sister is still stumbling over words when I turn to my papa and follow him out of the front door.

"Are you sure you know what you're doing, making your sisters crazy like that?" he asks as the girls hurry behind us.

"Don't worry, Papa. It's all in good fun."

I throw a smile over my shoulder at my sisters and am met by Masha's intense glare. By simply wearing this outfit, I've already riled up her plans. With the way I'm going, I can get things on track and return to Gavriil before the deadline. Once the curse is broken—and it will be because I am determined—I might ask if I can bring Papa to live with us. He can do the businessman thing in Skazka and then I won't have to worry about him. Or what the organization might do.

But first things first, I need to get through tonight.

I wish I had time with Papa before we left, alone, so I can gauge where everything is. He truly did entrust the running of the business to me while he did the traveling and the meeting with the people bit. Now he simply looks tired. Masha looks smug, and Olga looks disinterested. Those last two haven't changed much. Except Masha carries a twinge of anger within her too.

We arrive at the house, riding entirely in silence. Having raised three daughters, Papa knows when it's a good time not to say anything. When the door is opened by the valet, Masha and Olga are out in a flash. Pretty sure Masha is pulling Olga with her at this point. I open my own door and wait for Papa to come around and offer me his arm.

"What am I to expect?" I ask.

"I haven't been working, *dochenka*," he admits as we walk—very slowly—toward the front of the house. "They want me out."

"Why?"

"I was looking for you. I felt guilty, and I had no idea where you were and—"

"Papa." I pull him to a stop, turning him to face me. "Gavriil is not a monster. He is a good man in a bad situation. He knew I was worried about you, and he let me come see you."

Papa studies me for a long moment before his lips curl up in a sad smile. "You're not staying, are you?"

"I was going to tell you. But he needs me. His people do. His kingdom does."

"He's a royal?"

"A prince in line for a throne. There's so much there, Papa. The castle, the people—their time is running out. I only have three days with you and then I must return." My voice grows distant as I think about it all. I realize I miss them already.

"Will you tell me about it?" Papa asks.

"Of course I will. But first, we need to fix your position with the Bratva. Before Masha fixes it for you."

"Your sister—"

"I know you're going to defend her because you are a good papa, but she would throw you under the bus if it meant power. It's just who she is. But I can do my part and make sure you survive."

He doesn't argue with me, even though he wants to. Another valet walks past us, and we turn back to the house. Papa is a strong man with a good heart. People like him are eaten alive by the Bratva. He didn't choose this life for himself, but he did the best he could. Then, I came along, and I became the driving force behind our family.

Now, I need to prove to everyone that we are still a powerful family, and no one should think about crossing us.

⚜

WHEN WE STEP INSIDE THE HOUSE, THE WHOLE FOYER full of people freezes. My sisters are near the Balakins, and they know the moment the attention shifts to us. Masha throws a glare my way as Ilya pushes past her and walks toward me.

"Nikita, is that truly you?" He stops a few feet in front of me, his eyes taking me in. I don't miss the way they scan my body or the places they linger, before he finally meets my eyes. I send him the most subtle flirty smirk I can before replying,

"Eat your heart out, I have returned."

He moves toward me then, and I think he would've hugged me if Papa didn't extend his hand for a shake.

"*Dobrey nochi*, Ilya," Papa says. The other man tears his gaze away to shake papa's hand.

"It's good to see you, Artur Ivanovich. It's good to see your daughter as well. Returned to us, unharmed." His eyes find mine again.

"Yes, the business has been taken care of, and you can enjoy my company once more," I say, keeping the tiny smile on my lips.

"Mr. and Mrs. Balakin." I greet our hosts next, shaking hands with both. "It's good to see you."

"Nikita, traveling has done you good." There's an appreciative gleam in Mr. Balakin's face that makes me want to punch him in the face. No one in the room misses it, especially not his wife.

"Magical lands are good for the soul, I suppose."

"We should really go in," Mrs. Balakin announces, motioning for the rest of the people to file into the dining room. I move to follow when I feel a pressure on my arm. Ilya's hand pulls me back as he nods to his family.

"We'll be right in."

I'm too curious to simply brush him off. But also, I can feel Masha's glare burrowing into my skin from afar. I can't pass up this opportunity to rile her up some more.

"What's going on, Ilya?" I ask when the guests have filed into the room and we're left alone.

"I just—I can't get over the fact that you're here. And look at you. Eighteen looks good on you."

"Ah, yes. It is now legally acceptable for you to leer at me," I say, keeping my voice light. Thankfully, Ilya laughs.

"I'm only a few years older, Nikita. Hardly inappropriate."

"Well, leering usually is."

He laughs again, and I'm wondering if I'm wearing a clown suit instead of a dress. Or if he's trying so hard because this is going somewhere.

"We—I missed you. Were you really held against your will by an evil bargainer?"

"Where did you—never mind, Masha."

"She was worried about you."

"Oh, I'm sure." Or she simply used every opportunity she could to strike up a conversation with Ilya. He's an attractive guy; she's an attractive girl—who wants a powerful husband. The stars would align if he had any interest in her at all.

"I know you've been gone, and you probably don't know this, but your family is in a lot of debt. I can help you with that."

"And how do you propose to do that?" I don't point out that we've always been in a lot of debt. It's the only reason we're still in the Bratva. Not that leaving is all that easy, but there was a moment when we could've. Before Mama.

He glances at the closed doors to the dining room, taking a tiny step forward and lowering his voice.

"If we were to unite our two families, all debt would be forgiven."

"Ilya Balakin, are you planning on proposing to my sister?" I feign shock, placing a hand over my heart. His eyes narrow, clearly not appreciating my sarcasm any longer.

"You know she's not the one who holds my heart."

"Oh, please." I have to laugh at that one, all pretenses

forgotten. "You have to have a heart for someone to hold it, Ilya."

He takes a step back. For a second, I think he might actually slap me for that. He wouldn't be the first in the Bratva to talk with his hands. But then his mask falls back into place, and the happy go lucky spoiled mafia kid is back.

"We could be good together, Nikita."

"I think I'll keep my options open," I reply, turning toward the dining room.

"We'll see about that."

He doesn't wait for a response but pushes the doors open so we can walk in. Going our separate ways, I find my seat near Papa, smiling in that businesslike way to those at the table around me.

But my mind is still on Ilya. That last part seemed like a promise. It's not a promise I want him to keep. Maybe I should've played my cards closer to the chest, but I'm not here to marry into this awful family.

"Are you okay?" Papa asks, leaning over.

"Absolutely," I reply with a smile. This is going to be a long evening.

※

ONCE THE MAIN COURSE IS FINISHED, MOST RETIRE TO the sitting room while the family heads break off to their private meeting. I don't hesitate to follow Papa when the time comes, but Masha intercepts me.

"You have already done enough," she snaps, keeping her voice low.

"I haven't done anything yet," I reply with the same intensity in my voice. She's taken back for a moment, narrowing her eyes at me.

"You really have changed. I'd say not for the better."

"Well, it's a good thing your opinion never matters much anyway." I rip my arm out of her grip and push past her to hurry after Papa. I reach the study right as the doors are about to close but manage to squeeze through. Even though I know they know I'm here, no one pays me any attention. Ilya is sitting in the corner, purposefully ignoring me.

"We all know why we are here tonight," Balakin begins from his position behind the desk. I've always hated this room, but now it feels near suffocating. The cigar smoke and expensive *konyak* smell makes it that much worse. My gaze takes in everything at once. I don't have a good feeling about this.

"Artur, you have been negligent in your business dealings. We have missed out on payments."

"As you know, Balakin," my papa begins, an air of nonchalance around him. He's just as good at playing this role as any of them. "Skazka's borders have been shut down for weeks." My stomach coils in warning as I wait for Balakin's next line.

"Yes, it seems they're having a bit of a problem. But you have been distracted. You were missing deadlines, even before the portal shut down. We believe it is time for you to step down and have someone else take your place." Of course, I'm not even surprised. Balakin would have every seat in the syndicate if he could.

"My daughters are—"

253

"We're not talking about your family. My son is more than capable to run your affairs, while you—"

"*Nyet.*"

Every eye turns to me as that one word escapes me. I step closer to the center of the room, shoulders back and chin up. My blood is boiling inside of me, and the desire to reach for my knife is overwhelming. I'm not about to stand and watch my family's name disgraced by this weasel.

"You may have forgotten your place, being gone and all, but you are not here to speak for your family, Nikita."

"And why not? Because I am a woman? Because I am young? Give me a good reason, and I'll think about it." I cock my head to the side.

"You will show me respect." Balakin's eyes grow hot, but I'm not about to flinch in front of him, or any man.

"Respect is earned. My father deserves it. Not you." I snap, keeping my voice controlled and not raised. It has a much more desired effect. So do the words that I've had in my arsenal for years, which I utter next. "He has saved your neck more than once. Or have you forgotten the fiasco of 2005?"

"How do you—"

"I know all kinds of secrets, and so does every man in this room. So, in truth, they hold the power. Not you." Balakin's face grows red, his eyes throwing daggers.

"You should keep your daughter on a leash."

"You should show her respect." Papa stands, his face intense on Balakin's. "She's not wrong, and she doesn't even have all the pieces. I could've taken the organization from under you a long time ago, but I have allowed you to stay in power so I can focus on my family. If you bring them into this, I will not hesitate to play my hand."

Balakin's face pales just slightly, but enough that I know Papa isn't bluffing. I knew there were layers of beef between them, since our families have been in the Bratva the longest. But the way Balakin is looking at Papa—well, there's more there than I could even imagine.

"Pa." Ilya stands, coming over to his father's desk. "What does he mean?"

"It is of no concern to you." Balakin seems to snap out of his moment of panic.

"What does—"

"You will leave our family in place." I interrupt whatever Ilya was going to ask. "You will keep your noses out of our business. And you will make sure to keep Papa invited to all of these parties. We really appreciate your hospitality."

There's a moment of silence in the room as every man turns to stare at Balakin. This is the point of power, who will succumb and who will rise victorious. And because everyone is watching, I give them a show.

"You all know I have done the work to be equal with you." I turn to the other men in the room, a comfortable smile on my face. "You have taught me how to be strong and how to be cunning. Really, it is a testament to your example that I am who I am today. Will you honor that, comrades? That is up to you."

I turn back to stare at Balakin, who is as red as my dress, sweat running down his temples. He hates me, that's clear to see, and he hates that I put him on the spot.

"I think you should listen to the girl," one of the men

says, his face shrouded in shadows. "Nikita Arturovna has earned her place here."

"Aye," a few others agree, and my chest wells up with pride. Not for myself, but for my family. For the way I have represented them all this time. In a way, that is obvious to these men. The Bratva may not be the cleanest organization, but it is an organization of brotherhood and family. I was counting on that when I began speaking, and I'm glad I took that gamble.

"I appreciate your candor, Nikita...Arturovna. We will leave the dealings as is."

He doesn't say it, but the 'for now' is there. I don't even say 'thank you.' Nodding my head in the direction of the men, I loop my arm through Papa's and walk out of the room with others filing out behind me.

This is nowhere near the end of that battle, but at least Papa will be okay for now.

❧ 38 ☙

The next day and a half goes by in a blur of paperwork and ledgers. Papa's business isn't as bad as the organization—or should I say Balakin —was making it out to be. When the Skazka borders are open, one of Papa's main areas of work is smuggling magical items across the portals. People on this side pay a pretty penny for anything—even a stick from the Skazka forest. Some of the numbers being off is definitely because of Balakin trying to take my papa out of his position, so he can give it to his son.

I still can't quite believe Ilya nearly proposed to me. It's not as if I've ever made it unclear just how much I don't like him. But he's encouraged by that? Some people. Seriously.

"Will you be in the office all day today?" Masha waltzes in around dinner time. Papa and I glance up from where we're sitting on the couch. We haven't been working for the past hour. I've been telling him about the castle and everything that transpired there. He agrees with me in that I need to go back, but of course, he isn't exactly thrilled I'm leaving. Masha will be.

"Not all day. I need my beauty rest before tomorrow."

"Oh, are you planning on causing more problems?"

"No, I'm planning on going back."

"To Skazka?" She actually seems shocked for a moment. I'm surprised she hasn't been listening at the door, or maybe she's become a better actress in the last five months.

"Yes, I am needed there."

"In your big castle with your pretty jewels."

"Don't look now, Masha. Your jealousy is showing."

"Girls," Papa admonishes. "You should learn to get along."

"This is us getting along. I'm just joking with her," Masha says. "Would you like to eat your dinner in here?"

"No, we'll have dinner at the table as usual."

Masha gives me another long look and then she's gone. Papa also gives me a look, but I simply smile. After dinner, I head to my room, tired. My mind is filled with so many things, but a small nap will do me some good.

I wake up slightly disoriented, my head feeling heavy. Glancing at the clock, I see that only about an hour has passed, but I don't remember falling asleep. The pressure of everything that's been going on must've caught up with me. Placing my feet on the floor, I run my hands through my hair, untangling the long mess. It needs to be braided, but not yet. I leave it down as I push myself to my feet, heading for the kitchen. My throat is dry, as if I've slept for hours instead of less than one.

A slight vertigo overtakes me as I walk the first few steps. I stop, leaning a hand against the wall, taking a few deep breaths in the process. Maybe I'm more dehydrated than I thought. I give myself a minute or so to reorient myself before I feel steady enough to continue.

The house seems extra quiet as I make my way to the kitchen. After pouring myself a glass of water, I take my time, sipping it slowly.

It's almost time for me to return to the castle. It seems crazy that only two days have gone by. It feels like an eternity. I've become attached to the place—and to him—in a way I never would've imagined.

My lips curl into a small smile as I take another sip. I'm eager to be back within those walls, eager to discover more of who Gavriil is. This is an unusual curiosity, an emotion I never knew I'd experience. But it's not unwelcome. Maybe that's the biggest surprise of it all.

Once I finish off my glass of water, I feel steadier. Rolling my shoulders back a few times, I stretch my arms over my head. I don't want to wait any longer. I'm not needed here. My papa is taken care of, and I'll find a way to return in a few months. I'm needed back at the palace. I don't need to wait another ten hours before I return. I'm ready to go now.

First things first, I head for my papa's office. He's probably in there, going over numbers or planning his next business trip. It'll be nice to see him when he comes through Skazka. Hopefully that will happen soon. It's nice that Papa understands that even though Gavriil no longer holds me hostage, I'm not leaving until I help him and his people fight off this curse. Not when his very humanity is at stake.

Hurrying down the hall, I push the door open without a knock. When I step inside, I come to a halt.

Instead of my papa, Ilya sits behind Papa's desk. Masha and Olga are both present, and so are a few of Ilya's goons. They all turn to look at me as I step through the doorway. My eyes are searching for Papa, but I don't see him anywhere.

"What's going on here?" I ask, and then jerk a bit as the door slams shut behind me. I turn in time to see one of Ilya's henchmen take his spot in front of the door.

"Where's Papa?"

"Resting comfortably." This comes from Masha, so I turn my gaze on her. She's reclining on one of the chairs. Her dress, dark green and flowy, is spread around her like she's a queen on a throne. Olga mirrors her pose, but she's not as polished.

"What's going on? Why are you here?" I turn to Ilya.

He doesn't answer right away. Instead, he stands, walking around the front of the desk and leans against it.

"It appears that you have my father scared of some secret, which puts me in a position. A difficult one."

"I don't see how that has anything to do with me."

"Well, if you hadn't come back, I doubt your father would've paid enough attention to fight against him. You really had him all tied up in knots with worry."

"Oh, but I thought you were worried too? You said something about missing me?"

"When was this?" When Masha speaks up, Ilya's smirk grows bigger. He knows what I'm doing.

"You are one of a kind, Nikita. That's for sure."

"You said that already. When you nearly proposed to me."

"What?" This time, Masha stands up, marching over to Ilya. "What is she talking about?"

"Don't worry yourself with that," he replies, tearing his gaze away from mine and sending Masha one of his charming smiles. His arm wraps around her waist, bringing her against him. All of my inner alarms go off at once. "She's exaggerating."

"Where is my father?" I ask, ignoring whatever it is going on between the two of them.

"Taking a nap. Like you were."

The way she says that—my heart sinks.

"What did you do, Masha?"

"Only added a little something to your dinner."

"I've been asleep for an hour."

"You've been asleep for twenty."

I twist around, my eyes finding the clock on my papa's office wall. In my room, my clock said it was only seven in the evening. But this shows it's three in the afternoon. She changed the clock in my room.

"No." My chest feels heavy. I suddenly can't breathe.

"Yes. Don't you have a deadline? Oh, wait, *had* a deadline."

I stare at my sister in shock as she wraps herself more fully around Ilya. They make such a striking pair, both beautiful on the outside but rotten on the inside. The panic I feel threatens to overwhelm me. They did all this just to spite me, just to hurt me because I what? Rejected Ilya? Helped papa with the business?

"Don't worry, Nikita. I'm sure nothing bad happened to

your beast," Ilya says. Clearly, Masha spilled everything. I'm not even surprised she knows about the deadline. She probably had someone listen in at the party when Papa and I talked. I take a step back from them, horrified. But still fighting.

"So, what now? You're going to threaten papa into giving up his position?"

"No." Ilya laughs. "I'm going to take my father down. Then, your father will have no choice but to listen to me."

"And all this?" I wave my hand around.

"That was just a bit of fun."

Masha takes that moment to reach over and place a kiss on Ilya's cheek as he keeps his eyes on me. I move back another foot, and his eyes narrow, trying to figure out what I'm going to do.

"You have nowhere to go, Nikita. Your father will be awake soon and then we'll make a deal. You'll fall in line, just like everyone else."

I place my hands in my pockets, keeping my eyes trained on him. He really is the villain here, isn't he? But at least I know he won't hurt papa. Right now, I have to hold onto that because I have a prince to save.

I turn to leave. His goons are there, but I don't hesitate. Kicking out, I take them by surprise, sending them flying backward as my foot connects.

"Stop her!" Ilya shouts, but I'm far enough that I take the ring off my pointer finger, place it on my ring finger and then I'm gone.

❧ 39 ❧

When I materialize on the other side of the portal, darkness greets me. It's as if the whole castle has been covered in a blanket with barely any light shining through. It reminds me of how things were when I first arrived here, but also, it's darker somehow. And more menacing. There is no indication of the warmth that started to grow here.

"Gavriil?" I call out because he should be here to greet me. He would've known I've used the ring, and there's no way he wouldn't come. I know I missed the deadline, but he has to be here. He does. But even as his name leaves my lips, I hear nothing but the echo of my own voice. "Gavriil?"

My heart squeezes in fear as I make my way through the shadow-filled hallways. Panic sets in the more I call out his name. When I finally reach his room, I pause.

It's a place I've never been to before. I only know this is his room because he mentioned it in passing one day. It's near the music room, and the doors always stay shut. Yet, I know I have no choice but to check here. My only two options are here and the garden.

"Gavriil?" My voice is but a whisper as I slip through the crack in the door. The temperature in the room drops a few degrees, as if it can feel the worry inside of me. I move slowly, glancing around, hoping to see him sulking in the corner. Only two candles are lit in the whole room, leaving most of it in shadows. The room itself is similar to that of where the king's statue is situated, only longer. When I reach the balcony, I see that the view opens up to the garden. Hoping there's a light there, I lean over to see, but it's just as dark as the rest of the castle.

I'm late, and he's nowhere to be found.

That's when I feel it. The back of my neck prickles. Slowly, I turn just as the first growl reaches me. A wolf stands in the middle of Gavriil's bedroom, his teeth bared at me. I've seen the signs of him changing before, in the shifts I've witnessed, but this...this is another level.

"Gavriil, it's me. I'm so sorry I'm late. I—" My words die on my lips as there are no signs of recognition in his expression.

The wolf stares at me. The eyes I know so well are overshadowed by pure animalistic drive. He stands at eight feet tall, and he's long—longer than a horse. His fur is deep blue, the color of the midnight sky, just like his eyes. He's beautiful and terrifying, and he's no longer mine.

"Gavriil?"

He growls again. My heart thuds in pain against my chest because there's no doubt in my mind—he's gone.

I can see it plain as day. There's no Gavriil behind those

eyes, no warmth I've come to know in the last few months. The man I've come to call a friend has been erased, and in his stead is a beast. Beautiful and dangerous. He crouches down, nose close to the floor as he continues to watch me.

Tears pool in my eyes as my heart breaks into a million little shards.

I lost him.

Somehow, I lost him before I even truly had him.

When he launches himself at me, I scream.

⚜

MY BODY REACTS BEFORE I CAN THINK ABOUT IT. Rolling out of the way, I slam into a dresser. He growls again before he raises his head into the air and howls. The noise he emits shakes the very floor beneath me. I have to be quick. It won't take him long to reach me, not when his one leap takes him across the whole room.

Even though I don't want to, I'll have to fight him. I have no other choice. Desperately, I look around for anything I could use as a weapon. But his room is as empty as if he never even lived here. Of course, my own knife is back in my bedroom at Papa's house.

The growl sounds again, this time lower and more menacing. I move slowly toward the door, staying close to the wall to feel my way back. If I can get to the door, if I can close it behind me, maybe I can buy myself some time. But it's as if he knows what I'm thinking. He looks at me and then at the door. His growl is more pronounced as saliva drips from the side of his mouth.

I don't hesitate. I run.

My hand wraps around the door handle just as he grabs me by my pant leg. I'm yanked back. I twist in the air, landing hard on my back as the wind is knocked out of me. He reaches me then. I kick out, doing my best to scramble back at the same time. I've been taught fighting skills but never against an animal as big as a horse. It doesn't matter. I won't outrun him.

I kick at him again, this time connecting with his side. He grunts from the impact. Jumping to my feet, I try to get past him, but there's no use. His paw reaches out, swiping my legs from under me. There is no time for me to find my footing because he's on top of me in seconds. One paw pins me to the floor, his nose sniffing into my neck and hair.

"Gavriil." Tears run down my cheeks freely. My body feels heavy and bruised, but I reach my hands up anyway, placing one against the side of his face. If he's going to tear me to shreds, I at least need him to know that I didn't do this on purpose. That I came back to him.

I kept my promises. I would never abandon him.

My touch freezes him, his hot breath fanning over my face. I sob, my body shaking from the pain of seeing him like this. Of losing him to this curse.

"I'm sorry I couldn't find a way. I'm sorry I couldn't save you." I push the words out, my throat raw from the waterfall of tears. My hand curls into his fur, holding him in place, so I can see his eyes. If I have to choose the last thing I'm going to see, then I want it to be his eyes.

He brings his face level with mine as I slide my body up to lean against the walls. We're face to face now, my hand still buried in the fur on his cheek. One bite, and I'm gone.

I can see it all play out in my mind. He opens his huge mouth, teeth gleaming with saliva as he rips the skin off my bones.

But he doesn't move.

His eyes are trained on mine. I flex my fingers, half petting, half holding on.

"It's me, Gavriil. I won't leave you again. I won't."

We stay like this, locked together in a battle of wills or destiny, I'm not sure which. I don't dare to move, and he doesn't seem to want to. My tears subside as I watch him. When I reach with my other hand to wipe at my cheeks, he head butts me, but not in a mean way. It's almost gentle. My breath catches. I forget my tears as I bring my empty hand to cup the other side of his face.

"You're still here, aren't you? Fight it, Gavriil. Fight it for me. Fight it for yourself. We're not done, do you hear me? You and me? We're not finished yet. Fight it."

He growls again, a low rumble in his chest, but it's no longer menacing. It's almost like a question. I reach for him then, bringing my forehead against his. He lets me. We stay like that, girl and her beast, and I send every possible intention his way, every ounce of strength I have left in my body. I can't imagine him gone. I need him to fight.

And I will fight with him.

We could've stayed like that for an eternity, but then, suddenly, he steps away, ears back, as he turns toward the balcony.

Then, I hear it too.

❧ 40 ❧

The shouting from outside grows closer. I rush toward the balcony so I can look down. I am greeted by a group of people entering the castle. Even with the shadows, I know these people. Or at least, who is leading them in.

Ilya.

"They must've done something." I have no idea what. I turn to Gavriil and see that he's ready to leap down from the balcony and attack. "Let me talk to him. Please. I don't want blood on your...hands." He growls again but doesn't move. "I need a weapon." He turns his head to the side, and I follow his gaze. Moving forward, I'm at the wall. That's when I see it. A display with three daggers is hanging there. I take one, feeling slightly better with it in my hand. I give him one last look and then I race for the stairs.

I'm at the top of the staircase when I hear Ilya shouting.

"Take anything of value. Leave no place unturned."

"Bastard!" I snap. The goons freeze, surprised.

"Ah, there she is. I should offer up some thanks."

"What did you do?" I walk down the stairs slowly, the blade gleaming at my side.

"I found someone who can piggyback on spells. All you had to do was use your portal ring, and here we are. I even got to bring some weapons. Fun, right?" He's so smug, so sure of himself. The anger inside of me is coming to a boiling point. I have to focus on my breathing to keep in control.

"Greedy and sleazy, just like your father."

"You know nothing about me!" he snaps, anger making his face red. Men like him truly are so predictable. Wanting power and wealth and with no conscience in sight.

"I know you will scheme your way into anything, including a kingdom that does not belong to you." I'm close enough to the bottom that I see his goons hiding in the shadows at the sides. There's no way I can't take on all of them. There are at least eight, and maybe more, hiding. Although, I truly have no idea how many passengers he could've bought.

"And this belongs to you?" He waves his arm around. "Where is your prince? Your knight in shining armor?"

"I come carrying my own sword," I reply, my grip tightening on the blade. Ilya's eyes narrow.

"Don't stand in my way, Nikita."

"Or what? You're going to kill me?"

"If I have to."

A single nod from him, and his goons descend. Two

come from each side. I swing in one direction while I kick out in the other. None of these men expect me to know how to fight, but I didn't pay attention in training for nothing. I'm not afraid, and I'm not backing down. I go low as another one reaches me, swiping my blade over the top of his knee. When he drops down to his other one, I slam my own blade into his face on the way up. In the next moment, arms wrap around me. I'm lifted off the ground, my dagger cluttering to the floor.

Using the momentum of my attacker, I push off the one in front of me, sending us both to the floor as well. Someone grabs my hair, yanking me to the side. I scream. That's when my scream turns into a roar.

Gavriil leaps down the stairs, right into the group of men. He doesn't hesitate, clamping his teeth on those closest to him and tossing them right out the door or against the wall. He must've held back from me, even before I got through to him, because I hear a crunch of bones as the men land against the hard surface.

I get to my feet slowly, my eyes on Ilya. He's hovering near the door, ready to bolt, but I'm not about to let him leave like that. He meets my gaze and then he's reaching inside his suit coat. I know what it is before he even takes it fully out.

"Gavriil, watch out!" I scream as hard as I can, but I'm still not fast enough. The sound of a shot fired fills the air and then Gavriil is howling, his blood spraying all around. He lands hard. I'm rushing to him before I can even think about Ilya's gun. Gavriil whimpers, pushing me away as he tries to stand. He's moving toward the door, and it's like I can see what he's thinking.

"I'll get him," I say, and then I reach for my dagger and rush out the door after Ilya. He's only a few feet in front of me, the last one standing. He hears me behind him and turns, gun raised.

"Is that your beast?" he screams, spit flying everywhere. "You chose him over me?"

"Come on, Ilya. You never actually wanted me. I was just the one thing you couldn't have." I shrug, exhausted to the highest degree. My heart is back there with Gavriil, but once again I'm hopeless. Because I can't save him. I saw the blood.

"We could've been good together. Powerful."

"No, we would've killed each other anyway."

He stares at me as he contemplates my words, and maybe, finally, on some level he agrees. Then, he drops his gun and reaches for something else. When he takes his hand out, he's holding a knife. Immediately, I raise my own.

"I suppose we should just get it over with now."

He lunges at me then, but his form is sloppy. Even though I'm exhausted, I sidestep him easily. He swings his arm down, trying to catch me with his knife, but he's flailing. While he might not be good with a knife, he does know how to box. He punches me with his other hand, and the blow lands in my stomach. I stagger back but stay upright. He comes at me again, and I do my best to block him. He is stronger than I am. I jump back as he comes at me again. The only advantage I have are my legs. I use them to kick him in the side. The kick lands, sending him to the ground, and then I'm on him.

I raise my hand, bringing it down hard, driving my

blade straight through his dominant hand. He screams, thrashing to get me off him. I jump off as he tries to pull the knife out of his hand and the ground. I kick him while he's down, and he screams profanities my way.

The hatred inside of me is hot and nearly overwhelming but if I kill him now, I'm no better than he is. He's been calling Gavriil a beast, but in reality, that's who I'll become if I succumb to Ilya's ways. So, I pick up his gun, pointing it straight at him before I speak.

"Leave, Ilya. Leave and never come back. You have one chance."

He stares at me as if he's never seen me before. For the first time, there's real fear in his eyes. He rips the blade out of his hand, holding it close to his body as he reaches into his pocket. He comes away with a pouch. I hold the gun steady as I watch him rip the pouch open with his teeth. Items spill out all around him. Then, without a word, he disappears.

I stand there for a second longer, to make sure he doesn't come back, and then I'm racing back toward the castle. But when I step inside, Gavriil is gone. I see the blood trail and immediately know where he's gone.

Turning around, I race back out to the gardens.

❧ 41 ❧

I find him in the middle of the secret garden, surrounded by his favorite roses. Dropping to my knees, I check his wound. Even before I touch him, I can tell he's losing too much blood. His dark fur is covered in blood. When I push against the bullet hole, his whimper breaks my heart all over again. I will never be able to put the pieces back together.

When I thought I lost him to his beast form, I still had a shred of hope. Now? I have nothing left in me.

He moves his head so he can see me, those midnight eyes full of so much pain. I'm crying again because I can do nothing else. Everything is my fault. I left, I ended up bringing Ilya here. I caused this.

When I lose him, it'll be on me.

The bickering, the fights. Our long conversations after he saved me. He's become a part of me, and now, that part is dying.

"I'm so sorry, Gavriil. It's all my fault. I thought I could save you, but I did the opposite, didn't I? I am worse than your curse. I doomed you to die. I—" He reaches over, nuzzling his snout against my bowed head. I glance up, reaching out with one hand, running it over his fur. Nothing is going to be the same without him.

Not the eggs and toast breakfast. Not the long talks about magic. Not the music.

He nuzzles me again, as if telling me everything will be okay. I just hold onto him tighter. I don't care that I'm now covered in his blood; I simply wrap my body around his and hold on.

He has become someone to me, someone I never expected but wished for. He has become my family, my whole heart. Is that truly possible in such a short time? My mama would say yes. She would say she knew within the first week of meeting Papa. It took me longer with Gavriil, but I know. I know now and *now* is too late.

His body shudders under mine. I feel his heart beat slow more and more with every passing second. I reach over, taking his face into my hands, so I can look into his eyes one last time. His latch onto mine, full of unspoken promises and dreams that will never come true.

"You are the melody of my heart, Gavriil," I whisper, giving him my very soul with those simple words. He shudders one last time and then the light goes out of his eyes, leaving me hollow from the inside out.

I scream, hating myself for failing him. Hating him for leaving me. I scream until my throat is raw, and then I collapse on top of him, holding his lifeless body to mine.

There isn't comfort to be found here. There is only pain.

A rush of wind comes through the garden, and it pulls me away from his body. I yelp, surprised, as I look up to see the roses fly off the vines. One by one, they fall on top of Gavriil's body, as if pulled there by a magnet. I scramble back, pushing myself to my feet as I watch the shower of roses descend upon him. The whole garden comes alive as the roses twirl in the wind before falling on top of him. The wind tears at my clothes, slapping my hair against my face, but I can't bring myself to move as I watch what unfolds in front of me.

Then, just as suddenly as the wind comes, it disappears. Gavriil's body is entirely covered in scarlet roses. I stand frozen with no idea what to do. Then, the roses move.

Unable to tear my eyes away, I watch as the roses shift. It's as if something is growing restless underneath them, and then, they're falling away. A man stands where the roses used to be. He turns toward me. There's a moment when his eyes first find mine that he looks relieved, as if he didn't think I'd be here.

"Nikita," he breathes. My heart swells at the sound of my name on his lips.

"Gavriil."

There's no doubt it's him. Even though he looks different, his features are no longer distorted or hairy, I'd know him anywhere. I could never forget those eyes, not for as long as I live.

"I like it when you say my name all breathless like," he says, taking a step toward me. "I also liked when you said you loved me."

Immediately, I'm on the defensive. "I did no such

thing. I think a man should be the one to tell a woman he loves her first. It's the old fashion—"

"Nikita?"

"What?"

"I love you. Now, shut up."

In the next moment, I'm in his arms. He lifts me straight off the ground as his lips crash over mine. There's no hesitation in our kiss. Soon, we're drowning in each other. His taste fills me as his arms surround me. I hook my legs around his waist, needing to be closer still. His arms cradle me to him as his mouth explores and devours.

If we live for a hundred years, I will never get tired of this man kissing me. He fills my heart and mind, and I never want to let go. I wrap my arms around his neck, needing him closer and closer, until we're one flesh—when something occurs to me.

I pull back slightly, looking down at him. "Did you just tell me to shut up?"

"Do I have to do it again or will you kiss me already?"

I grin, pulling his face up to mine as I claim his mouth once more.

❧ 42 ❧

A noise reaches us, a hundred voices talking all at once. We spring apart, staring at each other in shock. He slides me gently to the ground, giving me another quick kiss, before taking my hand.

Hand in hand, we race out of the secret garden and toward the castle. What we see takes my breath away. The darkness that has lived in this place like a bad roach is gone. Sunlight streams down, blinding me for a minute.

But it's not the beauty of this place, or the way the garden is coming alive that shocks me. It's the people coming out of the castle. So many people, feeling the sun on their faces for the first time in years. When they notice us, they bow immediately. That's when it hits me that I'm holding hands with a king.

Because if the curse is broken, the king is dead, and Gavriil can now rightfully take the throne.

"Gavriil!" The shout comes from behind some people. They move to the side as Larisa rushes down the stairs and into Gavriil's arms. He drops my hand to hug her, holding her close. My eyes once again fill up with tears. Dina and Yevgenii reach us just as Larisa steps away from her brother and hugs me.

"You did it. You saved us."

"I did nothing," I reply, but I hug her anyway. Then Dina steps in and hugs me as well.

"We felt your love," Dina whispers into my ear. I pull back in shock.

"What?"

"Love conquers all," Yevgenii says. I stare at them, not quite understanding. "Turns out Baba Yaga did give us a way out of the curse. She just made that the first memory that went. We remembered the moment you told him how you felt. We could feel it even before we were human again."

I shake my head, my mind and heart overwhelmed, blushing profusely. If I ever meet that sorceress, and I hope I never do, I kind of want to give her a piece of my mind. Or something along those lines.

"Do you want to explain the bodies in our foyer?" Yevgenii asks, back to his captain of the guard duties just like that. He's looking at me.

"Not really?" I reply. Gavriil chuckles beside me, reaching over to tug me to his side. But then more people are there. They're bowing to him, but he waves them off and reaches over to hug instead. I stand beside Larisa. She takes my hand into hers, holding on tightly. Glancing over, I give her a smile that she returns, and I see that she's crying quietly. She even does that like a princess. Yevgenii and Dina move with Gavriil as he greets his people. My heart swells with the possibilities of the kind of king he will be.

There is so much to figure out, but we're here and we're together and this doesn't feel impossible anymore. It feels more than doable.

I never could've imagined I'd be the key to breaking this curse, and not in the way any of us expected. But one of the lessons Mama taught me when I was a child is that you cannot outrun your destiny. It finds you no matter what. Somehow, someway, being here is my destiny. It's such a small amount of time, if I'm to think about the rest of my life, but it's long enough to show me who I am and where I belong. I belong here in this kingdom with these people. I don't just love Gavriil, I love them all. And clearly, so does he.

Watching him greet his people, my heart swells. Now that his father isn't here to influence him, the true Gavriil can shine through. He is a beautiful, kind soul.

"Nikita!"

I glance up as he comes back, taking his hand in mine.

"You can't bear to be away from me for a second, huh?" I tease, through my own tears that threaten to overwhelm me.

"Not even for half of that."

I grin up at him, and he kisses me again, in full view of everyone. The cheers ring out all around us, as if every single person in this place knows who I am and what this means. He pulls back, grinning down at me as he links our hands together.

"Come on. There's much to do."

❧ 43 ❧

The next week goes by in a blur. There is a constant flow of activity throughout the castle as people leave to visit their loved ones and return. Not everyone does but the majority do. Gavriil is there for everything. He is no longer a standoffish prince. He is now a very hands-on king, and the people love him. He's learning every day, and so am I.

Being royal isn't something I ever had on my list of things I wanted to be. But running a kingdom is kind of like running the syndicate. It takes patience, organization, and communication. Thankfully, I've had practice in all. The communication part is still a work in progress. Just because I love Gavriil, doesn't mean I don't fight with him.

And I do love him. I didn't think love happened like that, sneaking up on you when you're not looking. But here we are. He's become a part of me, and as sappy as it sounds, I wouldn't want it any other way.

"You really think this is a good idea?" Gavriil asks me as I look over the paper in front of me.

"Of course it is. Don't argue."

"Why? Because that's your specialty?"

"Absolutely." I glance up at him, grinning. "And don't you forget it."

He grunts in response, very un-king-like. "Is there a way I would be able to win this one?"

"No." I chuckle. "It truly is a waste of your time. And mine."

"You're impossible." He rolls his eyes.

"It's one of my most charming qualities," I say as I reach over, pulling him down to my height, so I can leave a kiss on his lips. He doesn't hesitate to grab me right off the bench I'm sitting on and into his arms. I squeal, wrapping my arms around his neck as he holds me close.

"Ah, put me down."

"Nah. *This* is not an argument you're winning," he replies before he claims my lips with his. Kissing him feels like coming home, every single time. We fit together like we were made for each other. No matter how much time we spend together, I can't get enough of him and he of me. Mama told me once that that's how love feels. I told her that's not possible. She simply chuckled instead of arguing, because clearly, she knew she was right.

As Gavriil and I come up for air, I slap at his shoulder playfully. "Put me down. We have to finish this."

This, of course, being the melody we've been writing together. We've been arguing about the bridge for a few days now. We argue about all the important things.

A knock sounds at the door, and Gavriil places me back

on the bench as my papa steps in the room. He's officially out of the organization and living in the castle with us. My sisters have been banned from Skazka entirely and so have Ilya and his goons. Gavriil still knew some people to make it happen, and as he rebuilds relationships, or builds them for the first time, this kingdom will become safer and safer.

"I only wanted to say goodbye before I head off," Papa says, giving each of us a smile. He's accompanying Larisa back to her family's kingdom. Part of his position at the castle is that of an ambassador. He's good at people relations, so it only makes sense. I stand quickly, walking over to give him a hug. He holds me tight.

"I'm so proud of you, *dochenka*." He places a kiss on my head before stepping back and shaking hands with Gavriil. Then, he gives us both a long look and walks out of the room. We'll be heading down to say goodbye to *Princessa* Larisa soon, and I'm glad he's going with her. It's good that Papa has something to do. It's not easy for him to let go of his daughters. But Masha has been scheming to get rid of Papa for years. She had an assisted living home all lined up for when she claimed him as incompetent. I know it hurts for him to walk away from them, but they have to answer for their actions. Olga is Masha's righthand helper. Power truly does corrupt, and my sisters are no exception.

I had to talk Gavriil out of going to the human realm and ripping Ilya apart. Instead, he bought out a lot to Ilya's contacts, leaving the man bankrupt and in trouble with the organization. He'll be unraveling that situation for years to come. It serves him right. He nearly killed my Gavriil.

"Shall we leave this for later?" Gavriil asks, bringing me back to the present. I look up at him and nod.

"Let's go see your sister."

We descend the stairs together, hand in hand, as the staff moves around us. I have learned that Gavriil and I have to always be touching. Maybe it's to make up for all the touches we missed before, but I don't mind. The way my hand fits in his makes me think it was made to be there.

Papa is already in the carriage while Larisa says her goodbyes. She'll be gone for a while, and I can't blame her. She has her own family to return to. Her eyes meet mine as we step out of the castle, lighting up like they always do when she sees me.

"*Sistra*," she calls, walking over to take my hand in hers.

"You know, technically, we're not sisters."

"Well, we would be if someone decided to finally make an honest woman out of you." Larisa gives Gavriil a look and I chuckle.

"There really is no use in that," I say, squeezing her hands before pulling her in for a hug. "Please return to us soon. He is insufferable when you're not around."

She holds me tight, and I feel her chuckle before she steps back. Giving her brother a hug as well, she looks us over with a small smile on her face.

"Be good to each other," she says before walking over to the carriage. Papa sticks his head out briefly, waving. We return the gesture. Once the carriage begins to move, I turn to Gavriil.

"I'm off to help Dina with some official business."

Gavriil chuckles, lifting my chin so he can drop a kiss on my lips.

"And by official business, you mean you're practicing with a sword."

"Well, yes. But we're trying to be secretive about it."

I melt into him, eager to pull him back to me, but I resist. We'd never get anything done if I gave in to every impulse. It's difficult to be away from him. I've become an absolute sap.

"Meet me in the garden later?" he asks. I nod, standing on my toes as an invitation, and he drops another kiss on my lips.

"See you then!" I call out, stepping back and hurrying back up the stairs. Practicing combat with Dina helps me keep an edge, and I don't want to miss out.

Even though Gavriil and I plan to have a peaceful kingdom, there is one lesson from the Bratva that I will take with me: a girl must always be prepared, for every situation.

I FIND GAVRIIL HOURS LATER, HIS BACK TO ME AS HE tends to the roses. I stand there quietly, watching him work. His hands move across the vines expertly, and I smile to myself. A big man but such a gentle touch.

"If you keep looking at me like that, we're going to get in trouble," he says before he turns around and gives me one of his sexy smiles.

"I'm always in trouble. What else is new?" I reply, stepping farther into the garden. There's a bench in the middle of it, and I take a seat, watching as Gavriil continues to prune the vines. I love watching him work.

Well, I love watching him do anything. He's such a contradiction to the kind of man I thought he would be when I stole the ring and took papa's place in the bargain.

In my mind, I was already planning an escape and a murder, but then Gavriil changed all that by bringing his walls down and showing me the kind of man he could be. Even though he looked like a creature from one of those fairytales.

"What are you thinking so hard about over there?" he asks, not bothering to glance at me.

"You're not even looking at me. How do you know what I'm doing?"

"I can tell. Plus, I'm always looking at you. I'm just sneaky about it."

I chuckle at the prideful way he says that before I shake my head.

"It's nothing huge, just thinking how different things have turned out."

"From what you planned?"

"*Da.*"

He knows my tendencies to plan; he understands how my brain works. I'm not going to lie, I like this version of events a lot better than what I came up with originally.

"You know I like to be prepared."

"Does that mean surprises are out of question?"

I narrow my eyes at the nonchalant way he asks that. His eyes are still on the flowers, but I notice the way his shoulders are tense, and there's a bit of perspiration on his temple.

"What is it you're planning, Gavriil?" I ask, my eyes on

him. He glances up in surprise, opening and closing his mouth.

"How can you always tell?" He moves in front of me, getting back down to his knees, so he's eye to eye with me.

"I'm not sharing my secrets," I say, folding my arms in front of me as I glance down at him.

"Not even with your husband?"

At first, I don't think I hear him correctly. But then, the hopeful look on his face registers and so does the ring he's holding between his fingers. A big diamond set on a simple silver setting sparkles up at me. I stare at it as if I've never seen a piece of jewelry before. Everything in me wants to scream yes, but I'm much too controlled to do that.

"Are you asking me what I think you're asking me?" I say instead.

"Nikita Arturovna." He's on one knee now, pushing himself up so that we can be face to face. "I am asking you to be my wife. To share this kingdom with me, to bind our love into a bargain for the world to see."

Everything in me ignites, my heart ready to burst at the seams. His eyes are filled with love and hope, and his lips are curled up in that sexy smile I love so much. When I answer, I answer from the heart.

"Yes, I want to be your wife," I say. His grin nearly blinds me. "But not yet," I hurry to add. He's not even fazed as he chuckles.

"Of course you're going to argue about this." At least he's still grinning.

"It's not an argument. Just some stipulations."

"Okay." He does not move away, keeping his face inches from mine. "What are the stipulations?"

"I want Papa to walk me down the aisle, just like they did in the olden days. I want Larisa here as my maid of honor. And I want Dina to do my hair."

"That's all?" This time, I do shock him. Maybe he was expecting a huge list or different terms, but it's not about me being too young or not ready. He is my world. What we've been through, it's just an outward result of the love we already share. It saved him. It saved this whole kingdom.

I think he might've saved me too, after I learned how to save myself.

And while I know he is the man for me, I also know that I want to do things right. I've never been one to dream about my wedding day, but now, I see the possibilities. And I want people that I love around me.

"You drive a hard bargain, Nikita Arturovna," Gavriil says, leaning closer still.

"Better get used to it," I say, right before he claims my mouth with his. Just like always, there's no hesitation when we connect. It's only him and me and the magic that our love creates.

There is no other way I can ever explain what we are to each other but this: our love is magic, and it gives us power to do the impossible.

Even when the impossible is a mafia heiress falling in love with a beast.

EPILOGUE

S EVEN MONTHS LATER

"THIS KINGDOM IS BY FAR MY FAVORITE," I SAY AS WE walk through a city near a palace. The forest spreads out around us, but it's not menacing in any way. It's magical in the way fairytales talk about. The flowers that peek around the buildings are bigger than I am, and I see the tiny creatures known as fae flattering around them.

As with our other visits, we could've simply stepped through the portal and ended up in the courtyard of the palace, but Gavriil wants to experience all the things he's missed out on. So, we start in the cities and villages.

We go to lunch at the local restaurant, and we walk through the bazaar.

"You sure this isn't something you are dying to own?"

he asks, picking up one of the gorgeous turquoise bracelets. He really just has to buy me every gift on the planet apparently.

"I will definitely live without it," I reply, pushing his hand down and stepping up on my tippy toes to give him a kiss. He's distracted immediately, pulling me toward him, his arm around my waist. What starts as a simple peck becomes so much more in a matter of seconds. We hear a throat being cleared and pull apart. Yevgenii and Dina are beside us, trying not to laugh. I'm not sure how they're not tired of our public displays of affection, but they don't seem to be. They only make sure we don't take it farther on the streets of a kingdom we're trying to make our allies.

"Back to business then." I pat Gavriil's chest with the palm of my hand, a smile on my face. He leans down and places a soft kiss to my forehead before he leads us away.

We arrive at the palace right on time and are greeted at the doors by none other than the queen of the *Zelenoye Korolevstvo*. I'm a little surprised and very overwhelmed because she is beautiful and powerful all at once.

"*Zdrastvuite, dorogii*," she says, a blinding smile on her face. I feel completely inadequate next to her. But then she opens up her arms, and I step into them to be hugged and feel right at home.

"Queen Calista, it is so good to finally meet you," Gavriil says, bowing. She waves that away and hugs him as well.

"Please, call me Cali. This is my husband, Brendan." She motions to a handsome man beside her, and he sticks out his hand for a shake. They seem so regal and royal but also approachable and kind. They are exactly the kind of rulers I want Gavriil and I to be. "We have heard congratulations are in order," the queen says. I can't keep a grin from spreading on my cheeks.

"Yes, thank you," Gavriil replies, giving my hand a gentle squeeze.

"When is the wedding?" Brendan asks.

"Once our tour of the kingdoms is over. We would love to rebuild our relationships with our allies, if we can still call the kingdoms that."

"You can definitely call this kingdom a friend," Queen Calista replies. She takes a step forward, lowering her voice as if she's sharing a secret. What she says next brings tears to my eyes. "You are a brilliant and kind king, Gavriil. I knew your father, and I am happy to see that there is none of him in you." There is a moment of stillness as Gavriil lets her simple words, that hold so much power, settle over him. I can feel tension seeping away from him almost instantly.

"Then please accept this as our official invitation to the wedding. We would love to have you there." Gavrill bows as I curtsy.

"We wouldn't miss it for anything," Queen Calista replies. Just then, a young man, probably closer to my age than not, rushes from one side of the hallway to the other. "Oh, Luca. Please come here and meet our guests." Calista doesn't miss anything apparently, and the prince obeys right away.

"I apologize for the strange entrance," he says after we exchange pleasantries. "I've been in the midst of a conundrum all day."

"Our son has a tendency to forget that he doesn't have

to do everything himself," Queen Calista comments, looking at Luca with that mixture of pride and love that mothers wear so well.

"I understand that all too well," Gavriil comments, and I nudge him on the side.

"Hey now."

"I said nothing!" he replies. Everyone laughs, and I realize maybe I should be acting with more decorum. But then I meet Queen Calista's eyes, and it's evident she's enjoying this moment just as much as we are. I have a million questions for her because I heard she actually lived in my home realm for a while and fought off the very Baba Yaga that cursed my Gavriil. I also want to ask her all the questions about being a queen and what I can do to best serve my people.

She smiles at me, as if she can read my mind, before motioning us down the hall.

"How about we break bread," she says, "and talk business?"

"We would love that," I reply with a warm smile. Gavriil and I follow behind the royal family hand in hand. I feel Gavriil slightly squeeze my hand, so I look up at him.

"You know what?" he whispers, leaning down closer to me.

"What?" I match his tone.

"I think you're going to be a great queen." He grins at me.

"Yeah? I think you'll make an okay king," I reply, and he rolls his eyes at me.

As we share a smile, I realize that sometimes it's okay when life doesn't turn out the way it's planned out. And people can truly take you by surprise. I thought I had a purpose for myself. I thought I had all the answers on what should come next. I never planned on Gavriil or the magic of Skazka. But here we are.

He stops me right before we follow the royal family into the dining room, placing a soft kiss to the top of my head. I soak up the gesture, just like I soak up every moment I spend with him.

I can't wait to be Gavriil's wife and share in a million more adventures that await us.

FIVE MONTHS LATER

As I step inside the study, my eyes latch onto the single scarlet rose waiting for me in a vase in the middle of the desk. My lips curl up with a smile as I walk over, picking the glass vase up and smelling the flower. It's such a Gavriil thing to do. He leaves me flowers everywhere. Sometimes with new sheet music he procured.

I glance down at the table, but this time it's not sheet music waiting for me. It's a note, with one word.

Ballroom.

Smiling to myself, I take the rose with me as I hurry out of the study. Passing others in the hallway, I give them a polite smile, which they return, but no one tries to stop me. I hurry my steps, eager to see what Gavriil is up to. Our wedding is still a few months away since Papa had to return to the human realm for some business. Normally, I would be concerned, but Dina went with him. There's no way the Bratva or my sisters can get to him when that woman is on the job. I miss both of them and can't wait for them to return.

The doors are slightly opened when I come up on the ballroom, and I slip inside easily. Gavriil is standing in front of the middle window, gazing up at the sky through the glass. I know I haven't made a lick of noise, but he feels me there, so he turns.

We are always aware of the other, and it always feels like we haven't seen each other in days. He doesn't hesitate, sprinting forward before he picks me clear off the floor. I yelp, wrapping my arms around his neck. He holds me across the thighs, so we are face to face, grinning.

"Hello, *krasavitsya*," Gavriil whispers, his breath sending goosebumps down my back. Instead of replying, I lean down, capturing his mouth with mine. He responds instantly, melting into me, even though he's the one who's holding us both up. I bring him closer, my fingers spread into his hair. We're spinning, lost in each other, and it's by sheer will that we break apart.

"Why the mysterious note?" I ask, still firmly in his arms. He has no plans of putting me down, that much I can tell, and I wholly agree with that decision.

"Because I'm mysterious."

"You're something."

He shakes his head, but his eyes are shining. I will never get tired of seeing him like this, carefree and loved. And loving. He's giving himself that gift of opening up, of caring about those around him. It's making him the greatest king this kingdom has ever known.

"I have something to show you."

"Oh yeah?"

He sets me back on the floor now, and I step back to smooth out my skirt. I don't have much time because he takes my hand in his and guides me to one side of the ballroom.

"Remember all those secret passageways you were so curious about?" he asks. I nod a little too eagerly. In all the time I've lived here, most of the castle still remains unexplored. "Well, I have something to show you."

He places his palm against one of the painted roses and then it moves back. The vines seem to part and then a doorway opens up in front of us.

"Gavriil?"

"Come on."

He leads me inside, keeping my hand firmly in his. There are a million stairs in front of us, and the staircase winds up. We walk in silence, hands clasped. All of those workouts I still do, including running, are showing up for me now so I don't wheeze like an old cow.

"A little more," Gavriil says, and then it seems we have arrived. Immediately, I see that we're in one of the towers that sticks out over the castle's design. We have three, but I've never been able to get into one. Gavriil leads me to one of the windows, and I look out to see the rest of our gardens spreading around us and then into the forest.

"This is beautiful."

"*Da*."

But when I turn, he's looking at me. I smile and then he's leading me toward a picnic he's set up, right there on the stone floor. Blankets and pillows neatly litter the floor, and there are food and drinks as well.

"Shall we?"

I sit on one side and he on the other, but I can't take my eyes off him. All this beauty around me, but he's the most beautiful creature my eyes have ever beheld. My fingers run over my engagement ring before it also caresses the portal ring I haven't taken off my pointer finger this whole time. Both are a reminder. Of the past and the future, two pieces that make up who we are.

"What?" he asks, running his hand over his face as if he's worried there's something on it.

"I like you, that's all," I reply, giving him a smile.

"Oh, too bad. Because I don't think this is going to work."

My mouth falls open in shock, but we both know he's kidding. He couldn't even deliver the joke with any seriousness in his tone. Leaning forward, he steals another kiss from me.

"You're never getting rid of me, Nikita Arturovna," he whispers against my lips. I don't have a sense to reply because once again I'm lost in him. His scent is intoxicating, his touch electrifying. If I'm to live for a thousand years, I'll never get tired of him kissing me like I am his.

"Happy birthday, Nikita." His lips move over my lips as he tugs me closer across the mountains of pillows. This time, I don't hesitate. Climbing straight into his lap, I sit with my legs on either side of him. His arms come around me as I reach to hold his face with my hands.

I let just the tip of my finger run over his skin, starting at his chin, going up toward his forehead and back down again. Then, I lean forward, placing a kiss on the right side of his mouth and then the next. He growls, tugging me closer, but I'm not done torturing him yet. I lick my lips as

I meet his gaze before I lean closer. There's barely any space between us, and his eyes are on fire as he watches me play my game.

I run my finger over his cheeks and his nose, circling his eyes. All this time, he doesn't stop watching me, that midnight gaze filled with pure desire. My tongue sneaks out again to moisten my lips, and the rumble in his chest is all I hear before his mouth crushes over mine.

His lips feel like they were made for kissing only me, his skin hot against my own. If I live a thousand years, I will never get enough of him. He is the melody of my heart and the song of my soul.

"I love you, my queen," he whispers against my lips, my heart beating in sync with his.

"I love you, my king."

I can't wait for our happily ever after.

~ The Skazka Fairy Tales ~

A Cinderella Retelling

THE GOLDEN SLIPPER

Book 2 in the standalone Russian fairy tale
series

Coming early 2022

Valia Lind

GLOSSARY OF RUSSIAN WORDS

Da - Yes

Nyet - No

Ruble - currency unit in Eastern Europe, largely Russia (among other countries)

Milaya - darling

Ne spoirit - no argument

Dochenka - my sweet daughter

Pirogies - dumpling

Umnaya devushka - smart woman

Capitan - captain

Malchik - boy

Udachi - Good luck

Sarafan - multicolored dress

Rubashka - shirt

Balalaika - Russian stringed musical instrument, with a triangular wooden hollow body, fretted neck, and three strings - similar to a guitar

Sistra - sister

Babushka - grandma

Dobrii den - Good day!

Zdrastvui, devochka - Hello, young woman

Pozhalusta - please

Dobroye noche - Good evening/night

Spasibo - thank you

Katleti - cutlet

Magnitofon - record player

Dorogii - dears (as in Hello, my dears)

Krasavitsya - beautiful

Konyak - a type of brandy, popular in Russia

KINGDOMS OF SKAZKA

Volkovskoye Korolevstvo - Kingdom of the Wolf - Gavriil's kingdom

Zelonoye Korolevstvo - Green Kingdom

Holodnoye Tsarstvo - Cold Kingdom

Korolevstvo Tsvetov - Kingdom of Flowers - Larisa's home kingdom

Oceniye Tsarstvo - Autumn Kingdom

Vodnoye Tsarstvo - Kingdom of Water

WHAT MORE FROM THE LAND OF SKAZKA?

Discover how Calista became the Queen of Zelenovo Korolevstva and learn more about the land of Russian fairytales in The Skazka Chronicles trilogy. Available now!

ABOUT THE AUTHOR

USA Today bestselling author. Photographer. Artist.

Born and raised in St. Petersburg, Russia, Valia Lind has always had a love for the written word. She wrote her first published book on the bathroom floor of her dormitory, while procrastinating to study for her college classes. Upon graduation, she has moved her writing to more respectable places, and has found her voice in Young Adult and paranormal cozy mysteries.

The Skazka Chronicles

Hardcover Omnibus - 4 books in one

Remembering Majyk (The Skazka Chronicles, #1)

Majyk Reborn (The Skazka Chronicles, #2)

The Faithful Soldier (The Skazka Chronicles, #2.5)

Majyk Reclaimed (The Skazka Chronicles, #3)

The Skazka Fairy Tales

The Scarlet Rose (A Beauty and the Beast Retelling)

The Golden Slipper (A Cinderella Retelling) - coming Spring 2022!

Hawthorne Chronicles - Each season can be read as standalone!

Season Three - The Fae Chronicles

Marked by Fae (prequel novella) - free to download

Shadow of the Fae (#1)

Blood of the Fae (#2)

Revenge of the Fae (#3) - Coming Winter 2021!

Season Two - Thunderbird Academy

Of Water and Moonlight (Thunderbird Academy, #1)

Of Destiny and Illusions (Thunderbird Academy, #2)

Of Storms and Triumphs (Thunderbird Academy, #3)

Season One - Hawthorne sisters

Guardian Witch (Hawthorne Chronicles, #1)

Witch's Fire (Hawthorne Chronicles, #2)

Witch's Heart (Hawthorne Chronicles, #3)

Tempest Witch (Hawthorne Chronicles, #4)

The Complete Season One Box Set

Crooked Windows Inn Cozy Mysteries

Once Upon a Witch #1

Two Can Witch the Game #2

Third Witch's the Charm #3 - coming Autumn 2021!

Blackwood Supernatural Prison Series

Witch Condemned (#1)

Witch Unchained (#2)

Witch Awakened (#3)

Witch Ascendant (#4) - Coming Summer 2021!

Havenwood Falls (PNR standalone)

Predestined

The Titanium Trilogy

Pieces of Revenge (Titanium, #1)

Scarred by Vengeance (Titanium, #2)

Ruined in Retribution (Titanium, #3)

Complete Box Set

Falling Duology
Falling by Design
Edge of Falling

Printed in the USA
CPSIA information can be obtained
at www.ICGtesting.com
LVHW040224171123
763960LV00007B/22/J